WOLF BITTEN

THE FORBIDDEN MATE TRILOGY
BOOK 2

JEN L. GREY

CHAPTER ONE

My head was pounding, and my mouth felt as if I'd been sucking on cotton balls. *This* had to be a hellacious hangover. What had I done last night to deserve this punishment? I'd better have had a damn good time.

I stretched out my hand, searching for Raffe. The bed felt softer than normal. I needed him to hold me. His touch always made me feel better, and I loved having his body wrapped around mine.

No matter how far I stretched, I couldn't find him.

My heart skipped a beat. Where was he? I hoped he was okay. He had to be.

Then I remembered.

I tried to open my eyes, but my eyelids and limbs were so heavy. My heart pounded harder as my blood tried to jolt but couldn't. My emotions seemed dulled, especially for me.

Right. Dave had shot a tranquilizer into my neck.

Dave.

I should've let Raffe kill him the night he'd struggled not to attack me while my blood had been humming. I'd asked Raffe not to do anything because Dave had fought his vampiric urges, especially after we'd learned that my blood humming made vampires crave me. Dave had told me how to get away without tempting the predator in him, and I hadn't thought he deserved to be punished or killed.

Had I known my imminent future, my request of Raffe might have been different.

Dave had shot me in the woods, and with the soft mattress beneath me, I had no doubt he hadn't taken me home. The thought should've alarmed me, but all I felt was mild concern.

Dammit, I had to focus. I couldn't wallow in should haves. I needed to get moving if I wanted to find Raffe. He hadn't been where he'd told me he was meeting Adam, Keith, Josie, and Lucy. Had something happened to them?

That spot in my chest that had urged me to leave the apartment to find Raffe was burning hot and frigidly cold at the same time as if fear and anger were taking root inside me, but I didn't have any strong reactions. I was struggling to think, let alone process the situation, and I felt lethargic and numb.

Yet another strange occurrence to add to my ever-growing list of fucking problems.

This time, when I tried to open my eyes, they lifted just enough to give me a slight sense of the room.

And what I saw was nothing like I'd expected. Finally, my heart quickened a smidge. It was enough of a boost to open my eyes wider.

The room was nice and not some sort of prison cell. Overhead, a large circular light was turned off. Because of that, I could see my reflection staring back at me from its glass. My tangled hair was spread across navy-blue pillows, and there were dark circles under my eyes. My complexion was paler than usual, further proof that I'd been drugged. I was still wearing the lilac sweater and jeans I'd put on after ...

At the bittersweet memory, my heart panged, nearly stealing my breath.

After months of turbulent interactions, Raffe and I had gotten together and had sex, cementing our fated-mate bond as much as we could with my being human. Of course, it was my luck that, within an hour, I'd be kidnapped and taken away from the one person who made me feel safe and loved and could help me calm my blood when it went crazy.

Apparently, surviving years of bullying and abuse from my peers hadn't been enough for me to earn some happiness. The love of my life had to be stripped away from me.

Between the emotions crowding my chest and my pity party, I was way too damn close to spiraling out of control and wasting the little bit of energy I had on something frivolous.

I had to get out of here, and I could only do that by focusing and using my remaining energy to move and burn off the drug faster.

Forcing myself to concentrate, I noticed one glorious thing.

Dave hadn't bound my arms and legs.

I had to use this to my advantage while I could. My chest expanded with hope, which I tried to squash. Hope wasn't a good thing—it could destroy you.

The cement ceiling looked similar to the one in the hidden coven library. Where the hell was I? Was this another secret location within the Evergreen Elite University campus? Was I even still in Portland, Oregon? My stomach churned as the realization settled over me.

I had no idea where I was, why Dave had taken me, or what he or whoever had made him drug me wanted from me. In other words, I had to get the fuck out of here while my kidnappers assumed I was passed out.

Straining, I moved my hand slowly toward the spot on my

neck where the tranq had lodged. My skin seemed smooth, as if nothing had hit me.

Strange.

The needle must have been small enough that I couldn't detect a wound.

Turning my head to the left, I took in the space. Wooden blinds covered a window that took up half the wall. A light-colored wooden dresser sat underneath it. A few feet beyond the dresser was a light-gray desk with a reading lamp on top and a white chair. A thick wooden door stood at the edge of the dresser, which I hoped was the exit but could be a bathroom.

When I managed to look in the opposite direction, I stared straight at the toilet. That answered that question and confirmed something else.

I'd never seen this place before.

Footsteps scuffed the floor outside the room, and a lump formed in my throat. Between that and my cottonmouth, I needed something to drink and fast.

One problem at a time, Skylar.

The doorknob turned, and I closed my eyes and returned to the position I'd been in when I woke up.

"That's what I thought," an older woman said. "She's still asleep. That vampire must have given her too large of a dose."

That thought scared me. Too much of something as strong as a tranquilizer could lead to death, so if they hadn't been sure of the correct dosage, I was damn lucky to be alive.

At least, there was that.

Someone huffed, and a man replied, "She could be faking. We need to check, and you can't blame Dave. We only have dosages for supernaturals, not humans, and he had to give her enough to knock her out."

The footsteps came closer, and a pineapple-and-mint scent invaded my nose.

A scream lodged in my throat, but I swallowed it ... or maybe I didn't have the strength to release it.

Someone touched the base of my neck, and I had to fight a flinch. The hand seemed big, so I guessed it belonged to the man. He brushed his fingertips against my cheek. My skin crawled, and I desperately wanted to move away from him, but I suspected that was the point. Somehow, I didn't move a muscle.

"I thought she was supposed to smell extremely delicious," the man said as he bent toward me, his nose brushing my neck. "Don't get me wrong, she smells great. Not human, but not like anything I've ever smelled before either. But I don't *have* to drink her blood."

Between his proximity and the pineapple-mint scent filling my nostrils, I almost gagged.

The woman *tsk*ed. "You sound disappointed that you aren't blood-crazed. Be glad because I will do *anything* to protect her, including hurt you. Just so we're clear."

Luckily, the lump in my throat remained, or I would've laughed. Her protective stance clashed with my captive situation—which she was clearly okay with. I wasn't sure how she didn't understand the irony.

"I don't want to hurt her. I was curious what all the fuss is about."

"Well, I don't want to hear that thought again." The woman cleared her throat. "Let's go before we disturb her. We don't want to wake her too soon."

The man stepped away from me. Not only could I hear it, but I could feel it in the air and the way his scent weakened. They must have doused themselves in cologne because I'd never smelled a fragrance that strong ... either that or being drugged had heightened my senses.

"You're right." The man chuckled grimly. "We wouldn't want that."

"Remember our goal," the woman snapped. "Or do I need to make a call?"

"No need. I remember." The man then hissed at her. Hissed. At. Her.

The two of them walked out, and the moment the door shut, I let out a shaky breath. With their supernatural hearing, I had to be careful, so I stayed put in case they decided to check on me again immediately.

I listened as their footsteps disappeared then waited a while longer.

After counting to five hundred, I opened my eyes again. Thankfully, this time, it was easier. I raised my hands in front of me, and they followed the command, if sluggishly. That was an improvement and meant the drug was wearing off faster than I'd anticipated.

Moving as slowly as I could so the mattress didn't squeak, I sat up, and the world slowly spun around me.

Dizziness was another side effect of tranqs and something I naturally experienced, thanks to my blood and its ancient power.

Focusing on my goal, I inched across the bed, trying not to make a sound. Luckily, the bed wasn't creaky, and the smooth cobalt comforter helped me move along easily.

When my feet touched the floor, I paused to make sure I didn't hear anyone coming.

Silence.

Each heartbeat rang in my ears.

I stood and wobbled but managed to catch my balance and stay upright. I had to get across the room to the window.

If I was in a basement and the room had a window, the floor must be at ground level. It would be easier to sneak out that way than via the hallway.

Using the desk for support, I made my way across the room. By the time I reached the dresser, my eyes burned with unshed tears.

Almost there.

I had to keep going.

Then, I could find somewhere to call Raffe and get myself back into his loving arms.

That thought alone was enough to keep me going.

I reached across the dresser and grabbed the string to lift the blinds. My hands shook, and I had to grit my teeth to stop myself from raising the blinds too quickly and making noise. I couldn't wait to get out of here.

When the blinds reached halfway, my heart sank.

It wasn't a window.

It was a painting of a blue sky, sun, and flowers.

Acid inched up my throat. This was a cruel trick. I'd thought I was so damn close to heading home.

My vision blurred, and a tear trickled down my cheek.

No.

I would *not* fall apart.

I refused, especially if that was what my captors hoped would happen. I wouldn't give them the satisfaction of breaking me.

Releasing a shaky breath, I took a moment to pull myself together. I still had the door as an option, and I couldn't hear anyone.

Carefully, I tiptoed over, nearly tripping over my own feet. I wanted to scream in frustration, but that would ruin my attempt at escape by alerting my captors.

I placed my ear against the wooden door and held my

breath, listening one last time to ensure no one was out there or coming.

After several long seconds, silence continued to greet me.

Now or never.

I turned the knob and opened the door slowly. I winced, hoping like hell it didn't creak. It hadn't for my captors, but that could change with me.

Each inch was more excruciating than the last, and when it was partially open, I looked out the door.

My lungs seized.

This further confirmed my suspicions. I was either in a basement or an underground bunker. I feared the latter, but I couldn't just sit here and give up. I had to do something.

No one was there. Fluorescent lights lit a long hallway, giving it a department store feel. Three doorways stood on either side of the hall, which ended in a well-lit open area.

I wouldn't even have darkness to shroud me.

If Slade or one of the other coven members had been here, they could have camouflaged me, but I was on my own.

I had to stop overthinking and focus on the endgame.

Raffe.

With that affirmed in my mind, I opened the door the rest of the way. The more the gap widened, the harder my heart raced ... and my blood jolted.

There.

The drug was almost burned off. Maybe I could get out of here.

I listened again.

Still nothing.

It was time.

I took a step forward and slammed into something.

CHAPTER TWO

My entire body bounced backward, and a sharp ache encompassed my front half, especially my nose and shoulders. A coppery scent overwhelmed me, and warm liquid trickled from my nose onto my lip.

My nose and shoulders throbbed with pain.

I pinched the bridge of my nose to stop the bleeding. As blood splattered my shirt and the beige floor, my breath caught.

There was no way I could get out of here.

The urge to stomp and scream overwhelmed me, but I pushed it down. The one good thing about getting hurt was that my body no longer felt sluggish. The pain and adrenaline burned through the remaining effects of the drug.

Giving up was easy, and when had I ever taken the easy way out? There was no reason to do it now, not after a lifetime of circumstances being stacked against me. This was just one more thing to add to the list. I refused to accept this fate and never see Raffe again, especially since we'd finally gotten our shit together.

Blood oozed from my nose, and I used my free hand to

close the door as quietly as possible. The plan hadn't changed. I needed to find a means of escape, and I couldn't act carelessly now.

Now upright and thinking more clearly, I scanned the room for another way out. I tried to ignore the strong sensation in my chest and the hopelessness that wanted to crush me.

The door and fake window weren't options. What else could there be? There had to be a way out.

Behind the bed was a wall, and across from it was a television and a vase of lilac flowers sitting on a shorter dresser. Nothing else appeared to be an exit—until my gaze landed on the air vent in the ceiling in the corner of the room. The hole was small, similar to a unit inside a house or building ... not commercial.

Fuck.

I was trapped.

The hopelessness I'd been holding off crashed over me like a tsunami, taking me whole.

Each heartbeat pounded through me, and my head throbbed again. I stumbled to the white chair and sat, leaning my head back to stop the bleeding.

My eyes burned, and tears threatened to spill, causing my nose to get stuffy, which was problematic when it was bleeding.

My blood fizzed, and I locked onto it. Maybe if I fell apart, my blood would help break me out of here.

Footsteps came down the hallway again, and the man scoffed, "I told you I heard something. She's awake. I can smell her blood from here, and it smells *delicious*."

I tensed. A vampire was on his way here, and I was bleeding. I stood and stumbled away from the door, wishing I could get out of my clothes and clean the floor before he entered.

"Blood?" the woman asked, her voice strained. "Is she bleeding?"

"Yes. Otherwise, I wouldn't be able to smell her as clearly from out here."

Footsteps quickened toward me.

Shit. This was bad, especially since my blood was fizzing. If he came in here, I would smell more alluring, though nothing like a hum. Still, if he attacked, I wasn't sure if I'd be able to fight him off. And I feared what would happen if the walls and floor cracked. I couldn't shake off the feeling that we were underground.

I hurried toward the bathroom. I could shut the door and hopefully lock it from the other side to put another barrier between us.

"Warin, *stop!*" the older woman shouted. "You're not going in there with her."

He laughed maniacally. "I'll do whatever I want. You're not my *priestess.*"

Releasing my nose, I slammed the bathroom door shut and found a lock on the door handle. I turned it even though I suspected it wouldn't hold up against the vampire. At least, it would buy me a few seconds.

I used my sleeve to wipe the blood gently from my nose and saw a door to my left that swung outward. It didn't have a lock. My mouth dried further, and my throat burned as my blood rose too close to a hum.

Was there another way to get inside?

I heard a thump outside. Warin and the witch were fighting.

When I looked through the doorway, some weight lifted from my shoulders. The room was a walk-in closet that was mostly empty except for a few pairs of yoga pants, underwear, bras, and shirts stacked in the far corner. By the doorway, a wire rack held white towels and washcloths.

A new plan formed.

I needed to clean up and calm down before the vampire reached me.

I removed my sweater, tossed it to the floor, and grabbed a washcloth and a shirt. In the bathroom, I went to the smooth white sink and turned the water on to warm.

The door to the bedroom crashed against the wall.

My time was running out.

"Don't make me do this," the witch gritted. "Because I will."

I held the washcloth under the warm water and heard Warin laugh. Chaos erupted on the other side of the door.

I gently wiped the blood from my face, neck, and hands. The sound of things hitting the wall and Warin's moans made focusing on my task difficult.

When the blood was washed off me, I turned the water to cool and splashed my face, imagining Raffe. I needed to calm down so I could find a legitimate way out of here.

With Raffe's image locked in my mind and the coolness of the water outweighing the warmth of my blood swirling within me, I managed to calm my blood to a jolt. I took deep breaths to center myself and then bent over and took several long gulps of water.

Almost back to normal, I straightened and opened my eyes, realizing that, in my haste, I'd forgotten to put on the shirt. As I slid it on, Warin hissed and said, "Stop, Glinda. I'm fine now."

I shut my eyes again to imagine Raffe's face. If I let my blood get the best of me, the vampire would go crazy again.

"Why should I believe you?" the witch challenged.

"Because the allure is gone." He sighed. "Apparently, her blood is like a siren's call."

"You need to leave. We can't chance you reacting like that again. I'll talk to her alone while you compose yourself."

He laughed. "If you think I have to obey you—"

"Don't force my hand because I will call *her*."

Silence.

Whatever threat she'd tossed out there had had an impact, and I wanted to know who *her* was. That had to be the person who could let me out of here. Wherever *here* was.

"Fine," he huffed, and I didn't hear anything else until a knock on the bathroom door startled me.

It didn't *sound* like a crazed vampire, but that could be part of the ruse. I hadn't heard anyone leave. I remained silent, listening for anything odd.

"Skylar, he's gone." Glinda knocked again. "Come on out. It's safe."

Laughter bubbled out of me. "Is that what you call being kidnapped and held against my will? Safe?" I was dealing with people who didn't see the world clearly. I'd heard some people had fantasies like this.

"That's fair." She sighed. "But I promise you this isn't what it seems. We're doing this to protect you."

That was an angle I hadn't expected. "You drugged and kidnapped me for my own benefit?"

"Exactly. Can you please come out? I swear I won't let anything happen to you."

She sounded sincere, and it wasn't like I could stay in here forever. Blowing out a breath, I unlocked the door and opened it.

I wasn't sure what I'd expected, but the room was in complete disarray. The dressers were toppled over in the middle of the room, and the bed had shifted against the far wall, the comforter wadded up on the floor and the pillows scattered around. The lamp on the desk had fallen over.

More surprising was that only one person was standing there. Warin was gone. I lifted a brow. "I didn't hear the vampire leave. How is that possible? Are you cloaking him?"

Glinda raised a hand, and wind whipped past me to the bed. It pushed the bed back into the center of the wall. "I didn't cloak the bloodsucker." Her nose wrinkled, and the skin around her warm brown eyes tightened, bringing out her crow's-feet. "He did the blur thing when he left, so you didn't hear him. That's all."

"The ...blur thing?" I rocked back on my heels, feeling like maybe my head was still foggy.

"Their vampire speed." She continued straightening the room but turned to me. "Oh, you don't know. The older vampires become, the faster they can move. Warin is one of the oldest alive today."

Good to know. "How old is that exactly?" If she was being forthcoming, I would pump her for all the information she was willing to share. "Or is that rude to ask of the supernatural?" I wasn't sure what the social norms were in this world.

She threw her head back and laughed. "Oh, it's so refreshing to talk to someone who doesn't know how the supernatural world works." She brushed a strand of silver hair from her face.

My blood jolted. I didn't like the way she was mocking me, especially when it wasn't my fault that I'd been raised by humans. "Glad I can entertain you."

"Oh, child." She frowned and placed the comforter back on the bed. She'd restored the room to the way it had looked before Warin came along. "I'm sorry. That was rude. I didn't mean to insult you. I was actually being sincere. In this world, everyone acts like they know everything about all the species and how they work, so it's refreshing to talk with someone who's open to learning."

I did want to learn, but it wasn't her place to teach me. I had Raffe, Lucy, Hecate, Slade, Gavyn, Cade, and Zella—someone from each species so I wouldn't learn only prejudices from the others. "Are you going to answer my question?" I raised a brow.

"Vampires like to flaunt their age. The older they are, the more influence and stamina they have compared to the younger ones." She lowered her hands and wiped a bead of sweat from her brow. She had to be in her seventies or eighties—at least, if she'd been human, that would have been my guess.

A sour taste filled my mouth. "The complete opposite of humans." Humans were already physically weaker than supernaturals, and knowing that supernaturals got stronger as they aged made things worse.

"And witches and wolf shifters." Glinda leaned against the dresser that held the television. "It's a good thing you got your magic under control, or I might not have been able to hold off Warin. I was about to knock him out, which wouldn't have boded well for our alliance."

"Alliance?" I tilted my head. "In what, kidnapping me?"

She ran a hand over her brown dress, smoothing out the wrinkles from the two pockets sewn into it. "We brought you here to protect you." She straightened and took a few steps toward me. "We have to ensure your mind remains untainted."

Uh ... *what*? I could think of a whole bunch to say to that, but one thing I'd learned from being bullied throughout my childhood was when to hold my tongue and keep my face neutral. *This* time, it was harder than ever before because of what I suspected she was talking about. One of the people she thought would "corrupt" me was *the* most important person in my life. My blood fizzed in tune with the hot anger flowing through me.

Mashing her lips together, she steepled her fingers. "You're upset."

Great. My mask must have cracked. "Why would you think that? I'm just very confused about why you would consider me corruptible. Is there a problem with the EEU board?" I couldn't help but make the jab, though I tried to sound as innocent as possible. The supreme priestess was the head of the board.

Glinda's shoulders drooped, reminding me of Mom whenever I disappointed her. She said, "I know you're upset because your magic surged, and I've been informed that your magic is linked with your emotions. And no, the supreme priestess would *never* taint your mind. She's the closest thing to a goddess the coven has, and she loves all her children."

If that didn't sound like a cult mantra, I wasn't sure what did. It sounded like something Glinda had heard repeated over and over until there was no thought behind the message. "Then who would corrupt me?" I batted my eyelashes, my blood inching closer to a hum.

"Wolf shifters, especially one in particular." She scanned me. "What happened to your nose? Did you hurt it against the barrier when you tried to escape?"

The gloves were off, which meant she would be careful about what she said, and she was testing me to see if I'd lie. "Yes. I didn't realize I couldn't leave the room, and I ran into what felt like a wall."

"That's a perimeter spell. I couldn't cast an aversion spell because it wouldn't work if you were determined to leave." She lifted a hand. "Do you mind if I check to see whether your nose is broken?"

I shook my head. "I'm fine. It stopped bleeding, and I'd hate to have it accidentally start again."

She pursed her lips. "You're making this situation difficult."

A warning tingle surged up my neck, and my blood hummed.

"Shit. Warin won't be able to resist if he smells you right now. I can *feel* the power radiating off you." She reached into her pocket and pulled out a syringe.

What the—?

Then she lunged.

CHAPTER THREE

Before I could move, the needle hit my arm, and her thumb pressed down on the plunger, injecting the drug. My T-shirt had given her an easy target.

Still, the floor shook underneath me from the hum of my magic.

Glinda yanked the needle from my arm, and the door handle to the room twisted. With her free hand, she lifted her palm toward it just as a vampire charged in. A gust of wind slammed into the attacker and tossed him back into the hallway.

With her other hand, she slid the desk against the door.

Between the floor shaking and my heart racing, I almost lost my balance as the drug kicked in. My legs became dead weight.

Multiple vampires banged against the bedroom door, and enough adrenaline pumped through me to keep me upright. Luckily, the hum didn't intensify, and soon, my blood eased into a fizz, and the floor stilled.

I groaned, hating the fear and anger that remained

constant in my chest. The intensity was nearly overwhelming now that everything else had calmed.

Each second, my blood calmed more, and the vampires' frenzy quieted. I hated being drugged, but at least the vampires were no longer making noise at my door. I hoped that meant they were gone.

I wobbled, and the world tilted underneath me as the drug got into my system.

"Let's get you onto the bed," Glinda said and moved to place her arm around me.

I jerked out of her reach. I'd rather fall than allow her to touch me after she'd drugged me. I teetered but stayed upright.

Weird.

I'd never been graceful before. That was new.

"S-s-stay back." My words slurred like I was drunk.

She raised both hands and stopped. "I'm sorry, but we're underground, and any structural compromise could jeopardize all of us. There are also five vampires down here who covet your blood when your magic is out of control. I had to do something before chaos erupted."

I snorted. "Every villain is the hero in their own story, but I'm not buying it. This is the second time you people have *drugged* me against my will."

"If I'd asked, you would've consented?" She arched a brow.

"That's not the point." My breathing slowed, and I anchored my focus on the strong sensation in my chest. It was the only thing I could feel with the drug in my system. "Don't try to paint a picture that's not real."

"We did it to help you so that you can see the truth of the brutality of the wolf shifters and how they control us." Glinda shook her head. "Believe me, I know this isn't ideal, but it is necessary."

I closed my mouth. Anything I said would be a repeat. I needed to stop expending energy arguing with her and focus on my goal. I kept waiting for sleep to take me, but I was able to remain standing.

She licked her lips. "Get some rest. I'm going outside to ward these vampires from entering your room. It'll be best for all of us if you can't get out and they can't get in. I'll come back with your dinner." She lifted a hand and removed the desk from the door.

Her words sank in.

Dinner.

Odd. It was right around that time that I'd gone into the woods looking for Raffe.

When she opened the door, I asked urgently, "How long have I been here?" If it was the same day, that meant I was close to campus. I'd been dead weight, so maybe Dave hadn't been able to carry me far. There was no telling how many secret locations these witches had on or near campus. Maybe Supreme Priestess Olwyn and Slade would find me.

"It's been a day." Glinda's shoulders sagged. "You were given too strong of a dose, which wasn't our intention. That's why you need to eat, especially after I gave you more of the same drug. I'll be back soon."

She exited and shut the door behind her, leaving me alone.

I'd thought I understood what isolation meant, but I'd never experienced *this*. Even with the drug numbing my emotions, my chest ached from the sob building inside. I closed my eyes, wishing I was back at the campus apartment with Raffe, Lucy, and Cat-Keith. The need was so desperate that I didn't think I could take being here anymore.

There was no way I could survive this without the drug in my system. My blood probably would've hummed and killed us all like Glinda feared.

Maybe drugging me had merit, but I would never admit that ... especially not to her.

With nothing else to do, I lay on the bed and let tears slide down my face as sleep overtook me.

"ONE MORE SIGN of losing control, and I swear, Warin, I will do whatever is necessary to protect her." Glinda's terse statement stirred me from sleep.

The scent of pineapple and mint clung to my nose, and my eyes popped open.

A man with gorgeous dark, wavy hair stood at the edge of my bed, his coal eyes narrowed as he stared at the older woman. "I'm fully in control. I won't be caught off guard again."

This was Warin? The two-thousand-year-old vampire? He appeared to be in his early thirties, if that and had scruff on his chin like so many men of that age. The only thing that set him apart was the way he held himself, but other than that, he wore an ordinary black button-down shirt and black slacks you could find anywhere. Even his skin was a nice tan color, as if he'd spent time in the sun, quite a contrast to Dave's and Zella's paleness. I would've thought he was human. Granted, his handsomeness was on par with the supernatural world.

"You didn't seem in control earlier today." Glinda rolled her eyes and placed a tray of food on the desk.

My stomach grumbled, and Warin's steely gaze swung to me.

Even with the drug in my system, my heart rate increased.

"How very human." He wrinkled his nose. "You'd think you'd learn to control yourself better than letting your stomach make all those noises."

His condescending tone got the best of me, and I snapped, "Like you controlled yourself earlier when you tried to drink from me?"

Jaw clenching, he flared his nostrils but didn't say a word.

"She has you there." Glinda chuckled and smacked Warin out of her way while pulling out the black rolling chair from behind the desk. "Come and eat."

Though I didn't trust either of them, I needed food for energy. If I wanted to keep up my strength to seize my chance for the first opportunity to get out of here, I had to be smart, not stubborn. Besides, I hadn't eaten in two days, and I had used a lot of power.

Sluggishly, I stood and made my way to the chair. As I passed Warin, a shiver ran down my spine.

He smirked, obviously noticing his effect on me.

And here I thought I'd never find someone I disliked more than Raffe's best friend, Keith.

There had to be a higher power with a horrible sense of humor who liked messing with me. I'd bet whoever it was called the game "How Can We Prove Skylar Wrong?"

Straightening my spine the best I could, given the circumstances, I slid into the seat and examined the food—a turkey sandwich, chips, and a bottle of water. Basic items that almost anyone would enjoy. I took a bite of the sandwich, trying to prove that Warin's presence didn't bother me.

Glinda sat in the white chair. "I hope the food is to your liking."

It was the best damn sandwich I'd ever had, but I wasn't sure if that was true or just the hunger talking. "It's fine.

Thanks." I figured I should be somewhat polite to see what information I could glean from them.

I tried to eat slowly, but I took a second bite as hunger clenched my stomach. The two of them watched me as if I were a freak show.

Now, *that* was something I was familiar with. That's the way Lizzie and the other kids I'd gone to school with had treated me.

I refused to fill the silence. They'd brought me here, and the more desperate I seemed for answers, the more control they'd have over me. That was how bullies had worked back in school too.

"You must be curious about why we brought you here." Glinda crossed her legs.

I swallowed my latest bite to make sure my words were clear. "You already told me the reason. To get me away from —" His name caught in my throat.

Raffe.

My fated mate.

I couldn't say it without letting them see how much he meant to me.

"Oh gods, did the drug kill her brain cells?" Warin crossed his arms and glared down his nose at me.

He must have thought the drug was the reason I'd stopped speaking. For once, something had gone my way. I blinked, playing the part. "What?"

"Wolf shifters, dear." Glinda lifted her chin, staring the vampire down. "We needed to get you away from the wolf shifters before they tainted your mind."

I opened the bottle of water, making sure the seal was intact. Not that it mattered. They could've put whatever they wanted in the food. But it gave me a sense of control. "Right."

Warin tapped one dress shoe on the floor. "Shouldn't we

talk to her when she's not drugged? It would make the conversation easier."

"So she can panic and her blood can make you lose your mind?" Glinda tilted her head. "Not happening. If you want to be here, this is how you get her."

He hissed but didn't say another word.

Interesting. She was the one in charge, and he didn't like it. Typical alpha male.

I opened the bag of chips and popped one into my mouth, then chewed loudly. As expected, Warin cringed, giving me a little satisfaction.

"Wolf shifters are amazing manipulators, especially when stringing someone along." Glinda pressed her lips together. "They're power hungry and use their influence to control everyone."

Unfortunately, the drug left me too loose with my reactions, and I laughed, nearly choking.

"My gods, what is she doing?" Warin took a step back, staring at me like I was scum.

That made me laugh harder.

"She's choking." Glinda grimaced. "I think."

I cleared my throat and took several gulps of water to get myself under control. "I'm sorry. I just find it hilarious that you called the wolf shifters power hungry and controlling when you kidnapped me and imprisoned me in a room. Isn't that the pot calling the kettle black?"

Neither one of them cracked a smile.

"Humans are so stupid." Warin lifted both hands. "We should just kill her. That would solve our problem." His fangs extended from his mouth, and I stilled.

He wasn't joking.

"Say that again, and I'll make sure you leave immediately." Glinda stood, her breathing rapid. "We're supposed to be working together. You may move faster than me, but all I need is to be quick enough to force you from the room and spell it so you can never reenter. And I will do it."

"How would killing me solve the problem?" That was something I needed an answer to.

"It doesn't *solve* the problem. He's trying to scare you." Glinda pursed her lips. "But you are important, which is why we did what we did."

My heart thudded. Please tell me she didn't know. "What do you mean?"

"You're the arcane-born we've been waiting for."

She *did* know. Word must have gotten out among the coven. "If you know that, why do you have vampires anywhere near me? You know how my blood affects them." That made no sense unless she wanted to make me dependent on her.

My stomach churned, and the food I'd eaten sat hard. Was this an act they'd concocted to make sure I trusted the witch more than the vampire?

"Because, in our circle, vampires and witches are equals and work together for a common cause," she replied simply.

Wait. "Circle? As in the supernatural world?"

"No, the organization Warin and I are part of. The Veiled Circle. It's a secret society that formed centuries ago with one goal. To diminish the power and influence of the wolf shifters so witches and vampires can have an equal say in matters, especially within their own species."

"Witches and vampires?" A lump formed in my throat. I didn't like the way that sounded. "What do you plan to do with the wolf shifters?"

Warin smiled so big I could see every tooth in his mouth. "Oh, they'll still be around, but the royal family and anyone who opposes us will be imprisoned, if not killed, for dissenting. Those *savages* have been in control for way too long, killing thousands of vampires needlessly just because we exist."

My skin crawled. Something about him was horribly off, but I supposed living for as long as he had might put his sanity at risk.

Worse, the idea of Raffe dead or imprisoned had my blood jolting despite the drug. "Why haven't you done that yet?"

"Because our organization is small but mighty. We include only those who are most trusted, which was why, when we saw the sign of your birth, we were excited." Glinda rubbed her hands together. "With your power, you can help us regain our rightful place, and vampires and witches can once again embrace who they truly are without hiding."

My heart froze. Knowing what I did about animal behavior, I assumed most of the wolf shifters would be against this secret organization. "You do realize that wolf shifters won't support the mistreatment of their alphas. There'll be too many rebellious shifters to take them all prisoner." They'd be talking about genocide.

"Good riddance." Warin shrugged. "Fewer wolf shifters to monitor."

Oh, I was sure the vampires would be more than happy with that. Fewer people around to kill them when they stepped out of line.

Glinda glared at him and said, "We're hoping that won't be the case, but we're aware of the possibility. Either way, the wolf shifters have proven to be able to reproduce effectively. Their heritage will survive, and the next generation will be more accepting of the change in leadership since they won't have lived with the present power structure."

Acid burned my throat. They wanted to mistreat people for mistreating them. Their whole mission was tainted, and they'd be perpetuating the same cycle, but I knew better than to say that out loud. "And what if I don't agree to work with you?" I had no doubt they wouldn't let me out of here alive.

"I'm not worried." Glinda lowered her hands at her side. "You're the arcane-born. The restorer of balance in the world. It's your duty and the whole reason you're alive here and now. With time, you'll see the truth and believe in our mission."

A faint knock sounded on the door before it opened.

A man with light-tan skin stepped inside, his eyes a light brown that contrasted with the thick eyeliner around his eyes. "Priestess Glinda, I hate to interrupt, but we have an issue. Can you come with me outside?"

She tensed and glanced at Warin.

Warin placed a hand over his heart. "I promise I'll behave. I won't harm her. Like you said, we're a team."

"You have two seconds." Glinda walked to the door and assured me, "I'll be right outside the door."

I wanted to beg for her not to go, but that would only give Warin more power.

When the door shut, Warin blurred the five feet toward me. His nose touched my neck, and he inhaled.

I tensed.

"Just to be clear, if you don't join our team, I *will* kill you," he whispered in my ear.

I gritted my teeth. "Back away. Glinda will return any second, and she won't like this."

He laughed, grabbed me by the neck, lifted me, and pressed my back to the wall.

CHAPTER FOUR

H is fingers dug into my neck, causing my blood to jolt, the worst thing possible around a vampire. At least it wasn't a fizz. I wasn't sure how I could protect myself if it came to that.

"I may be part of the society and must get along with the members, but that doesn't mean I must obey them." A sinister smile slowly spread across his face, and his thumb pressed harder into my artery. "If I think you're a risk, I'll eliminate you. For now, you get a pass, but know it's because *I* choose to allow it."

I hated how helpless I felt, and I missed the hum of my blood. Even if I couldn't control it, at least it did *something* to protect me—apart from the few times I could have died from it.

Raffe seemed to make that all better.

Warin leaned forward, raking his teeth against my neck. I jerked away, and he chuckled.

Dammit, I needed to not react, but how was that possible? I bit the inside of my cheek, and he leaned his head back so I could see his face once more.

His nose wrinkled, and he smacked his lips. "You taste faintly of wolf shifter, which lessens the allure of your blood. How is that possible?"

I swallowed hard, ignoring the increasing pressure of his hand. My blood must taste different because of my partially completed bond with Raffe. He'd bitten me when we'd had sex. He'd mentioned that his scent would change since he'd mated with me, but being human, I hadn't expected mine would as well. However, the thought of people knowing I was his thrilled me, especially if it made vampires pause before biting me.

The door opened, and Warin released his hold. My body slid down the wall until my feet touched the floor. Luckily, I somehow didn't crumple to the floor.

At least I'd kept a little dignity.

My throat throbbed where he had clutched it, but I forced my hands to remain at my sides. I'd already given the jackass too much power by reacting to his threat. My skin crawled as I thought of his teeth on me in the same place Raffe's had been. I wanted to wash the area and erase him tainting it from my mind.

"What in the stars do you think you're doing?" Glinda asked as she strode into the room. Her gaze settled on my neck, which was probably red.

Warin rolled his eyes. "Don't be so dramatic. I didn't *bite* her. I just wanted a little taste, which was greatly disappointing. She tastes of *wolf*."

"That makes this a whole lot more challenging." Glinda huffed and ran a hand through her hair. "I suspect she's Prince Wright's fated mate. He must have bitten her already."

I hadn't expected them to figure that out so quickly, but there was no way in hell I'd be ashamed of it. "Yes, we completed our bond before Dave kidnapped me." I lifted my chin, refusing to cower. My blood began to jolt as my emotions resurfaced, but I didn't want them to know the drug was wearing off. Glinda wouldn't hesitate to use a higher dose.

Warin hissed, and his fangs extended. "Then we kill her. If she's already loyal to the wolf shifters, she's a threat to us."

A gust of wind slammed into Warin, lifting him into the air, over the bed, and into the wall that connected to the bathroom. He was as far away from me as he could get.

It still wasn't far enough. He might be handsome on the outside, but he was ugly within. Before this was over, I vowed I would hurt him in any way possible. Nothing was off the table.

"We will *not* kill her. Yes, their connection complicates things, but this is a good thing. The goddess wouldn't allow her to be born at this time if she wasn't meant to make things right for our people." The wind ruffled the comforter, but the bulk of it remained directed at Warin. "If you can't behave, I'll get another vampire representative. We can use their bond to weaken the royals further."

"I won't help you." The last thing I'd ever do was cause Raffe problems. Clearly, Glinda didn't understand how fated mates work. "I can't live without Raffe."

"*See?*" Warin gritted out, his words muffled by the wind. "Have you ever seen a connection between fated mates? With your limited life and how rare they are, I think not, or you would feel differently about her."

"There's an easy solution to the problem." Glinda nodded at me. "We'll make sure that, once the power imbalance is resolved, Raffe stays close. We would never want to hurt you in any way, Skylar. You're the one who will help us make things better, and we wouldn't want you to be miserable. We can spell a room like we've done here, so you can have relations with him at your choosing."

She thought making Raffe available so I could have sex with him would make things okay? Warin was right. She had no clue how fated mates worked, but one thing was clear—I needed to get the fuck out of here.

"Warin, we need to talk." Glinda lowered her hand, cutting off the wind. "Skylar, finish eating, and I'll be back in a few minutes. There is something Warin and I need to discuss."

I nodded. I'd much rather be alone than with either of them. They were both awful in their own right. Glinda seemed nice, but she was the one drugging me and had made the stupid comment about keeping Raffe at my disposal. Warin was evil, but he was up front about how he felt. I needed to remember that I wasn't safe here with anyone.

Warin rolled his shoulders and ran a hand through his hair. His lustrous locks were tangled, but other than that, he stood straight and confident.

Something I was certain I'd never be able to muster.

When the door shut and I was alone again, I sat at the desk. I didn't want to eat, but I needed my strength. I took a sip of water and forced bite after bite down.

The strong emotion in my chest heated to a boiling rage, the likes of which I'd never experienced before. It was so strong that it nearly took my breath. If I smelled like a wolf, maybe my bond with Raffe had strengthened more than we'd realized it could because the essence inside me felt like Raffe. If it was him, he was upset, and that made me more desperate to get to him.

Taking a ragged breath, I closed my eyes and focused on the sensation.

"This isn't good," Glinda murmured.

My breath caught. The words were damn near inaudible, but with my eyes closed, I could make out Glinda and Warin's conversation as if my hearing were enhanced.

"Wolf shifters are coming into the woods." She huffed. "How is that possible? She's human."

"She's more than human. I keep telling you this." Warin huffed. "Their bond exists, at least partially. She smells of wolves, but you've spelled the outside, so they won't find the entrance. I'm not sure why you're worried."

Of course they'd hidden the entrance, same as they'd done with the coven library, but at least I knew Raffe was near and searching for me. If I could find a way out, I wouldn't have to go far to find him. A little bit of that hope surged within me.

"If he's anything like his father, he won't give up. I need to step up the timeline. I'd planned on letting Skylar get some rest, but we need to show her everything that the wolves have done to us in case something happens."

She was getting nervous, which was both good and bad. Good that the threat of Raffe finding me had her on edge, but bad because that could make them desperate. I couldn't have Warin attack me with the drug affecting my blood. There was no way I'd survive.

"Go keep watch while I talk to her alone," Glinda said. "You make her uncomfortable."

"If you want to waste your time on her, be my guest."

The doorknob turned, and I opened my eyes and took the last bite of my food. I didn't want to come off like I'd heard anything, so I tensed and glanced behind her as if I was expecting Warin to follow her.

"Don't worry." Glinda smiled and shut the door again. "Warin has some duties to handle, so it's just the two of us." Her gaze settled on the empty plate. "I'm glad you ate."

"I was hungry." I forced a smile. If I wanted them not to

get desperate, I had to play along. Besides, it would be good for me to see their side. They had followers, and there had to be some merit to their grievances. I suspected I already knew some of them, based on things Hecate and Zella had told me.

She licked her lips. "I understand that being kidnapped makes it more difficult for you to trust us, but I swear we don't mean you harm."

I sank back in my seat, wanting to appear sluggish. "I find that hard to believe. Warin has threatened to kill me several times."

"He's the pessimist of the organization." Glinda took a seat. "And vampires are known to lose their empathy over time. What the wolf shifters have done to them doesn't help. In fact, it's encouraged the vampires' withdrawal and isolation."

That was how she was going to spin it. It physically hurt to keep my eyes from rolling. "I've seen vampires on campus. I even stumbled on one feeding." I left out what had happened to Edward, knowing that would lead her in a certain direction. I wanted Glinda to guide the conversation.

"They can't eat in the cities anymore because the wolves ran them out." Glinda shook her head. "Vampires do best in large, populated cities. A vampire requires a substantial amount of blood, but the wolf shifters don't care. They think vampires are at risk of outing the supernatural world despite their hunting skills. Wolf shifters began killing vampires who hunted in cities, forcing them to live and feed remotely, which caused many vampires to become bloodthirsty. At first, vampires resorted to keeping human prisoners to help with their needs, but the wolf shifters began patrolling vampire households and killing any that held hostages. They said humans would be searching for the missing people. So now, most vampires live on the verge of being blood-crazed and can be near snapping."

The memory of Dave fighting his lust for my blood surged into my mind. Even though he'd helped kidnap me, I remembered the pain and hunger in his face when he'd fought for control while my blood was humming. "Is that why vampires struggle so hard when my blood hums?"

She nodded. "If they weren't on the verge of starvation, they wouldn't struggle as hard even though you would still be tempting."

Although the thought of a vampire feeding off someone didn't sit well with me, starvation wasn't good for anyone. "If the shifters lose their influence, the vampires will flock back to the cities and resume their feeding practices?" I suspected it wouldn't be that easy. If they were starving, they might go back and lose their minds and kill people.

"Of course. And if they're no longer underfed, vampires will start reproducing again. Since this change, they've struggled to reproduce, and there hasn't been a child born in fifty years." Glinda clasped her hands in her lap. "And the covens could again gather and perform rituals to strengthen our magic and practice our craft together." She inhaled dreamily. "I've heard stories of how all the covens used to meet and celebrate the solstices and scour the *Books of Twilight* to learn ancient spells and form new ones. So much of our history has been stripped away from us, and people who do visit the Evergreen Elite coven library must be careful and come in low numbers to prevent detection. The information isn't easily accessible, thus giving the wolf shifters more control."

"Wait ... vampires don't turn people?" If that was true, my heart ached for them even more. It wasn't fair if the wolf shifters were holding them back and keeping them from their history and their present potential.

Glinda mashed her lips. "No. Like wolves, vampires can't turn people with their bite. The books have it wrong."

Yet another element working against them. I hated that vampires were suffering and almost starving. "I understand. I want to know my heritage too, and I don't have access to any of that knowledge." Pieces of me were missing, and even though Raffe had filled a large part of the void, I needed to learn how to control my blood.

Glinda smiled. "See, I knew you'd understand. And the more we talk, the more you'll see things differently. We just needed to get you away from *them*."

My blood jolted, and I clenched my hands under the desk to hide my anger. "Raffe is different. If you'd talk with him and explain—"

She shook her head. "You're letting your bond cloud your judgment. Wolf shifters don't care about the covens and vampires. They care only about themselves and their packs' needs. They covet power. There will be no getting Raffe to *see*. He's a puppet for his father."

If I knew one thing about Raffe, it was that he thought for himself and didn't only do what his father told him. "He's not. He's a great man. If you give him a chance, you'll see—"

She stood and scowled. "That's enough. You need your rest. We'll continue this conversation tomorrow. I have evidence you need to see."

I wanted to yell, *wait*, but I swallowed the word. She was already annoyed with me.

The door shut, and I heard the click of the lock. Even though the drug was wearing off, I was exhausted. I crawled into bed and closed my eyes, pulling up an image of Raffe.

I'd do anything to be in his arms.

The anger in my chest molded into hurt, mirroring my

own. I clung to it, hoping it was a true connection to Raffe and fell asleep crying.

———

THE NEXT TWO days were the same as the last. The only difference was how much I was drugged. Warin was the administrator, and he enjoyed each injection time, using his vampire speed and strength to control me. I suspected they were using smaller and smaller doses because the medicine wore off faster each time.

I played the part of being very drugged, hoping they would eventually give me something that barely affected me and I'd have a greater chance to escape.

After the first day, I realized I had to change tactics. I stopped arguing on Raffe's behalf because, each time I did, Glinda became angry and left. I had to gain her trust. She seemed desperate for me to buy into her stories, probably because of what I'd overheard the other day.

I could also still feel the strange emotions within me, angrier and more determined every hour.

It had to be Raffe.

Today was the third full day of me being here conscious, and Glinda seemed more frenzied. I'd been forced to listen to her read various accounts of all the bad things the wolf shifters had done and were doing to vampires and witches. The stories were heartbreaking. Vampires dying from starvation. Covens isolated and not free to practice their magic the way the goddess intended.

I agreed that change was needed, but the problem was how the Veiled Circle wanted to handle it. They wanted to oppress the wolves and impose restrictions on them, such as not being able to shift and run and other things that would impact their health and happiness. The secret society wasn't about making things fair—it was about getting revenge for the injustices they felt had been inflicted upon them.

Both sides were in the wrong, but I couldn't do a damn thing about it right now. I was just a human with ancient magic, mated to a wolf-shifter prince. Glinda was treating me like I was the hope everything depended on.

Tonight, both Glinda and Warin watched as I ate my dinner. Warin didn't speak, just glared at me hatefully then administered the drug when he deemed I needed it. Controlling my blood by thinking of Raffe was becoming harder and harder when the medicine wore off.

I took a bite of the turkey sandwich, and Glinda paced in front of the desk, holding a manilla envelope in her hands.

Once I took my last bite, Warin grinned.

He rarely smiled, and when he did, it was invariably about something that would be to my detriment.

"I've been waiting for the right moment to share this with you." Glinda tapped the envelope in her hand. "And I think that's now—since you've become so open to listening to us the past few days."

I nodded slowly, acting as if the drug had taken effect.

"Now I need you to see." She removed a few photographs from the envelope and placed them on the desk in front of me.

My stomach clenched, and my blood fizzed.

No.

CHAPTER FIVE

I blinked, thinking the image would change, but it didn't.

A lump formed in my throat that was so large I couldn't swallow.

The first picture had been taken outside a small one-story brick warehouse that looked abandoned. Raffe stood at the back entrance by a beat-up metal garage door, waving toward the building with ten men stepping from the woods behind him, including Adam and Keith, which wasn't surprising. There was no telling how many more weren't in the frame. In their black clothing, they blended in with the night.

The next picture was from inside the warehouse. The garage door was opened, and a fight was underway. Raffe was stabbing a vampire in the heart while the other men were attacking fifteen vampires clustered together. I searched for captive humans but couldn't find anyone who looked scared or restrained. In fact, everyone there was angry. Everyone fighting looked supernatural.

Why were the wolves attacking? There had to be a reason.

"Why are you showing me these?" I understood that she

wanted me to see Raffe differently ... to see him as a puppet or an aggressor.

"This was a warehouse for a liquidation shop that went out of business five years ago." Warin tapped the image of Raffe. "Someone alerted the wolves that a group of vampires were staying at the edge of the city, and Raffe organized the attack. There were no humans there, and all fifteen vampires were killed."

Glinda removed another photo that showed fifteen corpses on the ground and puddles of blood across the cement floor. Blood was spattered over the eleven wolf shifters with Raffe being the bloodiest.

My stomach churned, the half sandwich I'd eaten not sitting well.

No. I scanned the shot, but all I saw was a door that led outside, nowhere for a human to be hidden.

I tried swallowing unsuccessfully. "There has to be a reason they did this."

"Oh, there is." Warin straightened and went still as a statue. Right when I thought he wasn't going to explain, he spoke, startling me. "They didn't like how close the vampires were to the city even though it was a smaller population outside of Silverton, Oregon. That was their 'reason.'"

Silverton was a small city about an hour from here, so proximity must be why Raffe had led the charge. With all the grievances the covens and vampires had against the wolf shifters, I understood how disheartening this could be, and worse, these photos made me wonder if I knew Raffe at all.

That had to be Glinda's plan and damn if it wasn't effective. Still, I refused to be manipulated. There were always two sides to any story. Though I wasn't sure how Raffe could have a good reason for *this* slaughter.

"Warin, we've shown her enough." Glinda clucked her

tongue. "Look at the poor girl. She's pale and shaking."

I glanced at my hands. They were visibly quivering. Shit. I clasped them together and straightened my back. "Seeing all those people like that ..." I shuddered. Though I was used to blood from my studies, it usually belonged to animals and wasn't the result of anger or maliciousness. Even though I wasn't looking at the pictures anymore, the glint in Raffe's eyes would stay with me. "It's ... hard." I'd like to paint the supernaturals as animals, but whether I wanted to admit it or not, humans had the same tendency toward violence, war, and power.

"Her blood has a hint of an intoxicating coppery smell." Warin sniffed, breathing it in. "It smells as if her medicine is wearing off." He smiled creepily.

Without pausing, Glinda lifted a syringe from her pocket. Just like the past few days, Warin's hand blurred as he snatched it, and I tried to stand to get out of the way, though it was pointless. But just sitting here and letting them drug me, as though it were inevitable, made me feel as if I was giving in or breaking. I needed to fight back, even only on principle.

The needle sank into my arm before I could put weight on my feet, and my blood fizzed. Warin's pupils dilated, and the rims around his irises turned a faint red.

Strange.

I'd never noticed that before. A chill ran down my back, and something warm churned inside me. I had this feeling whenever Warin drugged me.

He and Glinda felt proud of themselves, and I knew why. They'd made me doubt Raffe, and I hated that I'd allowed them to see that.

"Leave before you get out of control," Glinda commanded as she took the empty syringe from Warin's hand. "If you don't, I'll make you."

He frowned and swallowed, his Adam's apple bobbing. His breathing quickened from being near me, but the drug began to kick in, and my blood eased.

Soon, my limbs would be hard to move for a couple of hours. I'd be so lethargic that the two of them could do anything they wanted to me with very little fight.

"I'm better now." Warin exhaled. "Her magic is calming."

Between the drug and the pictures I'd seen, I didn't have the energy to keep up any sort of charade around them. I placed my hands on the desk and pushed back slowly, not wanting to lose my balance. "Thank you for the information and food, but I need to be alone."

Glinda touched her chest. "I'm sure you do. It must be hard, seeing the proof and then coming to terms with the fact that the wolf shifter you trusted has been manipulating you." She waved toward the bedroom door. "We should respect her wishes."

"There's so much more we could show her, though." Warin pouted and crossed his arms.

Even as my body calmed, my heart beat faster than it should've been able to. What else could they show me? I didn't want to know the answer because I feared their plan would succeed. Something inside me prickled with hot anger that I'd allowed someone to make me think differently of Raffe. Soul mates or not, we weren't perfect people, and maybe his dad had more influence over him than I realized. He'd wanted to keep me secret and feared retribution. Fear had a way of making you do things, and I understood that more than anyone.

"Look at her." Glinda *tsk*ed. "We can't do that to her. We'll show them tomorrow. We don't want to overwhelm her all at once."

Warin rolled his eyes. "Fine. She is *human*, or mostly, but

I will show her more tomorrow. She needs to see that we aren't in the wrong and the shifters need to be stopped."

My mouth went dry. I didn't want to see any more pictures, but I also needed to know what Raffe and his dad had been up to. There had to be a way to convince Raffe he couldn't follow in his dad's footsteps and needed to right the wrongs they'd done. No species or person deserved to be starved, slaughtered, and bullied, and I refused to be with someone who treated people like that, so I had to believe he could change.

I wanted to wrap my arms around myself, but I forced them to remain at my sides until the two of them left.

"I'll come back later for your tray." Glinda leaned over and patted my arm. "That will give you time to settle and eat."

After those images, I couldn't imagine having an appetite tonight. The food was still sitting way too heavily in my stomach. "No need. I'm done. I just want to sleep." I yawned, not even attempting to hide it like normal.

"Very well." Glinda took the tray as Warin exited the room. "I guess I'll see you in the morning." She left the water on the table and carried the items from the room.

Once the door shut, the weight of everything pressed on me. I couldn't believe that Raffe would do something like that to anyone, even vampires. At least the vampire who'd attacked me in the woods had shown he wasn't rational and could have killed me and other humans. I understood Raffe's decision to kill him. But vampires hiding out in a warehouse alone didn't sound worthy of execution. If the shifters didn't want them there, they could have told them to leave instead of *attacking* them.

Taking a deep breath, I spun the chair around and scooted closer to the bed. With the drug in full effect, moving those three feet took a few minutes.

Once there, I plopped onto the bed and rolled into the center. Now that I was here, I had nothing to do but stare at the ceiling and let my mind wander.

No matter how I tried to control my line of thought, it kept coming back to those pictures. My heart ached as doubt about Raffe crept in. A picture had a way of telling a story, but not the whole one. I wouldn't know more until I talked to Raffe and heard his side of things.

That was when I became more certain than ever.

I had to get out of here. They were poisoning me against Raffe, which wasn't right because he wasn't here to defend himself. They would continue to do that and show me more and more "proof" until I agreed with their side. That's how manipulators worked and why they were so effective.

The best thing I could do was sleep off the drug. Then I'd find a way out of here, no matter what.

My eyelids became heavy, and instead of fighting to keep them open like I usually did, I slowly succumbed to sleep.

———

THE DOORKNOB TURNED, and my eyes fluttered open.

"Let me *go!*"

The familiar male voice had my heart squeezing.

Slade.

"Shut up," Warin snarled. "And get in there!"

The door swung open fast and hit the wall with a bang. Light from the hallway streamed into the room, and Slade stumbled inside. Blood poured from his nose, and he was hunched over, clutching his stomach. "You damn bloodsucker, you won't get away with this!"

Warin blurred inside and kicked Slade in the stomach. A

strangled scream lodged in my chest as Warin spun and exited, slamming the door and locking us inside.

The drug was halfway burned off in my system. I moved more sluggishly than normal, but I sat up. Even in the darkness, my eyes adjusted, and I could see Slade slumped against the wall. "Slade," I whispered, my voice hoarse from sleep.

His head snapped toward me. "Sky?" His emerald eyes bulged, and he clambered to his feet awkwardly. "Is that really you?"

The two of us shuffled toward each other and embraced.

Tears poured down my face. Finally, someone I trusted was here with me.

"Hey, it's okay. You're not alone anymore." He rubbed his hands up and down my arms. His dark-blond scruff prickled my cheek, and the deep void inside me ached.

I wanted Raffe.

This moment suddenly felt wrong, and I stepped backward with a bitter laugh. "That's not *okay*. You shouldn't be here." I stared at his face and noted that his spiky blond hair was full of dirt, and blood had dried on his lip and congealed at his nostrils. "We need to clean you up." I took another step back and almost lost my balance.

"Whoa." He clutched my arms, stabilizing me, and winced. "Are you okay?"

"Yeah." I straightened, not wanting to put more weight on him while he was injured. "Just drugged. Didn't they do the same to you?"

He smiled then wrapped an arm around his waist and groaned. "They think they did. Warin snuck up on me on campus while we were searching the woods for you, and he tried to inject me with the drug. I managed to kick him away before he could empty the entire syringe in me, but it was enough to impact me. Then he beat the shit out of me." He rubbed his ribs and winced. "I'm pretty sure he broke a fucking rib. I can't breathe without my ribs hurting worse at this point."

There wasn't anything you could do for a broken rib other than rest. "You should lie down on the bed." I pointed at the spot where I'd been lying. "That should take the edge off the pain." At least, I hoped it would. I needed him to heal before Warin came back.

He shook his head. "I'm good. I don't want to lie down." He scanned the area.

"There's no way out." I shook my hands to help the drug wear off. "The door has a perimeter spell we can't cross."

Slade froze. "Perimeter spell? Vampires can't use magic." He turned to me, his face strained. "How is that possible?"

I swallowed uncomfortably. He didn't know. "A witch is involved. Her name is Glinda."

His face fell. "No fucking way."

Something like a faint eggy fart hit my nose. I held my breath, not wanting to smell it. He'd broken a rib and got kicked in the gut—he probably didn't realize he'd passed gas. The last thing I wanted to do was call him out on it, so I tried to focus on the conversation. "Yeah, why are you surprised by that?"

"She's Mom's most trusted priestess. No one's been able to reach her since before you disappeared." He ran a hand through his hair. "Why would she do this?"

I filled him in on everything I'd learned, leaving out the pictures of Raffe and the wolves killing vampires.

When I finished, noises sounded outside the door.

Slade and I stared at one another, waiting for the door to open, but the faint scuffle of footsteps headed away.

Slade shook his head. "Shit. This isn't good. This must be why Warin took me. We've got to alert Mom and Raffe."

I tensed and tilted my head. "You want to alert *Raffe*? I thought you'd be behind the wolf shifters losing control."

"Yeah, I am. But taking me gives Glinda control, and don't you think kidnapping people goes a touch too far? We need to stop whatever she's doing before it goes further."

On that, we were in agreement. "I'm not sure what we can do. I've tried getting out of here with no luck. The vent is too small, and those blinds just cover a painting of the outdoors." That latter part killed me.

"Seriously?" His brows furrowed. "So we're in some sort of underground bunker."

"Once you heal, maybe we can find a way out." I hated to think how long that would take and what they'd make me look at and learn about until then, but I couldn't escape and leave Slade behind.

"We can't wait." He shook his head. "They'll keep drugging us, and right now, I can use my magic. I'm also at my weakest physically, so our captors won't expect us to try."

His determination to leave had me more eager than before. "But your ribs ..."

"I'll be fine. It's important that we get out of here tonight." He went to the door and placed his ear to the wood. After several seconds, he pulled away. "The hall is empty, so we need to run. I can heal once we get out of here."

He turned the doorknob and raised his brows when it opened.

"Yeah, they don't lock it because of the perimeter spell," I murmured, heading toward him. He wasn't listening to me.

Turning to me, he grinned. "Watch this." He raised a hand, and I braced myself for the impact.

But something else happened.

CHAPTER SIX

H is hand passed through the threshold into the hallway. My breath caught. "How did you do that? I'm pretty sure that was Glinda outside the door a few minutes ago. The area should be spelled."

Slade winked. "There's a little secret that even most priestesses don't know. The supreme priestess isn't affected by her fellow coven members' magic. Since my magic is inherited from hers, I have the same immunity."

That damn hope expanded uncomfortably in my chest. "You need to go while you can and let the others know where I am." Even though I couldn't get out, Slade could, and then help would arrive. He could walk through whatever magic was hiding the entryway from them as long as his ribs didn't hinder his escape.

Some of that hope dissipated, but this was the best plan we had, even if Glinda and Warin took out their frustrations on me. "Hurry before they realize you're missing and move me."

"I'm not leaving you." He held out his free hand to me. "Take my hand, and we can get out together."

I could leave too?

My chest ached from the pressure, and without another thought, I stepped forward and took his hand.

"Don't let go of my hand until we're in the hallway." He moved without warning.

Thankfully, he was holding me tightly because he tugged me and I stumbled right after him. As I crossed the threshold, the magic surrounding it chaffed against my skin.

Weird. Why would it be that much more intense? I'd have to ask later when we didn't need to be quiet.

I scanned the corridor. My room was at one end. The two of us tiptoed down the hallway, and even at the slow pace, I wanted to smack Slade over the head. His shoes left a slight scuff mark with each step that would give us away. But I had to remember he had at least one broken rib. There was no way I could get angry at him, so I bit my tongue.

Noises came from behind the doors on both sides of the hall. I wasn't sure what those rooms were, but people were in them.

I grimaced and tried to remain calm. Even though I'd heard multiple vampires out here, desperate to drink my blood when it was humming, for the past few days, it had felt like Glinda, Warin, and I were alone. The others must be in charge of guarding the area, meaning we could run into someone at any time.

One thing at a time. My blood jolted, beginning to wake up as the drug wore off. I bit my bottom lip to expel some of my nervous energy. If I didn't control my blood, the vampires would smell me and attack before we made it out.

"I'm shocked to say this, but I have to agree." Warin snickered, the sound coming from an opening down the hallway to the left. "Skylar found the photographs of Raffe and his minions atrocious. I thought their bond would prevent her from seeing things clearly, but the others may very well be right. He might not have completely brainwashed her ... *yet.* When she sees the other pictures, she won't be able to look at him the same way again. Not even a fated-mate bond could fix that."

Acid burned my throat. I'd hoped they were full of it, but they were having this conversation when they didn't know I could overhear them, validating their claims. What had Raffe's father put him up to? Though, I couldn't blame his father entirely because, at the end of the day, Raffe was accountable for his own actions.

Slade touched my arm, bringing me back to the present. Shit. I had to pay attention and deal with the fallout of Raffe and his choices once we got the hell out of here. Even if the Veiled Circle's cause had merit, their execution was just as bad as that of the wolf shifters because I had no doubt they would do the same thing in retribution. As my parents said, two wrongs didn't make a right, and they'd coached me to handle my bullies with that in mind.

But here was the thing. They were right, but that didn't mean a third person shouldn't have intervened and knocked some sense into both sides.

Forcing the thoughts from my head, I followed Slade. Despite my slowness and Slade's scuffing, we somehow reached the end of the hallway, which turned only to the left.

"She's more open-minded than I thought a human could be," Warin said, his voice coming from the left of the room we were about to enter. "I don't like admitting when I'm wrong, but Glinda could be right. She could be the answer to our cause."

Turning to me, Slade gestured for me to come to him.

"We coven members may not live as long as your kind does, but we understand nature and magic in a way vampires never will," Glinda said proudly. "And you'd best recognize that and realize there are some things, like Skylar, that we inherently know."

I didn't like how she kept emphasizing me. For the first time in my life, someone found me important, and I didn't like it. Being an outcast had its perks.

When I reached Slade's side, my gaze landed on a dining room table in the center of the room in front of us with a kitchen behind it. Slade pointed to the dining room then to the right.

Some of the weight lifted from my chest. At least we were heading away from Warin. With his speed and strength, Slade and I couldn't take him. Not with the drug still in my system and Slade injured.

Slade moved forward, keeping to the right edge of the dining room. I followed, not wanting to be left behind.

Silence filled the space as whoever they were talking to responded. They must be on the phone.

A door shut somewhere in the kitchen, making my heart gallop. Of course, my blood inched to a low fizz, following my emotions.

"Do you smell that?" a female voice asked from the kitchen.

It had to be a vampire.

Slade glanced at me and flinched.

"Yes. It smells like *her*," a male responded.

Slade grabbed my elbow and began dragging me through a threshold on the right.

"Sire, she's *escaping*," the same woman said from somewhere close behind me.

We entered a mudroom, and my socked feet slipped on the tile floor. Shit. I hadn't put on my shoes. That was what happened when you'd been confined to a room for several days. You became spacey and dissociated.

The thick door we faced looked *promising*, like it led outside. My blood came alive. We were almost free.

A large hand gripped my free arm and yanked me away from Slade. I spun and kicked a dark-skinned male vampire in the stomach. His eyes bulged, and his mouth dropped open, revealing his sharp, extended vampire teeth as he stumbled back.

Shit, they were getting bloodthirsty, and my blood was at a high fizz.

A female vampire blurred toward me, her fangs extended as she aimed for my neck.

She wanted to drink my blood.

"Fuck," Slade groaned. He lifted his hand and shot a strong spray of water over my shoulder into the vampire's face, mere inches from my neck.

As the water pushed her backward, she clung to me, digging her long, black-polished nails into the skin of my upper arm.

"It's not working," I gritted out, the stinging pain stealing my breath.

Warin and Glinda appeared behind the male vampire, who was righting himself.

The water poured harder from Slade's hand. The female vampire gurgled and loosened her grasp. When her nails retracted enough, I yanked my arm back and broke free.

Flames flowed from Glinda's hands toward me.

My blood was humming, and Warin and the other male vampire gnashed their teeth and barreled toward me. The humming circulated through my body and pushed outward, causing the entire place to shake.

Heat hit my left arm moments before the flames burned

my skin. The throbbing pain took my breath away. Another spout of water shot past my other side, dousing the fire.

Slade.

"Get behind me so I can hold them off," Slade gritted out. "And open the damn door."

He didn't have to tell me twice.

Dust blew into my face as a few chunks of cement fell from the ceiling.

I was out of control.

I ducked under Slade's arm and went for the door.

As soon as I saw it, I realized we were screwed. It was a heavy-duty, metal, double-key door, where you had to have the key to unlock it from either side.

Fuck.

"Sky, you need to calm down and open that door before you bury us alive," Slade said breathlessly.

Between his injured ribs and using his magic, he wouldn't last long. If I didn't figure out a way out of this hellhole, we would be trapped here for the foreseeable future. They wouldn't make the mistake of underestimating Slade again. And if I didn't calm down, the vampires would drain me dry.

Unsure what to do, I stared at the lock. Glaring at it wouldn't hurt its feelings and get us out of here.

The walls cracked under the pressure, and the floor and ceiling shook and creaked in tune with my blood.

"I can't hold on much longer, and if you don't get your power under control, we're all going to die!" Slade shouted.

Die. No. That couldn't happen. I couldn't die without seeing Raffe one more time and giving him a proper goodbye.

Not sure what to do, I placed my hands over the lock and pulled up Raffe's image in my head, focusing on the one person I needed to see before I died. The only thing standing in my way was this lock, and I needed it to fucking open.

The hum channeled through my body and centered itself in my palms. The ceiling, floor, and walls stopped shaking, and the door took the brunt of the force.

"Sky," Slade rasped.

My pulse raced faster, and the metal warped in front of my eyes. The section of the door that held the lock was pulled away from the jamb, and the door began to collapse in on itself. I grabbed the handle and yanked hard while holding my breath.

Something miraculous happened.

The door gave way and opened, and my back slammed into Slade's.

He jerked forward and landed on his knees, halting his magic, and the world roared. I spun around to help him to his feet, but the vampires were on us. Teeth sank into my neck, and I gripped the back of the vampire's head. I wasn't sure who was on top of me, but another set of teeth sank into the other side of my neck. I fell onto my back as Slade screamed, "Skylar!"

The vampires sucked small gulps of my blood as a third bit into my wrist. They grunted as if they didn't want to drink but were compelled to. If I didn't get them off me, they would drain me.

My blood hummed stronger than ever before, and rocks clattered all around.

"No!" Glinda yelled.

"Run!" I cried, wanting Slade to get out of here while the vampires were distracted.

He must have realized that my death was imminent because he stood and ran past me.

At least one of us had gotten free, and I'd take my captors out with me.

I closed my eyes and focused on Raffe—his ice-blue eyes

that warmed only for me. With each sip the vampires took, their fangs dug in deeper to get straight to my blood and not taste my skin. The coppery scent of my blood nearly made me vomit. The pain was all-consuming.

Liquid poured over me, and my chest constricted. They must have nicked an artery.

This would be over in seconds.

Then something strange happened. The vampires at my neck slowly retracted their teeth and started to gag.

"Get up, and let's go," Slade gritted out as water rushed past.

He was running out of magic.

Warin and the other male vampires were hunkered over, choking on the water Slade was firing at them, leaving only one vampire for me to deal with. I reached down and gripped the long hair of the vampire at my wrist then yanked hard. The teeth retracted, but some of my skin shredded as she released her hold. I kneed her in the face and scrambled to my feet.

I was woozy, but I managed to stand up. Then I saw something that petrified me and made me forget all about my blood loss.

Three more vampires were trying to reach me, but Glinda was holding them off, protecting me.

Why?

The ceiling over the battered door shook harder. Slade shut off his water, grabbed me by the waist, and dragged me over the threshold as my blood hummed harder.

It was so strong, and I couldn't control it.

"Sky, move. Please," Slade murmured, sounding agonized. "Calm down and help me get us out of here. I can't pull you anymore."

Warin and the dark-skinned vampire recovered, and their

gazes homed in on me.

I got my feet under me and rushed out behind Slade, damn near slipping on the cold, wet, rocky floor as we exited a tunnel that hid the door to the underground bunker. Drops of water hit my face as the bunker ceiling crumbled, blocking the captors inside, but then the door suddenly morphed into a rocky embankment. The door had vanished.

Shit. They'd been cloaking it with magic. No wonder Raffe couldn't find me.

The ground shook from the impact, and I could only assume that the roof had collapsed, and I slipped again. Water pelted me in the face, forcing me farther back.

"Be careful, or you'll fall," Slade rasped, grabbing my shirt and pulling me to his side. "You need to calm down."

It hit me where we were.

Underneath a waterfall, on a ledge no more than five feet wide. The waterfall hit the edge where I'd been standing.

This kept getting better and better, and he was right. I had to calm down, or this small ledge would crumble away. I closed my eyes and pictured Raffe again.

My blood soothed to a high fizz, calming enough that we weren't in imminent danger. "How do we get down?"

"There." Slade pointed to the left. "We have to climb down the rocks."

It looked like a drop-off. Lovely. "You expect me to be able to do *that*?" I didn't do physical exertion—or rock climbing—for a reason.

He sighed. "That's our only option, and there's no way I can carry you."

I shivered, the adrenaline wearing off and the October chill setting in. Standing here wet wasn't doing me any favors. "Fine." He was right. There was no point in complaining. This was the hand we'd been dealt.

"I'll go first and help guide you." Slade walked slowly around me to the edge.

Fear curled its cold claw into my stomach, but I pushed it aside. Freezing up—no pun intended—wouldn't do me any favors.

"Slow and steady. I won't leave you behind." Slade touched my arm and forced a smile.

I wished it had given me more confidence.

He went over the edge, and I followed suit. I tried to place my hands and feet exactly where he did, hoping like hell that my clumsiness didn't kill us.

My arms and legs burned, but the climb wasn't as awful as I'd feared.

When we got out from directly under the waterfall, he started making his way down more quickly.

"I'll tell you when to move and help guide your feet." He climbed down farther.

I moved to where he'd been a second before and waited for his command. The wind picked up. I shivered, and my teeth began to chatter. I hadn't been this cold in a long time.

"Okay, lower your right foot six inches," he commanded from below. "You'll feel something smooth you can brace it on."

Gritting my teeth, I followed his instructions, but I couldn't find the groove. Then my fingers slipped. "Slade," I said urgently.

"You're almost there," he assured me. "Just keep moving."

That was the thing. It wasn't happening. "I'm slip—"

Before I could finish that sentence, my hands lost their grip.

Not wanting to land on him, I pushed off with my legs, missing him by mere inches, and fell toward the rocky and shallow edge of the pond over a hundred feet below.

CHAPTER SEVEN

I fell backward, my eyes locked with Slade's as the wind rushed past me. With death rushing toward me, I couldn't feel the cold anymore.

That strange presence churned inside me while my blood remained calm, mixing with the warmth of what could only be hope in my chest.

Slade lifted a hand, and his face twisted with fear as he focused on me.

He was going to watch me die.

Somehow, that made it worse.

I closed my eyes and imagined Raffe, not wanting Slade's face to be my last memory, and water surrounded me. My back stung from the impact, but the water forced my body to slope downward like I was riding a wave to the center of the deep pond.

Slade.

He'd used his magic to save me.

As my body became immersed in the water, the wave settled back without even a ripple. I wasn't sure how that was possible, but the respect I had for Slade and his abilities grew. There was no way an amateur could've done that.

In the still water, my body sank. The wounds on my neck burned, and my eyes smarted. I surfaced and gasped, treading water. My blood was eerily calm. Normally, it would've been fizzing. I feared that maybe my loss of blood was making me woozy.

How bad would it be to drown after what Slade had done to save me? I didn't need to help my bad luck out by forgetting to swim.

As I paddled to the bank, the wound on my wrist stung, but I bit the inside of my cheek, needing to make it out of the pond. There was no telling how fast the vampires and the witches could break through the rock, and Slade and I couldn't fight them off much longer, especially with Slade climbing down the rocky edge with broken ribs. I suspected if he could've used his magic, he would've used his connection to water to help us escape faster. He must have used up most of his magic by helping me.

I reached the edge of the pond and clutched onto grass, roots, and weeds to hoist myself onto dry land. My limbs felt like heavy weights. My wrists and neck burned, and the fatigue from the blood loss and the exertion was catching up to me. Then, the sound of rocks jostling behind the waterfall had that presence inside me surging forward, forcing me up to my full height.

The vampires and Glinda were working on getting out. I didn't have time to rest.

I studied the waterfall. The water poured continuously, making the area behind it hard to see, but even if it hadn't, the illusion spell hiding the entrance meant I wouldn't be able to see what was happening.

Slade was close to the bottom, his movements jerky, revealing his pain.

The sensation in my chest increased in warmth, making my body ache. The yearning sensation was most definitely not my feeling.

I hurried around the pond to reach Slade. He needed assistance, and even though I was weak, I had to help him. He was the reason I was free.

As I reached the edge, he lost his grip and slid the remaining ten feet down. His face hit the rock, reopening the wound on his nose, and he tried to gain traction against the wall with his fingers, bloodying the tips.

I grabbed him and managed to slow him down by placing a hand on each ass cheek.

Lovely.

"You're at the bottom," I grunted as I tried to keep my balance and ease him down. When his feet hit the ground, I released him, and he crumpled. I managed to grab an arm and wrap it around my shoulders.

That was when rocks shot through the waterfall and splashed into the pond beside us.

Warin, Glinda, and the others were either out or too damn close for comfort. Slade and I needed to put distance between us and them, especially since the vampires could move faster than us.

"Go. You can run farther without me." Slade tried to jerk his arm free, but he moaned from the effort.

In hindsight, helping him like this wasn't good for his ribs, but it wasn't like he could get on my back. Even if he could, I couldn't support his weight. "I'm not leaving you. You got me out of there, and we're in this together." I refused to sacrifice someone else to save my own ass. I couldn't live with myself.

"Fine," he gritted out as we moved.

We started out awkwardly and out of sync. Every time I moved my left foot, he would move his right. But after a few steps and several whimpers, we found a groove.

"They're right there. See, I told you they wouldn't get far," Warin called from the waterfall's ledge.

My blood jolted. I had to keep it from activating.

"Dammit." Slade missed a step and grunted. "I can't use my magic much anymore. I'm too hurt and drained. That little bit I used to save you when you fell was pushing it."

His words weighed on me. Was that why he was struggling more than he had been? I laughed humorlessly. "And you thought I would leave you." All the hesitation I'd had about becoming friends with him again vanished. He'd tried to pressure me into a relationship, but maybe he'd thought that was the best way to protect me, and I'd read the situation all wrong. I'd felt like he didn't care about my wants or needs. I hadn't thought twice about it due to how Raffe had reacted and the fact the two of us had gotten closer. Regret squeezed my heart. I should've been willing to talk to Slade alone.

Howls sounded in the distance, and my heart leaped. Was it Raffe?

But they'd never reach us before the vampires and witches caught us.

We had to delay Glinda and the vampires.

The trickle of a spring caught my attention. Maybe the mud could hide us. I turned right toward the sound.

"That's not the way out." Slade tried to continue straight, but I pressed forward.

"There's shallow water running this way," I murmured, quiet enough that the vampires couldn't hear. "Maybe mud will mask our scent. We won't get far before they catch up." Animals like white-tailed deer and Tuatara lizards rolled in mud to mask their scent from predators. If it was good enough for the animal kingdom, where there was always a threat, then I'd follow suit in the hope of continuing the survival of the smartest.

Slade stopped fighting me and followed my lead. We passed through fir trees, and the stream came into view. It was a couple of feet wide but not deep enough to swim in.

The two of us plopped onto the embankment and slathered mud over ourselves. Luckily, there weren't too many rocks, and we made good time, but my wrist and neck stung from caking mud on my wounds. This would probably lower our core temperatures and cause infection in our wounds, but if we didn't do it, we might not live long enough.

"This way," the woman vampire said.

The voice was way too close for comfort, close to the end of the pond. I quickly finished covering myself and turned to help Slade, who had only covered his face and hands and was struggling to bend over.

Without hesitation, I worked from the bottom up. The mud stuck to us like oatmeal to a bowl, and chills racked my body.

Once he was covered, a twig snapped close by, and my heart raced.

The vampires were nearly on top of us.

More howls sounded, much closer than before. The odd presence inside me inched forward. We'd bought some time, but if we didn't move, the wolves would never reach us. I waved for Slade to follow me.

Warin stepped into view fifteen trees away, on the path where Slade and I had come from.

As I feared, they were following our scent.

"They're this way," Warin murmured. "What are the four of you doing?"

"Don't you hear the wolves?" the dark-skinned man asked.

"They're close."

"And so are we. We still have time to find them and leave."

Slade gritted his teeth and lifted a hand. Suddenly, a portion of the stream next to us hovered in the air and slammed into Warin. The water splashed down, obscuring our path.

Warin flew backward several feet as Slade and I climbed to our feet and ran away from the trail that led to the bunker.

Adrenaline had to be rushing through Slade because he kept up with me despite his injuries. Still, he was moving slower than normal, just keeping pace with a human.

Trees blurred past as we ran, but I could hear the pants of the vampires gaining on us. I shuddered, feeling very much like prey again. It reminded me of the first time a vampire attacked me.

Slade's feet dragged against the ground, helping the vampires track us. We had to hide before they were on us. Out of the corner of my eye, I noticed thick brush and snagged Slade's hand, leading him toward it.

He nodded, and we dropped to our knees and shuffled under the brush. I went in as deep as I could, the limbs digging into my back. Slade's front half stuck out. I grabbed his waist and yanked him as hard as I could, the brush limbs rustling.

The vampires' footsteps slowed.

"Did you hear that?" The shortest male vampire stepped into view, scanning the area.

A breeze picked up, rustling the branches and causing some needles to fall to the forest floor.

"It's the wind, Mylo." The woman vampire rolled her eyes and sniffed. "But where the fuck did they go? I can't smell them, and I don't hear them running anymore."

I breathed slowly, doing my best not to make any noise. I pulled up Raffe's face in my mind, picturing his strong jawline and full lips. As usual, my blood calmed, which was exactly what I needed so the vampires wouldn't sense me.

Warin stepped into view, his nostrils flaring. "How can we not smell them? That's impossible unless the warlock is using magic. But he's injured. Even fully healed, I doubt he could handle that much magic without his coven working with him."

My lungs seized. Of course the covens could perform spells together; I'd seen it in movies and read about it in books, though I'd yet to see the coven members I knew do it. When I'd watched them practice in the woods outside the apartments, they'd always used their magic separately. What sort of power did the covens have when they joined forces?

"So where *are* they, sire?" the dark-skinned man asked.

"I don't know, Demetris." Warin's nostrils flared as his cold eyes glanced everywhere. "You and Tatiana search the area behind us. Maybe they hid and circled back to the bunker. Mylo and I will focus our efforts on this side."

"But the wolves—" Mylo started.

"We have time," Warin snapped. "If they get close, meet at the vehicles. You know the emergency route. Glinda is already heading that way, preparing for our return."

I flinched. *Emergency route.* I shouldn't have been surprised. They were a secret society trying to take down the wolf shifters, so of course they'd have a backup plan. Their mission wouldn't go up in flames if this site was compromised. Our escape had only prevented them from using me against Raffe ... unless they found me again. Though I wasn't certain Warin wouldn't just kill me.

The two groups split, and my arms and legs started itching. The mud was drying. Not only was I turning into an icicle, but an itchy one at that. My wounds were the worst. They'd gone from feeling as if they were on fire to me wanting to claw my skin off.

I dug my hands into the ground underneath me, grasping anything I could so I wouldn't scratch.

I don't know how long Slade and I lay under the brush, but my eyelids became heavy, and my blood chilled. It could've been minutes or hours, yet I kept waiting for someone to grab us and pull us from our spot.

A howl sounded close by, but for all I knew, it was my imagination.

I snuggled into the ground, thankful I wasn't cold anymore. In fact, I was rather warm.

"Sky, we've got to go," Slade said.

I started, but my body didn't move. I didn't have the energy to jump. "Nuh-uh," I slurred and closed my eyes. "Nap."

"Listen, the wolves are close, and Warin and the other guy aren't coming back." Slade shimmied out from under the brush. "The wolves will know something's off if they smell mud here, and some of my mud is flaking off. We need to climb a tree or something to get off the ground so they can't find us as easily."

"Raffe," I rasped. If the wolves found us, Raffe would know where I was. Even if he'd acted questionably, he was my fated mate. He'd protect me, surely.

Slade grabbed my hands and tugged me out of the brush. "These wolves may not be loyal to Raffe. There are a handful of shifters out here searching for you that are part of Warin and Glinda's society. If they find us, we won't be safe."

Some of the fog in my brain cleared. "What? No. Only vampires and witches are part of that group."

"When they thought I was unconscious, I heard them

mention that some wolves loyal to them were out patrolling." He yanked me harder then released me and clutched his chest, wincing. "They wouldn't have told you about them because of your connection to Raffe. Think about it. Now move. I can't drag you, and I refuse to leave you behind."

Wolf shifters were part of the Veiled Circle? My heart pounded as determination fueled me. The spot in my chest warmed to scorching hot, adding to the warmth surging through my body.

If what Slade had said was true, I had to move and survive so I could warn Raffe. I struggled out from under the brush as Slade moved to the tree closest to us. He gestured and said, "Come on. Climb."

That strange presence inside me tried to surge forward. It seemed wild and feral, like nothing I'd experienced before. I pushed it down and rushed to the tree. Clutching the trunk, I tried to climb up, but I struggled to grasp any handholds, and my feet slid down, unable to find traction.

Fear settled in my chest, mixing with the heat and the strange presence.

There was no way I could climb.

Strange tingles spread across my skin, and I froze. We were being watched.

"Sky, hurry," Slade rasped.

There was no point. We shouldn't have left the brush. "They're here."

That strange presence grew stronger, but my blood remained calm. It hadn't been acting normally since the vampires had drunk from me, but no matter what, I was determined to die with dignity.

I turned around, ready to glare down my killer and fight with everything I had left in me.

CHAPTER EIGHT

My feet almost tangled underneath me, but when I turned, familiar crystal-blue eyes reflected back at me.

That strange presence in my chest inched forward, and my eyes burned as tears fell down my cheeks.

Raffe.

He raced from his spot in the center of the group, heading toward me, his dark fur ruffling with each stroke of his muscles.

"Sky, come on," Slade said urgently, tugging me away from my mate.

"No." I yanked away, enough energy coming back that my feet tangled, and I fell forward.

I tensed, bracing for impact, but Raffe reached me and broke my fall. My chest landed on his back, and electricity sparked between us. The presence in my chest churned harder. Between the spark of our connection, his warmth, and his sandalwood-and-amber scent, my body became uncomfortably warm, but there was no way I'd give up touching him. I'd been without him for so long.

He whimpered and lowered himself to the ground, then gently rolled so that my back hit the ground.

No. I needed to touch him. The presence in my chest tightened, making me more desperate to be with him. The strange emotions that didn't seem like my own surged with relief and happiness, contrasting with my devastation as Raffe moved away.

I reached out a hand, wanting him to come back to me. I wasn't above begging, but I still couldn't move well.

Four wolves emerged from between two thick firs, but I could see only *him*.

"Sky," Slade warned, the tension in his voice palpable.

I looked at the four coming toward us. Between their fur and eye color, I recognized them immediately. Adam and Keith stood in the center, with Lucy beside Adam and Josie at the other end. "These are our friends," I rasped as I shuddered. The warm buzz from touching Raffe had made me feel cold again.

Lowering her caramel-brown-furred head, Lucy kept her haunting gray eyes on me. I could see warmth and concern in them, but then Raffe pawed at my leg.

I turned to find him hunkered down again. He jerked his head sideways, and I understood.

He wanted me to climb onto his back.

Everything inside me urged me to do that. I needed to be next to him, as close as I could get, but I didn't want to burden him. "You don't need to carry me."

His large wolfy head turned toward me, and he scoffed. He inched back into me harder, essentially telling me to shush and get on.

I didn't fight because I wasn't sure how well I could walk.

"Just let him carry you." Slade shivered and moaned. "We need to get back and warm up."

He was right, and I didn't want Warin and the others to find us and attack. There were only five shifters with us. It wasn't like Slade and I could fight much.

My connection with Raffe snapped, yanking me toward my mate. Even if I'd wanted to fight longer, I was at their mercy. I still couldn't feel my hands and feet, but I managed to crawl haphazardly onto Raffe's back.

Keith rolled his milk-chocolate eyes at me, his look devoid of warmth.

Even my being kidnapped hadn't thawed his dislike for me. Lovely.

Once I was settled on Raffe's back, he chuffed, a sound I hadn't heard a wolf make but had read about in textbooks. The warm spot in my chest morphed into happiness, but it had an edge to it that screamed *worry*.

It was amazing how large Raffe was in animal form, even bigger than I'd remembered. Fitting perfectly on his back, I wrapped my arms around his neck. The warmth spread through me, making the mud even itchier, and the wounds on my neck and wrist burned again.

Raffe trotted off at a quick pace, his muscles rolling underneath me. I buried my face in his neck, not wanting to see the trees as we raced by. I wanted to get lost in his touch and the way our connection soared between us. The strange presence within me settled as well, and I'd have felt normal if it hadn't been for the discomfort of my wounds and the cold.

Little by little, my core temperature rose despite the freezing air brushing past me. My feet were still frozen because my socks were wet and dirty, but I was no longer on the brink of hypothermia.

Part of me was thankful. I hadn't realized how close to death I'd gotten. I started sweating everywhere Raffe and I were touching, but I shivered anyway. He'd soon regret having me ride on his back—I could feel the mud flaking off me and coating his fur.

Raffe's gait slowed, and I raised my head. The fir trees were thinning, but I didn't see any vehicles.

Ten wolves ran past us in the direction we'd come from.

I glanced over my shoulder, watching them go. Josie and Lucy were the only ones still with us. Adam, Keith, and Slade were gone.

My throat tightened. "Are the others okay?" I'd been so out of it that I hadn't considered that we'd been moving too fast for Slade to keep up. I was an awful friend.

Raffe nodded.

Not being able to talk to him frustrated me. I wanted to ask more questions, but when I faced forward, I noticed that Raffe was leaving the path. The ground was less level, and I had to hang on tighter to keep from falling off.

After a few minutes, he came to a stop and lowered himself like he wanted me to get off. I climbed down and stood, my feet frozen like ice.

He backed away, and I saw how much mud clung to his fur. No wonder he didn't want to be close to me. I hadn't showered in the bunker, afraid that someone would walk in on me, and I must stink on top of everything else.

I flinched, thinking how uncomfortable he must have been. "I'm sorry. I didn't mean—"

Bones cracked, and I inhaled sharply, realizing something was wrong. My blood jolted as I took a shaky step toward him. "Raffe—" I rasped.

His top half suddenly stood upright, his hind legs holding him up. More cracks sounded, and he stood taller—and realization settled over me.

He was shifting back into human form.

The strange presence inside me inched forward as if it

were just as fascinated with watching my mate change as I was. His dark fur retracted inside his skin, revealing his smooth olive complexion and muscular arms. My eyes focused on the wolf tattoo on his upper arm as it came back into view. Within a minute, human Raffe stood before me, every inch of him on display for my viewing pleasure, with no traces of mud on him. Something inside me expanded, and the *yank*ing had me stumbling toward him again.

"Thank gods." He closed the distance between us. He wrapped me in his arms, feeling warmer in human form. "I was afraid I'd never find you, and I'm never letting you out of my sight again."

"I'm okay with that," I responded with a half laugh. The past three-ish days had been hell.

"Good. I still can't believe you're here, and I never want to experience this again. I can't handle it," he murmured and tilted my head up to kiss me.

I flinched back, not wanting him to kiss mud, but he shook his head. "Your face is mostly clean from when you were riding on me."

My hesitation vanished, and our tongues collided. His minty taste washed through me and made me feel like I'd finally come home. The only thing different was the beard that rubbed my face.

When I threw my arms around his neck, my wounds throbbed, and I remembered I was covered in mud. I stilled, ending our moment together.

He pulled back, his eyes full of concern with dark circles under them like he hadn't slept. "What's wrong?" His deep voice sounded like music to my ears. His gaze went to one side of my neck, and he went still. "I'm going to enjoy killing them."

I had no doubt he meant it. Raffe was a killer. I shivered,

but his words thrilled a part of me. "It's nothing. And I'm making you filthy." I raised my injured wrist to cover the other side of my neck.

"I've been searching for you for three days nonstop. Do you think that fucking matters to me? I'm all about you getting me dirty." He homed in on the other bite before I could cover it, and he caught my wrist. I gasped and tried to jerk my hand away, but he turned it over.

His irises glowed, his wolf surging forward. "Why did the vampire bite you so many times? Is this why he took you?"

I shook my head. "It was different vampires."

If I'd thought that would comfort him, I'd been *so* wrong.

His entire body tensed, which was a huge distraction, given how his muscles became more pronounced. He growled, "How many fucking vampires *drank* from you?"

I quivered. "Three, but Raffe, you're fighting dirty, questioning me without any clothes on. How am I supposed to concentrate on anything you're *saying?*"

"Dammit, Sky." He sighed and placed an arm around my waist, gently pulling me to him. "You're freezing. Tell me everything while we get you home."

Home, away from the horrible past few days. Maybe I could forget everything and go back to my life like nothing had changed.

"Stay right here," he said and walked to some bushes. He pulled out a pair of jeans and a shirt.

I wanted to pout, but the thought of joining Josie and Lucy while he was naked had pressure forming deep within my chest. Though I wasn't thrilled about either woman seeing him like that, Josie was the only *real* threat. She'd been his fake girlfriend for *years,* and I wondered if it had all been pretending on her end. If she tried—

"Babe," Raffe said by the bush, pulling his jeans on. "Did you hear that noise?"

Blinking, I forced my murderous thoughts away. I surveyed our surroundings. "No. What?"

"I could've sworn I heard a faint growl." He quickly pulled on his black shirt and slipped his shoes on then came back to me. "But I don't sense anyone but the two of us here."

My face heated. Had that been me? I'd never growled before. "Let's get back to the others. I want to make sure Slade's okay."

His shoulders sagged. "We're officially back to that, even after—"

"If it weren't for him, I'd still be locked in there." I took his hand. "He's the only reason I got out. I think that earns him some forgiveness. Don't you?"

He scowled. "Maybe a little, but I still don't like him."

My cheeks tensed as I tried to smile, but the dried mud made it uncomfortable. "Just don't hate him."

A strong breeze rushed through the trees, and my teeth chattered.

"Keith and Adam stayed with Slade." His eyes glowed for a moment. "They're almost here. Thirty wolves are standing guard close by, so I promise you they're fine. You know I would never put my people in danger ... Slade either." The corners of his mouth dipped downward almost comically.

This right here was the amazing man I knew. Even when he didn't like someone, if they proved their worth, he'd protect them. It was such a contrast to what the pictures had depicted. There had to be more to the story.

Though I didn't want to leave, he was right. I was soaked, cold, and dealing with blood loss. The longer I stayed out here, the closer I'd be to hypothermia again.

"Here, I'll carry you—" he started.

"But the wolves." I bit my lip, but when I tried to walk, I almost crumpled.

Raffe bent down and lifted me to his strong, muscular chest—a place I'd feared I'd never be again. I snuggled into him, listening to his heartbeat. Somehow, mine synced up with his as he strolled back to the path.

"We were getting worried," Josie said from a few feet behind us.

Lucy snorted. "Let's be clear. *You* were worried, not me. I knew it would take those two a while to come back here."

My heart stopped. The last time I'd seen Raffe, he and I had partially completed our fated-mate bond, and he'd left, intending to tell Adam, Keith, and Josie that we were together. Had he not told them after all? Otherwise, Josie would have realized we needed a moment alone. Right?

The doubt about our relationship seeped back into my bones, making me question everything again. What if this fated-mate connection prevented me from seeing the real him, and I had fallen in love with an illusion? My heart ached at the thought, but it was short-lived.

"She's muddy and cold." Josie scoffed. "That should've hurried him up."

Raffe tightened one hand around me and reached into his pocket with the other. He tossed something at the girls. I tried to lift my head, but the bite wounds in my neck stretched. I whimpered, and Raffe kissed my forehead.

"Tell Adam to drive my bike back to campus. She can't handle it in this condition, so I'm taking the BMW. There's plenty of room in the other vehicles for the rest of you," he stated.

Lucy's rosy scent hit me as she replied, "Yeah, okay. Here."

"I could ride back with you two," Josie offered as the sound of footsteps drew closer.

"No," Raffe snarled. "You stay with them."

My pulse quickened at his rough dismissal, and I hid my face in his chest. In fairness, Josie had always been nice to me, but I was cold, uncomfortable, and needed Raffe.

"Uh. Yeah." She sounded disappointed.

Raffe didn't pause. He took sure, hurried steps, and before long, I heard the beep of a vehicle unlocking, followed by an engine starting.

He stopped. "I need to put you down for a second."

"Okay."

Slowly, he set me down, and I found myself standing at the passenger door of a black BMW sedan. He opened the door and helped me sit on the dark-orange leather seat.

"Raffe, wait." I'd never sat in a car this nice before. "I'm dirty."

He chuckled. "You're cute. I don't give a fuck if you get our car dirty. I'll get it cleaned later. You're going to get warm, and I'm taking you home."

My head spun, and in my shock, he got me buckled in.

The word kept spinning in my head. *"Our?"* I must have misunderstood him. All the things I'd gone through were messing with my head.

He shut the door, and my butt started getting toasty.

What the hell?

I glanced at the sleek buttons on the center dashboard to see that the car had seat warmers. Right. I'd heard about those, though I'd never experienced them. This was what they felt like.

Raffe got into the driver's seat and put the car in reverse. The car drove so smoothly that I couldn't be sure we were moving.

"Yes, *ours*," he replied, answering my question. "You're my mate, so everything that's mine is yours."

I snorted. "No, that's marriage."

He put the car in drive and pulled away from the few cars parked nearby.

Adjusting the controls, he turned the heat on, and the shivers shook me harder. I'd never been this cold before.

"Marriage is nothing compared to what we have." He reached over the center console and took my hand. "That's why I told you we didn't have to rush into anything. When I bit you, that made you *it* for me ... for my *entire* life. Our bond is unbreakable."

My heart hammered in my chest, and the warmth in its center exploded with love as the strange presence inside me jostled. Between that and the fullness in my chest, I'd never felt so happy and secure. His proclamation should've petrified me, but instead, it gave me peace.

No one would come between us.

Not only that, but his admission also felt *right*. This was how things should've always been between us. "I love you," I said, the words bursting from my throat.

"I love you, too." He squeezed my hand and smiled at me tenderly. Then his expression became stern. "I need you to tell me what happened."

So I did, leaving out the pictures. Once I started, the words spilled from my mouth. When I mentioned Dave drugging me, a murderous glint entered Raffe's eyes, but it turned to concern when I informed him about the Veiled Circle and the members I knew of. I added what Slade had told me and explained why we'd been scared when the five of them had found us.

When I was done talking, the moon was descending, and

we were twenty minutes from campus, which was saying something since I'd been taken to Silver Falls State Park, over an hour away.

"I'm going to hunt them down and teach every one of them a lesson." Raffe's knuckles blanched, and a growl laced every word. "I'll force them to give me the names of every member." His chest heaved and his nostrils flared. "They will pay tenfold for every twinge of pain they caused you."

Doubt crowded my mind. Though I didn't want the Veiled Circle to succeed, maybe not all the members believed in that same view and only the extremists had captured me. I wanted to calm him down. I hated seeing him this upset.

I turned to him. "Look, what they did was wrong, and the people who took me should pay." They'd drugged me, kidnapped me, and locked me up. No one deserved that treatment. "But the others ... they might not have known. You can't punish people who only want their freedom and the knowledge of their past and their heritage back at their fingertips. Besides, every group has extremists, and you shouldn't persecute them all based on a few."

His forehead creased. "I can see how it looks like we aren't being fair, but it's up to *us* to make sure humans never learn of our existence and keep the species in line." He glanced at me. "I would never do something to hurt someone just because I could."

My stomach tensed. He'd given me the perfect opportunity to ask him the question I'd been dreading. "Are you sure?" I murmured.

He glanced in my direction. "Yeah. Why would you ask that?"

"Because Glinda and Warin showed me pictures of you leading the slaughter of a group of vampires in an abandoned warehouse." I bit my lip. "And the picture didn't show any humans."

His expression became strained, and the color drained from his face.

Suddenly, I didn't want to hear the answer.

CHAPTER NINE

My blood jolted, and not even Raffe's presence could calm me. His answer would fundamentally change certain things between us, fated or not.

Now, I wished I hadn't asked the question. There was safety in not knowing, but that wasn't fair to him or me. The question would always linger in the back of my head. I wanted to understand who I was mated to.

He licked his lips and scoffed. "So that's what you think of me?"

A vise constricted around my heart, but the damage was done. "I'm asking you about it, right? Instead of taking their word."

"Because kidnappers are ethical and would never lie or bend the truth." He arched a brow as his eyes darkened with hurt.

The spot in my chest radiated his hurt and disappointment, which pissed me off.

"If I thought all of that was *true*, would I bother asking you about it?" I rolled my shoulders, the dried mud driving me insane by how badly it itched. "If someone would've told me that in August, I wouldn't have even *considered* asking you because I would've assumed it was true. Remember when you labeled me a social pariah in class? That wasn't out of the kindness of your heart." He didn't get to be upset with me for wanting his side of the story, and worse, the longer he deflected, the more I feared it *was* true. Why else would he be so defensive?

His hands tightened on the steering wheel, and his jaw cracked from how hard he was clenching his teeth. "I hated every second of that. Do you know what it's like to have to do something like that to your fated mate? Even then, I knew who you were. I knew it the second you ran out of the woods the night you arrived. I felt your presence as you jogged into the woods, and the only reason I didn't follow you was because you moved like a human. When you ran out, you became the very person that I *had* to protect from any pain and harm."

I shook my head, my blood increasing to a slight fizz. I needed to calm down, but he didn't get to turn himself into the victim. "Yet you did each one of those things to me."

"Dammit, Sky." He hit his palm against the steering wheel. "That's not fair. You weren't the only person struggling. It wasn't easy for me to want to be with you and have to pretend I couldn't stand you while you were being attacked every second or damn near imploding. Not to mention how Slade hovers around you like a dog in heat."

I tensed. I hated the way he spoke about Slade, but I was wise enough not to say anything about it. I didn't need to add to our already tenuous moment, but I felt like I was betraying Slade—especially after he'd risked his life to save mine—by letting Raffe talk about him that way. "I don't want to argue. I was just asking a question. I get that you're risking a lot to be with me. That's why I walked away from you when Keith found out we were secretly together."

That was the hardest thing I'd ever done, but I couldn't be with someone who was struggling over whether to stay with me. I didn't want him to resent me later.

I huffed out a breath. "I wasn't trying to dredge up the past, but clearly, that needs to happen. To be clear, I *wanted* you the entire time, even when you were being an ass. *I* wasn't the one fighting you or trying to make others view you as less than a person. You don't get to paint me as the instigator. That was all you, Keith, and your father."

Even after Raffe had claimed me and I'd been kidnapped, Keith still looked at me—even in wolf form—like I was worse than scum.

"But that picture looked bad, so I wanted you to be aware they'd shown it to me, and I need to hear your side of the story. If that makes me a bitch, so be it." I stared straight ahead, the familiar roads coming into view. We were about five minutes away from campus. I placed my hands on my ... well, mud since I couldn't even feel the jeans underneath with how thick the mud coated me. I tried to regulate my breathing. If my emotions got stronger, my blood would surge close to a hum while we were in a car. I did *not* want to find out how that would go.

He hung his head slightly. "I'm not trying to make you feel that way. I'm sorry. And yes, that's good information to know because they could be recruiting people by using that image depicting me as a monster. It also means they had someone watching and taking pictures." He grimaced and blew out a breath. "That particular attack haunts me." His voice thickened with regret, mirroring the heaviness in my chest.

I was *feeling* him.

How was that possible?

The strange presence within me churned, increasing my urge to reach out to him and take away all his pain. I hated seeing him this way and would do anything to alleviate his guilt so he'd never feel this way again.

I laid my hand on his, but he didn't respond, and his attention remained on the road. A sharp pain shot through me.

"The picture was right. When we reached the abandoned warehouse, there weren't any humans there. Only vampires," he said raggedly.

A gigantic lump lodged in my throat, but despite the horror, I didn't want to pull my hand away. He regretted that day, and I needed to be there for him. Whatever had happened was a burden to him.

I opened my mouth, unsure what to say, but he continued, "What the picture doesn't reveal is the five humans they were holding in a different location. They were manipulating their minds, making them want to remain blood slaves."

Mouth snapping closed, I swallowed, making a loud gulping noise around the lump in my throat. "Blood slaves?" I shivered; the thought was horrible. I'd been bitten by a vampire multiple times, and it had *hurt*. I understood people had their kinks, but the sensation of those bites was something I couldn't fathom anyone enjoying.

The black iron sign with the words *Evergreen Elite University* molded into the center appeared in front of us, held up by its two gigantic brick pillars. Usually, the campus felt like home, but not in this moment ... not with this horrible story.

"In the old days, when the human population was smaller, vampires would acquire blood slaves so humans wouldn't question why they had bite marks they couldn't remember getting." Raffe pursed his lips like the words tasted bad. "The vampires would usually have a human family live with them so they could feed off six or seven at their leisure. The families were ostracized because they would always wear layers of clothing to hide their marks despite the warm weather. They were deemed strange, and often, the family line died off because no one would marry their strange children, and the vampire would then move on to another family."

I inhaled sharply. That sounded similar to my experience growing up with people finding me strange and not wanting anything to do with me. Those poor kids. In a way, I understood why the wolf shifters had tried to keep vampires away from heavily populated areas.

We coasted into campus, the huge brick sports stadium where the football team played towering on our right and the student center straight ahead. The cherry trees around the lawn in front of the building, which students lounged under during the warm months, were bare in the cold weather.

Raffe turned left toward the apartment buildings, passing the soccer and tennis courts. "That's what a few of the vampires were attempting to do again, but they were living away from the family to go undetected."

Then it hit me. They'd picked a smaller city so they could feast on people without the wolves noticing.

"Dad got word of the situation through a supernatural intranet board monitored by an anonymous source who claims to be a witch. They were passing through the city and sensed the magical essence of mind manipulation on the humans at the local market."

I *hmmed*. "Is it normal to post anonymously?"

He nodded. "People reporting something like that don't usually share their identity. Supernaturals tend to be vindictive, and it's essentially a safety net to protect the whistleblower."

Made sense. My dad worked as an accountant at a large company, and I knew it had a number where you could report violations anonymously.

We passed the administration building, and Raffe pulled into the apartment parking lot. I kept my junky old Honda Civic parked in the back corner, but Raffe parked in a reserved spot in front of the path that led to the two five-story cement apartment buildings.

My focus went to the nearby woods, which were part of the Cascade Mountains forest that trailed up the side and back of the campus. I fixed my eyes on the tree line at the edge of the women's apartment building on the left, where I'd gone to find Raffe that fateful night Dave had kidnapped me.

I couldn't hold back a shudder.

Raffe took my hand, rubbing his thumb against my inner wrist. The buzz between us thrummed to life, and my pulse raced.

"We found the humans, and Lafayette removed the manipulations on them once the bite marks were healed. Adam, Keith, and I led a group of wolf shifters to the warehouse." He closed his eyes, and his face twisted. "When we arrived, we asked for the ones responsible to come forward. Said they were the only ones who needed to be punished, but all the vampires laughed."

My stomach roiled, but the weight of my concern lessened. As I'd believed, Raffe hadn't ruthlessly attacked these vampires. Pictures might be worth a thousand words, but they could also be deceiving.

"They told me to head back home ... that I didn't have the strength to do anything to them." Raffe ran his free hand through his hair, tousling it. "Then two of them attacked me. I was prepared, but Keith and Adam ... well, they believed their role was to protect me. The other vampires thought Keith and

Adam were attacking them, and chaos erupted. I lost control of the situation, and five of the men with me died, along with all the vampires."

I tried to pull up the photos in my mind because I only remembered seeing vampires dead on the ground. I counted the people who'd been standing behind Raffe—eleven wolf shifters. "The picture showed only dead vampires and all your men alive." Had the Veiled Circle photoshopped the picture?

He turned to me with glistening eyes. "By the time the vampires were dead, five of my men lay on the ground with them. I wouldn't lie about that."

His hurt seeped into me, and my vision blurred. I squeezed his hand. "I believe you, Raffe. I just can't believe they'd try to—"

"Drive a wedge between us?" He arched a brow. "Paint me as a murderer to further their cause?"

Those were fair points. "More the latter. It's going far beyond wanting their rights back and into some sort of perverse quest for vengeance." They were willing to do anything to take my mate down, and I wanted to make them hurt for what they'd done.

"I didn't realize how far things had gone, but right now, I want to get my mate inside our home, help her get cleaned up, then hold her in my arms." He turned off the car. "Can we not talk about all this for the rest of the night? I can't stand not holding you any longer."

His eyes glowed faintly, and that presence inside me stirred harder. With the *yank* strengthening in my chest, I had no qualms. "Of course."

He exhaled and smiled. "Good. I was hoping you'd say that."

He exited the car, and by the time I opened my door, he was already there, helping me out.

I smiled so wide that my cheeks hurt. "I'm feeling a lot better now that I'm warm. Well, other than being itchy." I glanced up at the half-moon, noting it was descending. It was around two in the morning, which was good, given how much mud was caked on me. It was the middle of the school week, and most people were asleep.

Wrapping an arm around my waist, Raffe shut my door, and we made our way to the building. The cold night air had me stepping closer to him. Maybe I wasn't as back to normal as I thought.

We entered through the double-glass doors and rode the elevator up to the fifth floor. In the light-gray hallway, we turned left. My mud-covered socks padded on the dark-gray carpet, leaving splotches of dirt behind. I cringed and stopped to remove the socks. A cloud of dirt swirled around me. Okay, that hadn't been the smartest idea, but I was committed at this point.

Raffe chuckled, and I turned to find him smiling at me adoringly. My heart sputtered, and we headed to the apartment at the end.

I entered the code to the door and paused. "Where's Cat-Keith?" The last thing I wanted was for my adopted cat from the animal shelter to attack Raffe as soon as I opened the door.

"She's fine." Raffe shook his head. "She and Lucy have come to an understanding while you've been gone. She's in Lucy's room."

Learning that the two of them had formed a connection made me smile. I would've never believed it based on Cat-Keith's reaction to Lucy the day I'd brought her home. "Good. I didn't want her to attack you." I wasn't sure I had the energy to fight her off.

I entered the apartment with Raffe on my heels and

headed straight into the one full bathroom in the middle of the small hallway that led to the two bedrooms.

Now that I could shower in my own place, I was eager to clean off the itchy dirt. I turned the water on in the marble-tiled shower and removed my clothes, trying to keep the dirt flakes to a minimum.

Raffe entered and grabbed a clean white towel from under the counter. He placed it on the sink for me.

He opened the glass door and pointed at my clothes. "I'll put these in the washing machine and clean up behind you." Something like sadness still shadowed his eyes.

I slipped into the shower and gasped, the water warmer than expected. I stepped under the spray.

The dirt still clung to me. I grabbed my vanilla-scented shampoo and started cleaning myself from the top of my head down. After I'd washed my body once, the water was still slightly brown. Not like when I'd first gotten in, but I had more work to do. As I washed the bites on my neck and wrist, I realized they were already scabbing over.

The sound of clothes dropping pulled my attention from my wrist. Raffe closed and locked the bathroom door and joined me.

My breath caught as I scanned his body. He was an amazing, caring person and built sexier than any god could ever dream of. I wasn't sure how I'd gotten so lucky.

He took the bar of soap from my hands and worked up suds, then guided me to turn around and washed my back where I couldn't reach. I could feel his anger swirling inside me as he growled, "Those vampires will die by my hands."

His strong hands kneaded my back, working out knots I'd thought would never disappear. The buzz of our connection and the way his hands worked my body had need flaring within me. I no longer sensed sadness from him. Maybe I'd been paranoid after our earlier conversation.

He spun me around, allowing the water to run down my back, and I stepped toward him, needing to kiss him. The yanking almost swallowed me whole. Having him here like this had the presence inside me urging me forward.

I needed him.

Before I could kiss him, he moved under the spray to clean himself. I wanted to help him, but I stood there transfixed by the way his muscles flexed as he washed his entire body. Somehow, this was more erotic than foreplay.

When he cleaned his already hard dick, something inside me snapped.

I surged forward and kissed him, and he pulled me against him. His tongue swooped into my mouth, and I reveled in his minty taste. I wrapped my arms around his neck, needing to touch him and also have him support my weight.

He spun us around, my back against the tile so we were both in the water.

I freed a hand and trailed my fingers down his chest, causing him to quiver. He groaned, taking a small step back, and growled, "You're injured. I'm trying to behave. Though my wolf wants to claim you all over again, we should wait."

I whimpered. "My wounds are already healing, and I'm clean. I feel fine, and I need you after being apart for so long." I closed the small gap between us and took him in my hand. Holding his gaze, I started to stroke him. "We can clean up afterward since we're already here." I waggled my brows. "You got into the shower with me."

His hand fisted my hair, tilting my head back so I could stare into his face as the water poured over him. He rasped, "I got in to get clean and wash your back."

"I'm not complaining." I stroked him again, and I watched as his resolve shattered.

"I need you too," he said and kissed me. He released my hair, and his hand brushed my nipple while he slipped his other hand between my legs. I continued to stroke him, and his fingers circled the spot between my legs at the same pace.

Unable to hold my head up, I leaned it against the tile wall, and his mouth went to one breast.

I moaned, unable to stop myself. I clenched with need so hard that I nearly combusted, but all that accomplished was making his fingers work faster as he sucked my nipple into his mouth. My hips ground against his hand, and he slipped two fingers inside me.

My body was on fire.

My muscles tensed as he moved his fingers and tongue faster.

Our bodies were slick with water and desire. His breathing turned ragged as his hips jerked in time with my hand. We worked each other's bodies into a frenzy.

My orgasm consumed me. My muscles tensed, and pleasure rolled through me, my body spasming around his fingers, urging him to go faster.

As soon as the ecstasy eased, I tried to pull away, hypersensitive to his touch, but he held me firm.

"I'm not done with you. Again," he growled, his words igniting something wild inside me.

With that, my body was ready for him all over again. "Not this way. I want *you*." After being apart for so long, I needed him inside me.

He shook his head. "You're hurt. I don't want to do anything that will cause you pain."

"Please, Raffe." I understood he was afraid that I wasn't well enough to take him. "I *need* you."

Something like relief crossed his face. "Gods, I need you too, Skylar. You swear you'll tell me if I hurt you?"

I increased the speed of my strokes and answered, "I swear."

"Thank gods. You still smell like vampires where they bit you, and my wolf can't take it. All I want to do is make love to you over and over again until you remember only me and how I feel." He stepped between my legs and lifted me against the wall.

I nodded. "I want that too. Please."

He pressed against my opening and slid inside, filling me. My head thumped against the cold tile, a slight discomfort that ebbed.

He placed one hand behind my head, keeping me from hitting the wall again, then pressed his mouth to mine.

With him inside me, I wrapped my legs around his waist, pulling him closer so his body pressed to mine, and he sank deeper.

Then he thrust inside me. Each time he completed me, our souls merged more. In my chest, I felt his love and desperation so strong that they only added to mine.

Soon, that knot of desire tightened again, my release imminent. Our kisses became messy and urgent as our pace quickened.

The presence inside me jerked, and I suddenly had the urge to bite him.

What the fuck was wrong with me? That couldn't be normal. What sort of human wanted to bite someone? Had Glinda and Warin done something to me when I was unconscious?

Raffe's mouth pulled away from mine, and he kissed down my neck to a spot above where the vampire had bitten me.

The urge to bite him intensified just as the urge for him to bite me crashed down even harder.

"Make their smell go away," I panted, using my free hand to grab his head and press it hard against my skin. "I want to smell like only you again. Bite me."

He groaned, his teeth raking my skin, pushing me closer to an orgasm. I shuddered against him and panted, and he bit gently into my neck, the experience bringing me closer to the end. Then he kissed the spot where the vampires' fangs had dug in.

"The other side too," I said, chasing my pleasure.

He didn't hesitate. As he moved to the other side, I saw his glowing eyes so bright it was breathtaking. He bit me carefully as he pushed hard inside me and stilled, and I writhed against him, ecstasy exploding through me.

His body quivered with his own release, and I dug my nails into the small of his back instead of giving in to the strange temptation to bite him.

Being with him like this, with our souls fully connected ... I needed this more than I needed to breathe.

He peppered kisses over my face then pulled away and stepped back into the water. I followed him, not ready to give up touching him. I pressed my lips to his, and our tongues tangled again.

"You don't know how crazy I was while you were gone. I didn't sleep. I was so determined to find you." He pulled away and stared deep into my eyes. "I love you, Skylar, and they'll never take you away from me again."

His love filled the spot in my chest, and the strange presence eased back as if it were pouting.

"I love you, too," I whispered. I cupped his face. "Which is why we need to dry off and dress so we can both get some sleep."

His eyes warmed to a cobalt hue. "You don't know how much better I'll sleep tonight now that I've claimed you again. I didn't hurt you, right? I tried to be gentle."

"You were perfect. I needed you to do it just as bad as you wanted to." I kissed his lips again. "Let's go to bed." Exhaustion inched up on me.

He grinned. "Now *that* is something I can do."

Raffe put on sweatpants and a shirt, and I headed into my bedroom. My lilac comforter was still askew from when we'd had sex the first time, right before I was taken. I bit my bottom lip, remembering that moment as I moved to the gray dresser and removed a pair of lilac pajama bottoms and a black T-shirt.

I climbed into the queen-size bed and stared up at the purple paper butterflies I'd made back home, which I'd threaded through the light fixture so that they hung down like a cascading chandelier.

When Raffe entered the room, a tender smile graced his face, but that sadness was back in his eyes. I hadn't imagined it earlier. I could feel the warmth of his love in my chest, but I could also feel hurt.

He climbed into bed beside me, and I couldn't handle it anymore.

"Raffe, what's wrong?" I asked, knowing I couldn't sleep with him feeling like this. I should've pushed him about it earlier.

"Noth—"

I sighed. "Don't lie, please." A faint odor drifted to me, but I didn't worry about it.

"You need rest." He kissed my forehead and stretched his arms out to me.

I shook my head. "I won't be able to." I suspected what it was, and even though he was still being loving and amazing, I hated that I'd hurt him. "Earlier, when I asked about the abandoned warehouse, I didn't really think you'd done something wrong."

He arched a brow. "But you weren't sure. You asked the question. If you knew, you would've just told me."

Shit. I had known better, and I'd let those people get inside my head. I wanted to punch myself. "I'm sorry. It's just—"

A loud knock at the front door caused Raffe to snarl and jump to his feet.

CHAPTER TEN

The spot in my chest infused with his emotions heated with anger and annoyance, which had my blood jolting and the strange presence in my chest dancing. "What's wrong?"

He blew out a breath and forced a smile, but it didn't meet his eyes. "There's someone I didn't expect at our door. Stay here. I'll be back." He left the bedroom.

A bitter laugh stuck in my throat. These were the times when I glimpsed the man I'd first met. The prince who expected to be obeyed and not challenged.

Well, he might be upset with me, but with his reaction to the person at the door, I wouldn't stay hidden. Something was going on, and he wanted to protect me. We'd seen how well that went last time.

The front door opened, but nothing was said. Of course, Raffe was using the pack link, so I couldn't overhear the conversation.

Not wanting Raffe to hear me, I tiptoed toward the door. Raffe growled, low and threatening, and when I e̶n̶t̶e̶r̶e̶d̶ the living room, my attention settled on the man standing in the hallway.

Holy shit. My jaw dropped. I might have been staring at Marcel Gerard from *The Originals.* The irony wasn't lost on me that he played a vampire on the show when he clearly was a wolf shifter. I'd had the largest crush on him as a teenager when I'd been sucked into that world.

His gaze settled on me, and he frowned. "That's the woman who caused *all* this trouble?"

"Of course she didn't listen," Raffe murmured, but it sounded like he'd thought it in my mind.

My entire body went rigid, and I shook my head. Exhaustion, healing from my injuries, and being drugged for days were catching up to me. I needed some real sleep and fast.

"Be careful how you speak to my mate," Raffe rasped, the muscles in his back tensing. *That* I'd definitely heard.

Butterflies took flight in my stomach. He'd claimed me in *all* ways now, and I couldn't fight the stupid smile stretching across my face.

Marcel seemed anything but amused. His jaw clenched. "A fact you failed to mention to your father. Does Josie know?"

Josie. Why would he—?

"That's a question for you to ask your daughter directly," Raffe retorted. "Not that it matters. My relationship status is none of your business."

I blinked. "You're Josie's father?" This man was best friends with the wolf-shifter king? Now that he mentioned it, I could see the resemblance between him and Josie.

He sighed and nodded. "I'm Aldric Spencer."

So ... not Marcel. Just a lookalike. That made much more sense, but I didn't want to be rude, so I responded, "Skylar Greene."

"I'm well aware." He adjusted the black tie around his neck.

Realizing a movie star wasn't at my door, I took in Aldric's suit. Who dressed so formally at three in the morning? Someone who didn't plan on sleeping anytime soon.

"And your *relationship status* is my business." Aldric's nostrils flared. "You're the prince and future *king*. All your decisions impact our species, something you've forgotten." His attention turned to me. "Skylar, I need you to talk sense into him. Ever since you arrived on campus, he's lost sight of what's important. The king needs to talk to his son, so release whatever hold you have on him."

Ah. That must be why Raffe had wanted me to stay in my room. He'd known that Aldric would insult me. I snorted. If Aldric thought I had influence over Raffe, he was sorely mistaken.

"Not happening," Raffe said and crossed his arms while sidestepping to block me partially from Aldric's view. "She only got back a few minutes ago after being *kidnapped* for days. She needs to heal and rest, and I'm not leaving her side. I'll link with Dad and tell him I'm not coming back. You don't have to be the messenger."

Aldric sniffed and looked down his nose at Raffe. "Her injuries didn't stop you two from having sex. Besides, she can sleep here. Lucy is on her way back with the pack and can watch her. You're needed at home."

My face heated from the fact that he was well aware of what we'd been doing minutes ago.

I didn't want to come between him and his father. "If your dad needs you—"

"He doesn't." Raffe straightened, standing as tall as possible. He had at least two inches on the older man. "He's not happy that I had so many wolf shifters searching for you, and there's nothing to discuss about that." He glared at Aldric. "It's done, and there's no way I'm going anywhere without *her*."

"The king is on a jet flying back to Seattle and has something important to discuss with you, *Prince* Raffe. Time is of the essence." Aldric's dark eyes glowed. "I'm not here asking. I will tell him to alpha-will you if it comes to that."

A snarl vibrated from Raffe, and he stepped closer to Aldric.

I didn't know how in the hell this problem would be resolved, and I wasn't certain what alpha-willing meant, but if they didn't quiet down, the neighbors would come out to see what was going on. I needed to calm the situation down.

I blinked, trying to find the right words. "If your dad needs you, then go. You heard Mr. Spencer. Lucy will be back, and I'm sure Adam can stay with us."

Raffe's head snapped toward me, and a patch of fur appeared on his arms. His jaw set as he growled, "No man but *me* will be staying here with you."

Shoving past Raffe, Aldric entered the apartment and shut the door behind him.

"Raffe, I may love you like a son, but you're about to go too far." Aldric pointed to the front door and shook his head. "You're being careless, and you're losing your cool when humans could be listening. You're also disobeying your father's wishes, all for a human girl."

My mouth went dry. I wasn't sure what to do or say, but my presence wasn't helping. Even though Raffe was my everything, it did seem like I wasn't the right fit for him.

"Imagine if your mate had been taken from you, drugged, and harmed for days, and you couldn't find her." Raffe's breathing quickened. "I *just* got her back, and you think I'm going to be rational when you're trying to get me to leave her?

What the fuck did you and Dad think would happen? I'm not acting this way because she's *human* but because my wolf needs to be with his *mate*. I'm not leaving her side. I'm not sure how much more fucking clear I can be. Dad can come here if it's that important."

"He can't." Aldric closed his eyes as if to regain control of himself. "There are things going on, and he needs to ensure that only certain people hear. You have to come with me."

I rubbed my arms. I could think of only one real solution, though neither of them would like the suggestion. But if Raffe didn't compromise, I suspected he would be forced to go home, causing more issues between him and his father. "What if I come with you?"

Aldric shook his head. "The king needs to talk to him *alone*."

Head jerking back, I tried to ignore the sting of his complete dismissal. Of course they didn't want me around other wolf shifters, but still … Raffe had chosen me as his mate.

Warmth spread through my chest, though the heat from his anger was still there. Raffe took a step back, coming to my side. He interlaced our fingers, the buzz of our bond strong, and said, "Either she comes, or he can call me to tell me this information. It's your choice, but I'm sure Dad won't be thrilled if he learns I would've been willing to travel to the mansion."

My eyes burned, and my vision blurred. I hadn't expected Raffe to support my offer to go with him. In fact, I was certain he didn't want me around his father, yet he was willing to bring me home like he wasn't ashamed of me. My blood jolted despite his touch.

Aldric's jaw twitched, and his eyes glowed.

I glanced at Raffe's and saw that they'd remained his normal blue, meaning Aldric wasn't talking to him.

He had to be talking to King Jovian.

After a moment, Aldric nodded. "Fine. Get your things and let's go."

"Now?" My heart skipped a beat. I was exhausted. I didn't want to ride in a car for the rest of the night and face Raffe's father in the morning. Seattle was over three hours from Portland, so we'd be rolling in around seven in the morning.

"My *mate* needs her rest." Raffe released my hand and placed his arm around my shoulders. "I won't fight going, but we will let her sleep until eight. We'll reach the Seattle house by lunchtime, and we'll both be in a better place mentally, especially if my wolf has alone time with her while she heals."

Aldric frowned but nodded. "Fine. I'll meet you at your car at eight thirty. Don't be late. You've almost pushed King Jovian too far."

Raffe smirked, not helping the situation.

"We'll be there." I didn't care what I had to do; I'd make sure Raffe got there. I just hated that I was going to miss more classes. I'd have a shit ton of makeup work to do when we got back, and I needed straight *A*'s to have a shot at vet school, given how competitive getting accepted into a good one was.

Footsteps sounded down the hallway, and I pressed closer to Raffe, uneasy about who was coming. With my luck lately, it could very well be a serial killer coming to finish me off.

The three of us were still staring at one another when the buttons on the keypad were pressed, indicating Lucy had returned.

The door opened, and I sagged in relief when Lucy, Josie, Adam, and Keith entered. They'd all made it back. Josie's expression seemed more serious than usual.

"How's Slade?" I probably shouldn't have asked that in front of Aldric, seeing as wolf shifters hated witches, but Slade was the reason I'd escaped. Annoyance radiated off Raffe, but he remained quiet.

Keith rolled his milk-chocolate-brown eyes. "Still breathing, unfortunately." He scratched his dark-brown scruff. "One less Wright would make the world a better place."

"Daddy." Josie smiled, her somber expression lightening. She tossed her long, dark, wavy hair over one shoulder. "I didn't realize you were here." She hurried to Aldric and pulled him into a hug. Her hair and eyes were the same shade as her father's, though her skin was a touch more bronze and her lips poutier, reminding me of a model.

Her lack of surprise at Raffe and me being here spoke volumes, and Aldric's deep scowl confirmed he shared the same thoughts.

Clearing his throat, Adam shoved his hands into his jeans pockets and strolled to the couch. His loose, curly brown hair hung slightly into his honey-brown eyes. "Slade's got some broken ribs, but we helped him to his apartment, and Supreme Priestess Olwyn was there, waiting for him."

That was one benefit of Slade's mother being on the board of directors at EEU. She was nearby when he needed her. I was thankful, but I wished witches had healing powers.

Lucy pulled me into a hug and grumbled, "I've been so worried about you. I'm glad you're finally home."

"And looking like a person and not a mud goblin." Keith wrinkled his nose. "I've never seen anything so disgusting. I'm glad Raffe had me drive his bike home, so I didn't have to be around you two."

Raffe snarled and took a hurried step toward Keith, but I grabbed his arm and held him beside me.

"So you'd rather I'd done nothing and died?" Bitterness

laced my words. "I didn't coat myself in mud for the fun of it. It was either that or Warin and the other five vampires finding us." If the situation arose again, I'd coat myself in mud without a second of hesitation.

"You made the right choice." Lucy pulled back and smiled. "I'm so glad you're home."

Aldric grimaced. He didn't like the way the others were acting toward me ... well, besides Keith.

Exhaling loudly, Aldric turned to his daughter. "Josie, let's head to your apartment. We need to talk, and I need to rest before driving back to Seattle in the morning."

"Sure." Josie pecked his cheek and hurried over to me. She hugged me and said, "I'm glad you're back. You had us all worried."

My initial reaction was to tense and step back, but that was mean. I didn't like her because of her connection with Raffe. I felt threatened by their closeness, but she'd never been anything but kind to me, and I refused to ignore that the issue was with *me,* not her. I squeezed her back gently. "Thank you for searching for me."

"You're one of us now." She beamed. "That's what we do for each other."

Aldric scowled at our interaction, but he looked more concerned than upset about it. I'd take that, especially since I was a human with powers ... an arcane-born.

"On that note, I'm taking my *mate* back to bed." Raffe snagged my hand, tugging me back to him. "She needs rest to heal, and we have an early start tomorrow." His displeasure festered in my chest uncomfortably. He led me toward my room, and I didn't fight him.

Raffe wasn't hiding what we were to each other anymore. Besides that, I was exhausted.

"Yeah, you need your rest too, with how you've been going

nonstop." Adam yawned. "I'm not far behind. It's been a long night."

That was when it hit me, and I paused. "Oh, do I need to feed Keith?"

"Aw." Keith placed a hand on his chest. "She's worried about me."

Oh shit. I'd forgotten that Keith hadn't learned about Cat-Keith.

Lucy beamed. "Not you, friend. Her cat. She's adorable."

Keith's expression froze, and his gaze darted around the living room, searching for the animal. "You got a female cat and named it *Keith?*"

"Oh my gods." Adam leaned over, his tan complexion turning red from laughter. "That's perfect."

I quickly filled them in, telling the story of the animal shelter owner naming her and why, along with how she'd wound up here.

Keith's face twisted in disgust. "We need to change its name immediately."

"Not happening," Lucy singsonged. "It fits her so well."

Raffe karate-chopped the air. "We can talk about this later. Everyone else, out of here."

"Yeah, let's see how you'd react if a cat was named for you." Keith pouted, but everyone headed out the door.

I mashed my lips together, trying not to laugh.

Raffe led me into the bedroom and shut and locked my door. The two of us cuddled on the bed. Though I enjoyed his touch, I eventually opened my mouth to talk to him about how I'd hurt his feelings.

But his breathing had steadied, and he was snoring softly.

He was out.

I closed my eyes and tried not to think about how badly I'd fucked up. Finally, I fell into a restless sleep.

A LOUD, piercing noise attacked my ears. I startled awake, sitting straight up and surveying the area for the threat.

Raffe groaned, his arm tight around my waist. He mumbled, "Turn that damn thing off."

It was his phone alarm.

I reached over and hit the off button, wondering why the noise sounded so different. Then, something else registered. "Shit. My phone. I need to call my parents." My stomach tensed. What did they think had happened to me?

"Lucy has it." Raffe tugged me back against his chest. "We'll get it from her before we leave. She's been texting them, pretending she was you."

Oh. I wasn't sure how I felt about that, but at least they weren't worried.

I kissed his lips, knowing we needed to go. "We've got to meet Aldric."

"Fine." He groaned, kissing me back. "Let's get it over with."

The two of us dressed, and I went into the bathroom to apply some makeup and brush my hair, hoping like hell I didn't look like death. The vampire bites barely showed anymore.

Strange.

I headed back into my bedroom and pointed at my bag. "How many days should I pack for?"

"We're not staying overnight. You won't need anything." Raffe's eyes glowed, and I realized someone was linking with him.

Probably Aldric.

I headed into the kitchen and found Lucy at the table,

eating some crackers. When I reached her side, she slid the pack toward me. "Here. You need to eat."

"Thanks."

"Be careful." Lucy touched my arm and frowned. "And remember that, no matter what, I support you two and your relationship."

That sounded ominous. A knot tightened around my stomach. I knew the king wouldn't like Raffe and me being together, but having it confirmed made me sick.

"Fuck," Raffe shouted from my bedroom, and his hot rage filled my chest. He hurried past us and ran out the door.

Something was wrong.

CHAPTER ELEVEN

That strange presence inside me surged forward, stronger than ever before. The new magic that swirled inside me was warm and feral, heating my body in a different way than my blood. Between that and the uncomfortable pressure where I could feel Raffe's emotions, I almost didn't want to know what the new problem was, but ignorance hadn't worked well for me in the past.

Not missing a beat, I followed. With his wolf-shifter speed, Raffe was already halfway to the elevator, but that didn't matter. He'd have to wait on it the same as a human unless he decided to take the stairs at the opposite end of the hallway.

As expected, he paused and pressed the button. The elevator tended to be fast, so we never had to wait long.

By the time the elevator arrived, I'd caught up and slid inside with him. I tensed, waiting for him to complain about me being here, but he remained quiet.

That was something. "You aren't going to tell me to go back to the apartment?"

He crossed his arms, his biceps bulging underneath his

evergreen EEU sweatshirt. "Would you listen?" He narrowed his eyes, waiting for my answer.

Fair question.

I shook my head. "Nope. Not a chance. Remember how well things went last time you left me behind?"

The way he flinched had me regretting the words.

"Yeah, I fucking remember, Sky," he rasped, and his crushing guilt stole my breath. "It's haunted me every moment since you vanished."

I wanted to yank my hair out. "That's not what I meant. I was trying to say that we're stronger *together*." The elevator door opened, and I moved to exit, taking his hand.

"Believe me, I don't plan on leaving your side unless someone I trust is there with you," he gritted out and increased our pace as we walked outside.

That was more than okay with me. I had no desire to get kidnapped again, and I was certain the Veiled Circle would try again or straight up kill me. I'd say I had about a fifty-fifty shot at either option. "What's going on?"

He led me toward the men's apartment building, and I realized I'd never stepped foot inside before. Every time Lucy and I hung out with the guys, we were elsewhere on campus, or they were at our place. I hadn't considered how odd that was until this moment.

"Dave," he said, so low I was surprised I'd heard him. "He's gone."

My steps faltered, but not long enough for me to fall behind, especially since he was pulling on me. "How do you know?"

"Did you really think we wouldn't hunt him?" Raffe shoved open the doors that led into the men's apartment.

The place was identical to the women's, down to the gray

walls. The two buildings must have been built at the same time.

Two guys got off the elevator, their eyes widening as Raffe shoved his way inside, not waiting for them to exit fully before we entered.

"What the hell—" the shorter, bulkier guy exclaimed, turning to us just as Raffe pushed the third-floor button.

The taller, more athletic one shook his head and tugged on the guy's shoulder. "Dude, that's Raffe Wright. Don't piss him off."

"You got something you want to say to me?" Raffe arched a brow, edging in front of me to block me from the guys' view. His jaw twitched, everything inside him on edge.

The shorter guy's jaw dropped open. "Uh, no, sorry we were in your way."

"Don't let it happen again," Raffe sneered as the doors slid close.

I pushed him gently in the back and sighed. "Seriously?"

Raffe shrugged, glancing over his shoulder at me. "He was running his mouth, and I have a reputation on campus to maintain. We don't need humans feeling tempted to hang out with us."

"Did you forget?" I pointed at myself. "I'm *human*."

"Don't smell like one much since I claimed you." He winked, a smug smile tugging at his mouth for a split second. When the elevator opened, the smile vanished like it had been a figment of my imagination.

Still, my heart pattered—until we stepped into the hall-way. On the right, four doors down, the door to an apartment was open. As soon as Raffe's gaze landed on it, he bolted to it.

I couldn't move as quickly as him, and by the time I entered, things were chaotic. The apartment had the same floor plan as ours but opposite, so I turned left toward the living room and found Raffe grabbing a guy I'd never seen before by the throat and lifting him high above an evergreen couch.

Adam and Keith stood at the sides of the couch, watching Raffe as if this wasn't a big deal.

My instinct was to close the door so no one would see what was happening and rush to help this random man I didn't know. I inhaled sharply. That wasn't normal. But Raffe had to be acting this way for a reason.

"Where is he?" Raffe spat, droplets of spittle hitting the guy's face.

The scent of honey hit my nose, and it took me a second to realize I was smelling a man I didn't know. His scent overpowered the woodsy smells of the other guys, suggesting he wasn't a shifter.

"I don't *know*," the man rasped, his wavy, dark-blond hair framing his face. "He left late last night to find something to snack on. He asked me if I wanted to come, and I told him no because I'd eaten earlier. I told these two the same thing when they woke me up around three this morning, and I don't know why you're here, asking *again*."

Adam flinched. "Yeah, about that, we—"

Snapping his head in Adam's direction, Raffe's eyes glowed. "We'll discuss that shortly. Right now, I need Jared to tell me where I can fucking find Dave."

I swallowed. This must be Dave's roommate. Vampires already hated shifters, and the Veiled Circle was using that to their advantage. Raffe's behavior would only help their cause. "Jared, I'm sorry we barged in, but Dave stuck a needle into my neck and drugged me." If we couldn't get his help via threats, I hoped he was a decent person—er, vampire—and would help because of the situation.

Jared's light-gray eyes focused on me, and I moved to

Raffe's side. I placed a hand on Raffe's arm and gently pushed down. The buzz of our connection thrummed, and I could feel Raffe's rage retreat a bit.

He growled, clearly unhappy, but he obliged me by lowering Jared.

Jared's legs hit the couch, and he caught his balance and stood in front of it. Raffe released him but didn't move back. He was prepared to grab Jared again if needed.

I continued my explanation. "After Dave drugged me, people who wanted to brainwash me held me captive." I wasn't sure how else to put it. "We need to know how and why Dave is involved. So it would mean a lot to *me* if you could help us find him."

Keith snorted, unhappy with me, but I understood what it was like to feel threatened by bullies, and that was how the witches and the vampires viewed Raffe and his pack. If someone had shown me kindness, it would've made a difference.

Jared lifted his hands. "Seriously, I don't know where he is, but before he told me he was going to eat, he got a phone call."

"Who was it?" Raffe seethed. "And what did they want?"

"If I don't tell you, will you choke me again?" Jared rubbed his neck where Raffe's handprints showed faintly.

Nostrils flaring, Raffe hissed.

He was going to ruin the progress I'd made. I tightened my hold on his hand, wanting him to get the hint. He needed to shut up and let me handle this.

I tried to shuffle him sideways so he wasn't standing right in front of Jared, but he refused to budge.

"Do you know who it was?" I asked gently.

"No." Jared sidestepped, so he was in front of me and not Raffe. "I don't have any idea. But this last month, Dave was acting weird, and it wasn't unusual for him to get angry after taking a call."

Raffe tilted his head and sniffed, his eyes on Jared's face.

That was interesting, but it didn't help us. I felt like an incompetent detective, and I didn't like it at all. "Can you think of anything else? Any places he'd go or people he'd visit?"

"His parents are dead, and all his friends are here on campus." Jared shrugged. "But I think he was heading out to meet someone he didn't want me to know about."

Keith stepped up next to Raffe, staring Jared down. "I don't know how he's doing it, but he's lying. He's found a way to conceal the smell."

Jared grimaced. "And you wonder why I don't want to talk to you."

"He's right." Adam shrugged from his spot a few feet away on my side of the couch. "You said he invited you to go with him. If he was meeting someone he was arguing with, why would he ask you to come along?"

Dammit. They had a point. But Jared had sounded sincere.

"Why not ask the question instead of accusing me of lying?" Jared wrinkled his nose. "Dave invited me because he *knew* I'd fed a couple of hours ago. I didn't need to eat again, and I was already in bed watching por—er, a movie."

My face flamed. Now, things were awkward. Images I didn't need to have of him flashed in my mind, and I pushed them away.

Of course, *now* Keith laughed. "Are you saying he walked in on you whacking off?"

Raffe shoved Keith in the shoulder hard, and he stumbled into the wall. Raffe bared his teeth and said, "Don't talk like that in front of my *mate*. Got it?"

Now, I was looking at the commanding Raffe I'd met on my first day here, but this time, his anger was directed at one of his own and not me. I gritted my teeth. I didn't like him turning on Keith, which didn't make sense because Keith made my life hell.

"*Mate?*" Jared's eyebrows rose almost to his hairline, and he focused on my hand on Raffe's arm. "Wait, I thought she was human." He sniffed, his eyes widening. "You've claimed her. Holy shit."

"Which is why, if you two don't stop talking about your *movie*, I may kill you." Raffe's chest heaved.

"Yeah, okay." Jared took a step away from me, moving closer to Adam. "Got it. Though, in fairness, he's the one who took it to the next level."

"Oh, I know," Raffe replied, glaring at Keith, who was yanking on the hem of his black polo shirt. "If anyone says anything that might make my mate think of someone else inappropriately, I will *hurt* them. *Happily.*"

I smiled a little then sobered. We were losing focus. "Dave entered your room."

"Which he forgot to lock, *clearly,*" Keith added with a smirk.

Raffe snarled, and my blood jolted. Keith was going to keep pushing Raffe. Did he *want* Raffe to kick his ass? I didn't want my mate to lose his cool, especially with his father already upset with him.

I had to fight to keep my smile from spreading. "And he invited you to join him in feeding, knowing you'd say no."

"Why would he do that?" Adam scratched the back of his neck. "If he knew you'd say no, he could've just left."

Pursing his lips, Jared tapped his foot on the floor. "One time, when he left without saying anything, I went searching for him. He probably didn't want that to happen again."

My blood was at a mere jolt, but I could faintly read something coming from him. He was nervous, like he wanted to hide something. From the way the guys were reacting, he was telling the truth. Jared had to be hiding something. "Was he meeting someone that time?"

Jared shook his head. "He wasn't, but seriously, that's all I know. He's probably in the woods somewhere, but you've had someone watching me all night, so I haven't been able to search for him."

He'd deflected my question, confirming my suspicion, but I doubted he'd be willing to tell me anything specific with Raffe, Keith, and Adam here.

"He's not there." Adam clasped his hands in front of his chest. "I recruited two other wolf shifters to help me canvass the woods. We didn't find him, just a faint trace of his scent that disappeared into thin air."

Despite my recent entry into the supernatural world, I knew what that meant.

A coven member had covered Dave's tracks.

I stopped breathing. "What time was the phone call?"

"A little after midnight." Jared's brows furrowed. "Why?"

That was around the time Slade and I had escaped from the underground bunker.

Raffe punched his palm. "That fucker ran. He was alerted about the escape."

I was still trying to reconcile Dave, the druggist jerk, with the nice guy I'd known up until he'd injected me. The night he'd fought so hard to resist my blood when I was damn near losing control had earned my trust.

Maybe he'd fought the temptation so hard because he knew the Veiled Circle wanted me.

Had I been wrong about him this whole time?

"A coven member must have helped him." Adam pinched the bridge of his nose.

"Reasons I don't like coven members." Keith pursed his lips as if he'd tasted something bad.

Jared huffed. "Because wolf shifters are so *great*."

I wanted to reach out and shake him. Was he trying to provoke Raffe? Could *he* be part of the secret society?

Glancing at the clock, I noted the time. We were already five minutes late meeting Aldric. "Raffe, we need to go." Though I was nervous as hell about going to Raffe's home, I didn't want to piss off his dad further.

"Yeah, okay. Come on, guys." Raffe took my hand and headed toward the door. "Let's go. Jared, contact one of us immediately if you see or hear from Dave."

I flinched at the barked-out order. Just asking Jared would have gone a long way.

"Sure. I'll get on that," Jared replied as the four of us entered the hallway.

Keith and Adam glanced at each other as Raffe and I headed to the elevator. More tension filled the air, which puzzled me. We'd left Jared—what else was there to be upset about?

A guy stepped into the hallway and paused when he saw us, then hurried back into his room.

Strange.

When the four of us got onto the elevator and the door closed, Adam cleared his throat and said, "Raffe—"

My mate released my hand and shoved Adam into the wall, anger pulsing off him. "Don't say another *fucking* word."

CHAPTER TWELVE

I jerked back, startled. I understood he was mad, but I hadn't expected his anger to be directed at Adam.

Keith ran a hand down his face. "Man, we—"

"*Shut up!*" Raffe bellowed, and something strong lacing his voice made my lips close.

What the hell? Something was wrong with me.

"Why did you wait until morning to tell me Dave had disappeared?" Raffe released Adam, stepping back to glare at both men. "I should've been notified *immediately* to search for him."

The strange presence in me nudged forward harder, and my body warmed inappropriately. Part of me always hated it when he got controlling and rude, but another side thought it was hot. Suddenly, I found it *extremely* sexy and wanted to jump him here in front of everyone.

"See?" Keith lifted a hand. "Told you he'd get all alpha-y. We should've told him."

Adam cut his eyes to Keith and scowled.

That was enough to take my hormones down a notch. I

swallowed my snort, not wanting to make the situation worse. Leave it to Keith to throw someone under the bus.

Raffe sneered. "That makes it worse. You knew better and still said nothing."

The elevator door opened, and for a moment, they didn't even notice. Raffe wore his displeasure in the form of a frown like he usually did around campus. Keith didn't seem fazed, standing tall and cocky. But Adam's forehead was creased, revealing his concern.

The four of us marched out the door and went into the parking lot to meet Aldric. Raffe took my hand, the buzz simmering between us, but his anger didn't ease.

Adam hurried up on Raffe's other side. He exhaled noisily and said, "What would you have done? You hadn't slept in days, and you had *just* gotten Skylar back. You would've been torn about what to do, and we were handling it."

Jaw twitching, Raffe didn't respond.

We passed a group of students heading in the direction I should've been going—to class. It was Tuesday, which meant I'd miss one day of every class. That wasn't a huge deal for statistics and economics, but microbiology and chemistry were a whole different ball game. It was easy to get left behind in science, and I'd need to get notes from someone and read the material in detail. I couldn't afford to let my grades slip, not with vet school on the horizon.

Keith caught up with me and rolled his eyes.

I suspected he blamed me for everything. In a way, I agreed. Until I'd come along, nothing like *this* had happened, and I was driving a wedge between the three of them. Though I hadn't intended to, it didn't matter. Intentions didn't mean much when someone caused problems.

"It was my right to be *torn*." Raffe puffed out his chest. "I'm your prince, and you don't get to decide for me."

Adam tilted his head. "Aren't I supposed to be your strategist? If I am, you need to trust me. What would you joining us have accomplished? Nothing. His scent had vanished, and not even a wolf of your strength could overcome that."

Raffe's car came into view with Aldric pacing in front of it. He noticed us as we approached.

"That probably changed when he decided to claim *her*." Keith wrinkled his nose and spat. "I bet she's been talking to him about how she should take our place."

My blood surged, and the jolt went straight to a low fizz. I understood why Keith resented me. I wasn't one of them, not really, but that didn't mean he could talk about me like that. I stopped in my tracks and prepared to tell him where he could go.

But Raffe beat me to it.

He tugged me behind him and shoved Keith in the chest. Even though I couldn't see his eyes, I had no doubt they were glowing.

In public.

Around humans.

Worse, in front of Aldric.

My lungs quit working.

"I've been more lax than I should've been with you." A growl laced Raffe's words, making them almost inaudible. "And it ends now. You've pushed me too far."

Adam touched my arm, tearing my gaze from Raffe.

He mouthed the words, *Calm him down.*

Like I knew how to do that. If I did, he wouldn't get flustered as often as he did. And since I'd returned, he'd been acting more erratic than before.

"Raffe," Aldric warned. "Now's not the time. You know that."

The warning fell on deaf ears. Raffe clutched the front of

Keith's shirt and snarled, "Say one more negative thing about her. I *dare* you."

Keith flinched, the first sign of fear I'd ever seen from him. He mashed his lips together and shook his head.

I froze. Seeing Keith like this affected me more than I would have thought possible. With his cocky demeanor gone, my heart quickened. This situation was worse than I'd realized.

A few girls stopped on their way to class to watch the show.

"Tell Skylar you're sorry." Raffe didn't release his hold; instead, his voice lowered to a more menacing tone. "And mean it, or I will kick your ass. She didn't mean for anything like this to happen, and the way you're trying to make her feel like shit on top of everything else is a dick move that I won't tolerate. She's my mate, so you either fucking accept it, or our friendship ends now. Got it?"

My stomach somersaulted and churned. I loved that he was standing up for me, but causing problems between childhood friends made me sick. The strange presence inside me squirmed while Raffe's determination and anger sat heavy in its spot. I hadn't had a friend since kindergarten when Lizzie had turned on me. I'd always wanted a true friend, and at EEU, I'd found three. The last thing I wanted was for Raffe to lose one because he'd chosen to be with me. "Raffe, he's just worried—"

"Don't," he replied but kept his gaze on Keith. "I have to handle this, or he'll keep escalating, and I'm at my wits' end. He needs to get in fucking line or get out of my life. You're my mate. I made that decision. It can't be undone or changed, so his attitude ends now. He needs to decide what sort of relationship he wants with me—friends or enemies."

Aldric and Adam exchanged terse glances. They weren't

thrilled with Raffe, but neither was I. I didn't know what needed to happen, but he'd better calm down before he made things worse.

"This is how it is? You're willing to throw away twenty-three years of friendship for *her*?" The area around Keith's eyes tightened.

"I'm not sure how much clearer I can be." Raffe released his hold and lifted his chin, coming off even more threatening. "I chose her. Our bond is unbreakable."

Keith scoffed, the warmth in his eyes fading to bleak pain. "Fine." He looked at me. "Skylar, I'm sorry, but to be honest, I'm struggling with Raffe's decision. Regarding everything that deals with you, he's more overbearing than normal, which makes me furious. But I'm taking it out on *you,* and that's not fair. I'm sorry."

Jaw dropping, I blinked a few times. Had I misunderstood him? But when Raffe's shoulders relaxed, there was no denying what I'd heard. He couldn't take his anger out on Raffe, which made me the easier target.

"I won't say it's okay, but for Raffe's sake, I accept your apology." That was the thing with bullies—if you allowed them to justify their actions, they'd never hold themselves accountable. They had to learn boundaries, and I wouldn't allow Raffe's actions to be in vain by mitigating what he'd done.

That strange sensation I kept feeling propelled me next to Raffe. "But, Keith ..." Hell, I wasn't sure what I wanted to say. "You make one rude-ass comment like that to me again, and it won't be Raffe putting you in your place." I lifted my chin, the strange sensation settling inside me. "It'll be me."

A cardamom scent hit my nose, and my connection to Raffe heated up. At the same time, Keith smirked, but the cruel lines that usually accompanied that look were missing. Instead, something strange crossed his face.

"Is that so?" He tilted his head. "I almost want to rise to that challenge."

Raffe growled, the sound threatening but low so the humans didn't hear.

Keith lifted his hands in surrender. "I said *almost*, but I get it. The two of you will team up and kick my ass. I'll try to behave."

That was more of a concession than I'd expected from *him*.

"We need to go," Aldric interjected, his voice dripping with disapproval. "Your father arrived home and wants to know our status."

"Since he refuses to ask me himself, tell him we're on our way," Raffe said and extended his hand to Keith.

Shoulders relaxing, Keith accepted Raffe's hand, and they shook, I guessed sealing the promise.

I was just happy for another small win, especially after Dave had vanished.

As soon as they dropped each other's hand, Raffe tensed. "And if you two *ever* leave me out of something important like Dave's disappearance again, we're going to have serious problems."

"Got it." Adam averted his gaze to the grass. "But honestly, we weren't trying to hide it. We were just making sure you rested and reconnected with Skylar."

Raffe sighed but nodded. "Still wasn't your call to make." He took my hand and led me toward the car. "I get it, but don't let it happen again."

"Understood." Adam hung his head.

With every step, my legs felt weighed down. It was time to head to Raffe's childhood pack home, and I feared what would greet us. He'd warned me there would be challenges to our mate bond, and that hadn't truly computed until now.

Meeting the king.

I'd met him only once at the one football game I'd attended. The man had screamed power and intimidation, and my blood had fritzed in his presence. He'd also forced Raffe to decry me so I would be ostracized by humans and shifters alike.

Raffe took me to the passenger side and opened my door.

"Uh ..." I chewed on my tongue. "Aldric might want to sit in the front."

"No, I'm good." Aldric gestured to a burnt-orange Bentley sedan parked beside the BMW. "That's my ride. I'm just waiting to follow you there."

In other words, he wanted to ensure we didn't change course. "Are all wolf shifters so trusting?" My mouth had run away from me once again. I'd never had a problem controlling myself before, and I needed to stop with the snark before we met with King Jovian.

"We were"—he arched a brow—"until you came into Raffe's life."

Touché. I told myself to get into the car and not drag it out, but my mouth had a mind of its own. "I haven't forced him to do *anything*. Don't make me out to be the bad guy."

Raffe placed a hand on my back and said, "She's right. Everything I've done has been of my own choosing."

"Her mouth is going to get you both in trouble, especially with you enabling her." Aldric crossed his arms. "I sure hope you know what you're doing. She's your mate and should be making things easier on you, not alienating you from your family."

"She's not alienating me from anything," he snapped then kissed the top of my head. "That's everyone else's doing."

My heart ached from the sweet gesture, and I slid into my seat.

Raffe marched around the hood while Aldric got into his sedan. The looks on their faces were of pure determination.

Both vehicles started, and Raffe backed out of the spot.

"What is all this about?" I asked. He had to know something. I had no doubt he'd been pack-linking his dad to get answers.

"I don't know." He glanced in the rearview mirror then drove to the road.

I stared at the apartments. Josie had joined Keith and Adam, who were still standing where we'd left them, watching us go.

A shiver ran down my spine.

Something was off. Or was that paranoia from being kidnapped and held captive?

"Hey," Raffe said and placed his hand on my thigh. He squeezed gently and smiled timidly. "Everything will work out. Besides, the two of us will be there together. It'll be good to get this meeting over and done with so my parents' reaction to us won't be hanging over our heads."

I wasn't so sure about that, but I wanted to address one thing. "Thank you for protecting me, but I don't want to cause problems between you and your family and friends." Unfortunately, I now understood why he'd struggled with our relationship. Given Aldric's reaction, I feared what we would face in Seattle.

"Like I said, you're not the one causing problems. Dad has a hang-up about wolves being the strongest species, believing we can't risk diluting our bloodline. He'll have to accept our mating, or we'll figure something else out."

The problem with powerful people was that, sometimes, they made others feel like they didn't have a say in their own lives. I suspected that was what we were going to walk into and one reason the king had demanded Raffe be there in person.

With that said, it would be best if we presented a united front. "Raffe, what I asked about after you saved me ... I want you to know—"

"Please, don't." He kept his hand on my leg. "We don't need to talk about it. I don't have the energy for it."

I bit my bottom lip. "But—"

"Seriously, Sky." He forced a smile that didn't reach his eyes. "We're more than okay. I'm over it."

A stench like eggs filled my nose, and I wanted to gag. Where was that coming from?

"Why don't you take a nap? You need it." He removed his hand and turned on Pink Floyd.

Not wanting to push him to talk, I sighed and did as he'd asked. I leaned my seat back and tried to go to sleep.

———

WE TURNED into a long driveway on top of Cougar Mountain. Raffe's pack neighborhood was nestled in a forest far from the main road.

A huge mansion appeared, the thick woods behind it. The house had stones around each window and tan siding for the walls. Various plants lined a stone sidewalk that led to six huge steps up to the wooden front door.

Raffe parked his car in front, and I noticed Aldric's Bentley continuing down a side road, deeper into the woods.

Strange.

"Let's go. Dad knows we're here." Raffe climbed from the car.

Following his lead, I headed up the stairs. My blood jolted

then fizzed close to a hum. I wasn't sure what sort of welcome we'd receive.

When we reached the covered porch, Raffe turned right toward a second door. He took my hand and opened it without pausing.

We entered an office, and my attention homed in on the man standing in the middle of the room on a fancy rug.

King Jovian's salt-and-pepper hair was messy, and he had dark circles under his steel-blue eyes. But it was the red hue of his face and the sneer on his lips—so noticeable even through his brown beard—that made me falter.

He rasped, "Do you know what you've done? Because of your choice, we've lost everything."

CHAPTER THIRTEEN

Raffe chuckled while inching in front of me as we came into the room. Despite the carefree sound, his body was rigid, and he took deep, ragged breaths to stay calm.

The hot presence of his anger returned inside me—a damn near constant emotion for Raffe lately, and I hated it because it was all due to me. My blood jolted.

"Don't be dramatic. I didn't ruin *everything*." Raffe scoffed. "You always say you leave the theatrics to Mom, so let's keep it that way. Only a handful of people know about Skylar and me, so you can control the message."

Control the message. I didn't like the sound of that.

King Jovian swung his gaze at me and glowered. The strange presence in my chest crept forward, pushing harder than before. The longer he stared at me, the more intense the sensation became, and when his eyes glowed, that presence churned until I thought it might leap from my chest.

I averted my eyes, taking in the nicest room I'd ever seen, especially for a study. That weird presence in my chest grew hot, a feeling similar to Raffe's anger. Now, it felt as if part of *me* was upset with myself for breaking eye contact

But breaking eye contact was the best way to handle bullies. When an imminent threat presented itself, like the king, you didn't escalate things with a challenging stare.

Silence descended. My skin crawled, and I focused on the wall to my right, where two gigantic wooden bookshelves flanked a small cutout.

"Anything you have to say, you can say it out loud to my *mate*." Raffe's voice deepened, determination bleeding through each word.

That must be why King Jovian's eyes were glowing. He was pack-linking with Raffe. A shiver ran down my spine, contrasting with the heat from Raffe's emotions and the presence.

"This is *wolf* business," King Jovian growled. "Which doesn't involve her, seeing as she's *human*. She may smell like a wolf, but that's only because of your stupidity in claiming her. Or is that something you've conveniently forgotten?"

A deep rattle rumbled from Raffe's throat. I kept my attention on the bookshelf and noticed a picture of King Jovian, Queen Tashya, and Raffe. The king stood in the center, wearing a black suit, with the queen on his left, her dirty-blonde hair pulled back and makeup emphasizing her fair skin and gray eyes. She wore a regal black dress that matched the king's suit.

My focus settled on the image of Raffe.

I'd never seen him look like that. He wore his typical blank expression, the one that was intimidating and screamed not to mess with him, but he was wearing a black suit that, even in the picture, showed off the outlines of his muscles. A little scruff made him look slightly older, but his piercing blue eyes held the type of man he truly was if you knew what to look for. The *yank* in my chest took hold and urged me toward the real Raffe.

My mate stepped in front of me, blocking me from Jovian's view.

My blood jolted again, and I clenched my jaw. Whether intentionally or not, by stepping between his dad and me, Raffe had removed me from the conversation, but I couldn't voice my concerns without King Jovian overhearing me, and I didn't want to contradict Raffe when we were supposed to be presenting a united front. I kept my mouth shut.

"I claimed her, Dad." He lifted his chin, a muscle twitching between his shoulder blades. "You'll have to accept this. She is my *mate*—my equal—so you might as well include her in the discussion because I'll share everything with her when we get out of here."

My chest relaxed. With everything he'd done for me and for us, I had to believe we would weather the storm and come out stronger.

"Your *equal*?" King Jovian spat. "If that's the case, why are you blocking her from my view? That contradicts everything you're saying and reinforces what I already know. You screwed up."

My breath caught, and I flinched. King Jovian was Raffe's father. Did King Jovian see regret in Raffe's eyes when I couldn't? Did being captured make Raffe question that I wasn't strong enough to be by his side? Or had me questioning him about the warehouse photo made Raffe question whether we should truly be together? If either were the case, he couldn't do a damn thing about it since he'd bitten me.

Acid burned my throat as the core question slammed into me.

Did Raffe feel *trapped* with me now?

Raffe fisted his hands. "I didn't screw up, and I don't regret my decision. The only reason I'm blocking her is because I don't want you taking out your anger on *her*. Smell the air, *Dad*, and you'll see that I'm not lying."

Some of the weight on my shoulders vanished. He didn't regret claiming me, though that didn't mean he wasn't hurt by it. Knowing I needed to be the type of woman who didn't hide, wanting to be worthy of Raffe, I placed a hand on Raffe's back to let him know I was there. Then I moved up next to him because his dad was right. If Raffe was proclaiming I was his equal, he needed to show it beyond words.

I squeezed my shoulder blades together so that I stood tall.

"If she's your equal, she can handle it," King Jovian sneered, and the hatred I saw in his eyes had my lungs seizing.

I'd seen numerous people who didn't like me or feared me, thanks to my strange blood, but *this* was something else.

Something more.

My blood fizzed, and I could read his disgust and rage clearly. If I'd been a bug, he'd have squashed me without hesitation. Between his disgust and the raw power he radiated, I wanted to step back, but I also wanted to march toward him to prove that I could. Once again, it was as if I had two personalities at war with each other. My mouth often got me into trouble, but I could usually control it when I knew saying something would go too far.

Then again, my mouth had a mind of its own. "Well, here I am."

"If you don't start talking, then Sky and I will go back to campus. We're missing another day of classes because you demanded that I come here." Raffe stepped closer to me. Our arms brushed, and the connection between us buzzed.

King Jovian grimaced and shook his head. "I should've known something was off when you pulled wolves from our pack and other packs on campus to find her." He waved a hand between Raffe and me. "But *claiming* her? Have you lost your damn mind?"

"I know it's not ideal," Raffe started, and I gasped.

Pain squeezed my heart, and the presence in my chest jostled, mirroring my shock and hurt. He sounded like he had when we'd been dating in secret and Keith had walked in on us in my bedroom. He'd made it clear then that he'd wished he *didn't* feel a connection with me, which was damn similar to what he'd said now.

Maybe my questions about the photos had done more damage to us than I'd realized.

"Not *ideal*," King Jovian parroted back. "That's putting it way too mildly."

"Let me finish." Raffe cut his eyes to me, hurt reflected in them once more. I swore I heard his voice in my head say, *Of course she thinks the worst.*

Before I could question it, he continued, his irises burning a bright icy blue. "It's not ideal, but I wouldn't change it for the world. It took Skylar leaving me to realize I never want to be without her again, and her kidnapping taught me that I don't want to live without her in my life."

My face burned, and my heart galloped. Once again, I'd thought poorly of him without giving him a chance to finish. He'd said exactly what I needed to hear, but I didn't deserve his loyalty after my horrible assumptions.

"There's more at risk than just your place as my heir." King Jovian pulled on the hem of his white button-down shirt, which was wrinkled. "I determined a way to appease the Eastern wolf shifters, only for you to ruin it the moment it was solidified."

Now would've been a nice time to be able to pack-link with Raffe to ask what this was about.

Raffe pulled me to his side. The warmth of our connection settled my blood to a low fizz, and the presence inside me eased back. Even the rage and hurt in the spot where I could feel Raffe's emotions lessened slightly. It was amazing how we both reacted to a simple touch between us.

"We need to put the East in their place. That's what you've said before." Raffe arched a brow. "Don't use something that's not a real threat as leverage to get between Sky and me. It won't work, and you should know that, seeing as you and Mom claimed each other and have a similar bond."

"I've sheltered you from the growing threat Eastern wolves pose." King Jovian paced in front of us, his bare feet barely making a sound on the rug. "They plan to separate from us and name their own king. That's why I was there—to mend the gap between us."

That sounded ominous. A knot formed in my stomach as I waited for the punch line. Whatever it was would be something King Jovian thought Raffe would listen to.

Raffe tilted his head and remained silent.

"You've been betrothed to the Atlanta alpha's daughter. You're to claim her and move to the city to integrate into their society. You are to learn the struggles they face and find solutions for their complaints."

A lump formed in my throat, making it impossible to swallow. I hadn't seen that one coming.

"It wasn't your place to make any such agreement." The veins in Raffe's neck bulged, and his arm clamped tighter around my waist. "You don't get to choose my mate. Only I can decide that, and I've chosen."

King Jovian's nostrils flared. "Raffe, this isn't about you. This is about our people. That's more important than anything else, and it should be an honor for you to do something to benefit our rule."

That presence inside me lunged forward again, and my

blood fizzed so high it almost hummed despite Raffe's touch. This man wanted to come between me and my mate, and the scary part was that it might work.

"There's one problem you seem to be forgetting." Raffe placed his fist to his chin. "I've already claimed a mate, and that can't be undone. Not that I would anyway. You promised something that wasn't yours to give."

"Like *fuck* I did." King Jovian marched across the room and got in Raffe's face. "I'm your *father* and *king*. Or did she make you forget that along with your *place* in our hierarchy?"

My blood inched a breath away from a hum. I couldn't control it, not with King Jovian trying to come between Raffe and me. The urge to hurt this man surged along with the presence inside me.

Raffe released his hold on me and stepped closer to his dad, their chests touching.

I thought when Keith and Raffe got into an argument, it was a pissing match, but nothing compared to this. Their eyes glowed as their wolves surged forward.

"*She* hasn't made me forget anything, but none of this matters. The choice was made, and I have absolutely no regrets. Besides, she's my *fated mate,* which trumps *everything.*"

His dad threw his head back and laughed. The sound was loud and unhinged. "I don't know how you managed to lie without the smell, but that's impossible, and we both know it. Fated mates haven't happened in *centuries*, and it would never happen between a wolf and a human."

"I'm not only human." I was so tired of everyone tossing that word around like I was *nothing*. "I'm an arcane-borne. My blood holds power." The words had slipped from my lips even though I'd been warned not to share this information with anyone. But maybe, just maybe, his dad would react differently with that knowledge.

King Jovian's face paled as his entire focus turned to me. "What?"

Raffe's brows furrowed. "You've heard of her kind?"

"She needs to go." King Jovian pointed at the door. "I don't care if she takes your car, but she needs to get out of here. You and I will go to Atlanta, where you'll meet your betrothed. There's no point in waiting until graduation. We'll talk to Supreme Priestess Olwyn so you can finish your courses online."

Something was off. He was angry, but fear was making him push Raffe harder. The thought of Raffe with someone else pushed my blood to a hum.

Raffe clenched his hands. "I'm not going. It would be pointless. Skylar is my mate. It's done."

"You can't claim the Eastern heiress, but you can marry her. Make it legally binding in the eyes of the humans and live with her far away from this *human* who's messing with your mind." King Jovian rubbed his hands together. "In time, you'll see that this was the right choice. Besides, your mate bond isn't complete yet and never will be because she's not a shifter."

My blood hummed, the power flowing through my veins as my anger, Raffe's anger, and the anger of the presence inside me blurred into one.

"Everyone will see that you made a mistake and rectified it, bringing peace back to the wolf shifters here in the States."

"No," Raffe and I bellowed. The presence inside me clawed at my chest while my blood went beyond a hum to a vibration, spinning out of control, ready to push power out everywhere.

Raffe's hands fisted like he was struggling to maintain

control. "I won't walk away from Skylar and *marry* some woman who will never hold a candle to *her*." He pointed at me and bared his teeth. "I don't fucking care if the East breaks away because being with Skylar is what's best for me and what makes me the best choice to lead our people into the future."

The vibration centered under my feet, ready to reach out and defeat the threat in front of me. Sounds grew louder, and I could hear Raffe's and King Jovian's every heartbeat.

King Jovian's eyes glowed brighter. "You don't have a choice." Power radiated from each word, stalling my blood for a moment. "Your alpha commands you to leave Skylar and go to Atlanta to do what's right for our kingdom."

"Don't you fucking dare," Raffe said through clenched teeth. "I will *never* forgive you."

"That's a risk I'm willing to take." King Jovian hovered over him. "Bow to my will as your alpha and king."

CHAPTER FOURTEEN

The floor shook underneath my feet, the power pushing from my body and into the ground, but even with my blood fritzing, King Jovian didn't tear his gaze from Raffe.

Strain and fear, both my own and Raffe's, constricted my chest, and with my magic this strong, I could feel King Jovian's anger, determination, and fear as he stared down my mate.

This had to be what alpha-willing was, and burning acid inched up my throat. Forcing someone to do something against their will was sick. At least my bullies had excluded me from things; they hadn't forced me to do something that would break me. What sort of father did this to his child? Even when my parents had encouraged me to go out and make friends, they'd never forced my hand. And *this* was way worse than them wanting me to have a chance at being *happy*. King Jovian didn't care about his son's wants or needs.

The ground shook harder in tandem with my rising emotions—guilt for not being there for Raffe when he needed me the most and driving distance between us.

My head screamed that I needed to calm down, but I also

knew that any attempt would be futile. It would be the equivalent of trying to get a dog not to play with a squeaky toy.

Pointless.

The immediate threat was King Jovian and his determination to come between Raffe and me. I couldn't calm down with that threat imminent.

I could think of one positive—if things got bad enough, King Jovian would have to break this standoff and handle the repercussions of my blood. Not that it would make things better between us and him. He'd eventually try to alpha-will Raffe again.

Sweat beaded on Raffe's forehead as he fought the command of his alpha. *I can't lose her. I can't let him win this battle.*

His words echoed in my head, faint but clear. I had to be imagining them and reading into the emotions that clung to him.

"Sky, you need to lock your magic down," Raffe rasped, but I could read and feel the concern pouring off him. "Fighting him will be pointless if you wind up killing yourself."

I snorted humorlessly. He was right—I ran the risk of dying—but the thought of him being with someone else hurt too damn bad, especially with our relationship under threat. "Sorry, but I can't control it, not when he's risking us."

"That's my point," King Jovian gritted out. "She's not only human but untrained and volatile. She can't stand next to you, and I have no other heir as an option. I need to do this for our people, and you will see it clearly in time."

My breathing quickened. Once again, I was unworthy in someone else's eyes, which shouldn't have been surprising. After coming to EEU and feeling a sense of belonging, this felt like Lizzie in kindergarten all over again. The pain was worse because the price would be Raffe.

I knew of one way to calm myself, and maybe if I touched Raffe, he'd realize I was there for him.

I took his hand, wanting to simultaneously stomp and yell because I couldn't think of a damn thing I could do to help him. I felt powerless despite the ground quaking, the family picture behind the desk crashing to the floor, the huge desk shaking as if it was about to splinter, and the wooden planks curling upward from the floor.

When my hand touched Raffe's, a shock sprang between us, stronger than any buzz from before. Raffe's discomfort ebbed as surprise took over, but he didn't avert his eyes from his dad. If anything, my touch increased his determination tenfold, which was what I wanted.

With all my animal facts and the classes I'd taken, I understood why. Wolves were all about strength and dominance, which revolved around fights, stare-offs, and hunting.

The ground shook harder, and the wooden floor cracked and popped. The desk broke apart. As if that wasn't bad enough, the odd presence inside me that was becoming more and more of a hindrance grew hotter. Strength pushed into my arm, easing my blood a bit, but not enough to keep the ground from quaking.

A door that led into the house opened, and two male shifters ran into the room. The taller one's eyes widened when he took in Raffe and King Jovian glaring at one another while the shorter one hurried to turn off the lights in the room.

Then I heard the creak, and I glanced up to find the chandelier in the middle of the room dropping a few inches before something caught it. But it wouldn't stay that way for long.

I jerked on Raffe's arm, knowing we needed to step back. Not only might I implode, but there was no telling how many people I might kill along with me. One being Raffe, which was unacceptable.

"I won't *leave* her," Raffe snarled, not fighting me and taking a few steps back. "Your alpha will won't work on me."

King Jovian marched toward us, either not noticing or caring about the chandelier swaying precariously over him.

"Leave," King Jovian barked and pointed at the doors the guards had gone through. "I need to talk to my son and Skylar alone."

"But sir, there's an earthquake happening only in this room. You should—" the taller one started.

King Jovian shouted, "Leave *now*."

The two guards listened, not hesitating, and my blood calmed to a hum, which was ironic, given the situation. How my blood had increased to more than that without leaving me on the ground dying was beyond me, but the power swirling through me was still too strong.

As if some higher being had a morbid sense of humor, the desk splintered like the coffee table had in Lucy's and my apartment months ago.

Still, the king remained focused on Raffe.

"You heard me," he rasped. "You will leave her. *Now*."

My heart sputtered. This was it. Raffe was going to leave me, and I'd never be able to apologize and beg for his forgiveness.

A cocky smirk spread across Raffe's face. "No."

I blinked, startled enough that my blood dropped to a high fizz. The floor quieted.

"What?" King Jovian croaked and blinked. "That's impossible. You *have* to bend to your alpha."

Raffe shrugged. "I don't know what to tell you, *Dad*, but it's not working."

My eyes burned as relieved tears flooded them. I'd been so

certain his dad would win, and a bitter taste filled my mouth. Once again, I'd doubted Raffe. What the *hell* was wrong with me? He was amazing.

Mouth opening and closing, King Jovian reminded me of a fish out of water.

"What's wrong?" Raffe tilted his head, his face slipping into the mask of indifference he wore on campus and around almost everybody. The look screamed *don't mess with me*, which was an amazing attribute on the football field. "Giving up?"

I loved his confidence, but I didn't want to antagonize Jovian into trying again and succeeding. "Raffe—"

"Stop," King Jovian snarled. He jabbed a finger at me. "You've done *enough*. I knew something was strange when Raffe avoided my questions about you, but I assumed he was focused on football and finishing his degree. Little did I know you were entrancing *him*."

I laughed then tried to cover it with a cough. But from the way his eyes narrowed, he wasn't buying it.

Fair enough.

Raffe moved forward, attempting to edge me out of the way again, but I moved with him. I wouldn't hide.

"You just accused me of being untrained and volatile, and now you're claiming I'm skilled enough to entrance him?" My voice rose higher than I wanted, but dammit, this whole visit had gone worse than I could've imagined. What if I hadn't been here to support Raffe when his dad had tried to alpha-will him? He might not have been able to push through on his own. "Is it even possible to entrance someone?"

"Centuries ago, witches had potions that could give them control over humans and supernaturals." King Jovian wrinkled his nose.

I didn't like what he was insinuating, and my blood

neared a hum again. "From what Slade says, wolf shifters banned those documents, so please tell me, how would I get a hold of one to even know what to do? And don't forget, I'm not a witch. I'm a mere *human*." I threw what he considered a slur back at him.

King Jovian lifted his head. "I should've run you off campus on that first day. Raffe and Aldric talked me out of it, saying it would make the witches pay more attention to you. I'm not sure that's possible, given how close you are to them. Your mere presence—"

"If you finish that sentence, it will ruin our relationship *forever*." Raffe's hands tightened, and his jaw twitched. "You demanded that I come here, which I did even though it was the last thing I wanted to do. I knew you wouldn't be thrilled about Skylar and me and our relationship, but I never dreamed you would try to force me to leave my fated mate, especially in such a disrespectful way."

My heart ached for him, and I hated that I hadn't been more understanding about his situation and why he had been so hesitant to come out about our relationship. Now I understood where he'd been coming from. His dad was determined to get his way even if he had to force his son to do what he wanted.

"You're a *prince*." King Jovian huffed, enhancing the sound of his lungs filling and emptying. "You don't get the luxury of choosing the way other shifters do. There are certain expectations—"

"Maybe I should leave the pack." Raffe inhaled so deeply that his chest puffed out. "Then none of this will be an issue."

"None of it will be an *issue* for me?" King Jovian yanked on the ends of his hair. "You're my *only* heir. Something I used to be proud of."

"For doing what you told him to instead of following his

heart and fighting for his happiness?" I asked, wanting the man to wake up and realize how selfish he sounded. "He wants to be with me."

King Jovian cut the air with his arm. "A royal doesn't get to do what he *desires*. He does what is required of him to keep his people strong and in line. Marrying the Atlanta alpha's daughter is the best way to do this." He stared Raffe down. "A year ago, you wouldn't have hesitated."

"I have chosen my mate." Raffe intertwined our fingers and walked backward, guiding us to the doorway leading outside. "I won't marry anyone but Skylar, and if leaving the pack is what it takes for you to listen to me, so be it." He turned on his heels and opened the door.

I swallowed. I hated leaving like this, but staying would only escalate the matter. The king would likely try to alpha-will his son again. I couldn't live with myself if I tried to get Raffe to stay and it worked.

Still, wolves were pack animals. They weren't meant to be on their own, and I wasn't sure what the consequences of Raffe leaving his pack would be.

Outside, the cool afternoon air circled us, and the misty rain hit my face, cooling my blood. Luckily, that presence in my chest eased too, and I breathed a little easier.

"Raffe, come back." King Jovian's heavy footsteps followed us. He said louder, "We aren't done here."

"We are. I have *nothing* left to say. You can figure out another way to get the Eastern wolves back in line." Raffe opened the passenger door of the SUV. "In fact, why don't you alpha-will them into remaining in the pack? You seem to be *really* good at that."

I mashed my lips together to hide my smile as I slid into the vehicle. Raffe made a good point. Why hadn't King Jovian done that?

When Raffe opened the driver's side door, King Jovian said, "If you leave, things will change between us."

"That already happened in your study." Raffe shook his head and frowned. "I hope losing me is worth it." He climbed in and slammed the door, then started the car and backed out.

I glanced in the rearview mirror and watched King Jovian's face turn bloodred. I could only hope his anger was mixed with regret.

Raffe placed a hand on my thigh, and for the next several miles, we rode in silence. I didn't want to push him. He needed to process everything that had happened. What his dad had done was shitty, but that didn't make it easier. I couldn't imagine having biological parents who wanted me, and I'd always tried to keep my adoptive ones happy.

"Babe, I'm so sorry about that." Raffe hung his head slightly while keeping his eyes on the road. "The stuff my dad did and said—"

"Hey." I placed a hand over his and squeezed gently. "You have nothing to apologize for. You did nothing wrong. Your father's actions aren't your fault. He's his own person, and you stood up for us and our relationship. I'm sorry you had to go through that. And I'm sorry that I wasn't understanding before when you didn't jump all in to be with me immediately."

He cut his gaze to me, the warm cobalt that made me feel like mush returning to his eyes.

"You had every right to be upset over that." He licked his bottom lip. "You're worth the risk, and I was foolish to hesitate. Don't feel bad about that. I needed a good kick in the nuts."

I snorted. "Nuts? Most would go with the ass."

"Maybe." He tilted his head with a half shrug. "But

watching you walk out that door was worse than that. It felt like I'd been neutered."

"When an animal is neutered, they're under anesthesia, so the pain is minimal when combined with medication and rest." I rolled my eyes. "A kick in the ass would hurt worse."

"This was a neutering done at one of those cheap places where they don't knock the animal out. They just cut off their balls." He removed his hand from my leg and booped my nose. "That's how painful it was."

"Maybe if you lived on a ranch, but fortunately for you, you live in a bougie mansion." I turned my body toward him and arched a brow.

He chuckled. "Fine. Let's say you ripped my heart out, but fortunately, you gave it back to me before I officially stopped breathing."

I placed my hands together and pressed one side against my cheek, batting my eyes. "You're such a romantic."

"I can be. Eventually, you'll see." The corners of his lips tipped downward. "If people can fucking leave us alone for a minute."

Like that, our reprieve from reality was gone. "So, did you just leave your pack for me?" I had no clue how it worked.

"Not officially, but I think I'll have to." Raffe chewed on his bottom lip. "I couldn't stay there. I didn't want my father to use alpha will on me again. I'm not sure how I resisted it. He's done it before, and I *had* to obey. The only difference between then and today was that I've claimed you as my mate."

"I doubt it was that, but I'm glad you fought him off. I can't imagine—" I stopped, unable to continue; thinking about him with someone else was horrible. But to say the words ... I couldn't.

Raffe took my hand again. "Babe, I swear I'll leave the

pack before I'm forced to do anything like that. You're it for me. No matter what. I understood the risks when I bit you."

The weight of his decision sat heavily on me. I asked, "Why doesn't he alpha-will the Eastern pack like you said?"

"Doing that would guarantee that the Eastern wolf shifters would split off from us. If it would work, trust me, he'd have already done it."

"Now we're facing threats from Eastern wolf shifters and a secret society that wants to use me." Being invisible did have its merits, but if I'd stayed invisible, I would've never met Raffe.

"The Eastern wolf shifters are Dad's issue. The only thing I'm concerned with is keeping my mate safe, which means taking down the secret society. We just need to figure out who the members are."

He was right. Dave had vanished, and I doubted Glinda, Warin, and the other vampires would be easy to find. We needed help to figure out who was involved. "Some of the wolves searching with you work for the Veiled Circle. I'm not sure how many, but that's a place to start."

"That's all we've got." Raffe pursed his lips. "I'll start working on it via pack link before we get back."

That was more than okay with me. Even though I wasn't as exhausted as I should've been, I laid my head against the seat to rest.

"Fuck," Raffe almost shouted, startling me. I opened my eyes and blinked, trying to determine where we were. I hadn't realized I'd fallen asleep.

My head cleared, and my eyes focused on a group of people standing at the edge of the parking lot.

Keith, Adam, Slade, Supreme Priestess Olwyn, Lafayette, Zella, and Hecate, in that exact order.

Raffe pulled into his spot, body tense. "Skylar, stay in the car."

Yeah, that wasn't happening.

When he opened his door and got out, I followed suit.

Supreme Priestess Olwyn hissed, "Have you lost your mind?"

CHAPTER FIFTEEN

I t was the equivalent of igniting a bomb.

The three coven members and two vampires stood in front of Raffe's parking spot, looking ready to toss shade at my mate when he was already struggling with everything else.

His hot anger sizzled into me.

Supreme Priestess Olywn edged toward the car. She made a faint duck face, her high cheekbones sharp, and scanned me with her emerald eyes that were so like Slade's.

That wouldn't go over well with Raffe.

"What the *fuck* is your problem?" His neck corded as he moved slightly in front of me. "Do you think I would *harm* her?"

"What do you consider taking her from campus?" Olwyn countered, straightening her shoulders. The breeze blew a stray piece of light-blonde hair that had fallen from her bun into her eyes. Normally, I had a hard time believing that this woman was Slade's mother, but with her face tense and lines creasing her forehead, I could see now that she was older.

My blood jolted, and that damn presence that plagued me swirled uncomfortably in my chest. I wasn't in the mood for fighting. All I wanted to do was head inside the apartment and just *be* and see Cat-Keith. "I don't see how staying on campus could be considered safe."

Lafayette chuckled. "Because I'm here, making arrangements with security to keep an eye on things, and the priestess is setting up perimeters to ensure that, even when people from her coven visit the campus, she's alerted." His golden eyes twinkled as he stared down his nose at me. His gelled, light-brown hair didn't budge despite the windy day, and he didn't look as stressed as Olwyn. I wondered how old he actually was. He appeared to be in his thirties, but after meeting Warin, I knew how inaccurate that might be.

"I'm with her." Keith nodded his head toward me. "A fucking student on *this* campus *drugged* her, and you witches did some sort of spell to prevent us from getting to her when we heard her screams. So, being *off campus* with *Raffe* is probably the safest place for her."

Silence.

My shoulder blades tensed, and I waited for Keith's head to start spinning to prove he was possessed. Any second now, he'd laugh at us for even considering he'd be on my side.

Instead, Raffe moved beside me, placing a hand on the small of my back. "*Exactly*. She was with me the entire time, and she's my mate. If anyone can protect her, it's me."

That presence inside me flinched, and without thought, I turned to Raffe and said, "I'm not completely helpless, you know."

"Thank you for saying that so I didn't have to." Hecate held out her hands toward me. Her thick, wavy hair swayed with her movement. "What is it with wolf shifters thinking a woman can't protect herself?"

The muscle in Raffe's jaw twitched, so I stepped closer to

his side. My nearness calmed him marginally, though his stare shot daggers at Lafayette and Olwyn.

"In fairness, Raffe saved her several times, including her first day here when someone was spying on her in the woods." Adam shoved his hands into his jeans pockets.

"So?" Hecate narrowed her jade-green eyes at him. "Things have changed since then."

"Did she not know what she was when she got here?" Zella rocked back on her heels, her arm brushing Lafayette's while she turned to him. "Dad, you were the one who first experienced the draw of her blood. Right?"

Dad? I bit the inside of my cheek to prevent myself from reacting. This whole supernatural aging thing confused the hell out of me. They could pass as siblings rather than him being her *father.*

"Not the first, but the first to *survive.*" Lafayette's nose wrinkled. "Unfortunately, the first vampire died at Raffe's claws and teeth."

The memory of Glinda and Warin informing me of how wolf shifters dealt with a vampire's first loss of control flickered through my mind. Even though I understood that Raffe had reacted out of fear of seeing his fated mate hurt, I wondered if Edward had lost his life because of my special blood. He'd been in control until I'd come snooping around.

I pushed away that concern and focused on the *biggest* issue. "Should we be talking out *here*?" However, I couldn't fathom a place where everyone would be comfortable, especially with how divided these three species were.

With all the mist and cloud cover, it seemed close to twilight, despite the time being a little after three in the afternoon. Humans were out and about, though they gave us a wide berth, with not even a handful heading toward the parking lot for after-class jobs and activities.

"Don't worry." Slade kept his arms close to his sides and spoke quieter than usual. His face was still swollen from whatever the Veiled Circle had done to him, and I appreciated him that much more. He tried to smile but grimaced. "Mom and Hecate cast a diversion spell, so no one can hear us."

Of course, I should've known that I could trust him to make sure things were handled. He'd always taken care of me, even when I might not have understood his methods. "Right. I'm still getting used to all this."

Raffe's hand clung tighter to mine, and the icky sensation of jealousy filled our bond.

Despite everything, he felt threatened by Slade. Part of me was annoyed, but between the way I'd made him feel since he'd found me and what had happened with his father, I understood him feeling insecure. After all, he might lose everything because he'd chosen me.

I also couldn't turn my back on Slade, not after he'd risked his freedom to help me.

"Everyone is tense and tired." I had no doubt that Supreme Priestess Olwyn had been up all night, worried about her son. "Slade should be in bed resting."

"So should *you*," Raffe rasped, his concern swirling in my chest. The deep edge in his voice had a shiver running down my spine.

"You're right." Olwyn scowled as if agreeing with Raffe caused her tremendous pain. "But you need to tell us when you're planning to take her off campus. The worst thing any of us can do is make the secret society think she's siding with the wolves. In fact, it probably would be best if she stayed with me at my house, away from everyone."

Hot anger pulsed from Raffe. "She'll be with me *every*

night. Besides, one of your most trusted was behind her capture. She's no safer with you than me."

"But she *is*." The supreme priestess sneered. "If they think she's aligned with your *kind*—"

"Don't forget your priestess and vampires kidnapped your son." A growl laced Raffe's words, indicating he was losing control.

This had to end now. This was *my* life and future that everyone was trying to decide on my behalf. "As much as I love how everyone is weighing in on my safety ..." I placed a hand over my heart, noting that the vampires hadn't offered their assistance, which was for the best. My blood had a mind of its own. "*I* want to sleep in *my* bed in *my* apartment where all *my* stuff is. Being apart from Raffe will only distract us, and the secret society already knows he's claimed me as his mate."

Raffe bobbed his head cockily.

Yeah, he wouldn't be gloating in another second. "I refuse to give the secret society more power. I will live my life the same as always, but that doesn't mean I won't be smarter and more cautious. Raffe can't be by my side all day long—he has a few different classes—but luckily, at least one of you is with me in every class. The only thing that might be challenging is Saturday mornings."

"Saturday mornings?" Lafayette's brows furrowed. "There's nothing happening on campus then."

"Nope, but I volunteer at the local animal hospital." I wrung my hands together. The fact that I'd missed last Saturday just hit me, and I'd bet the people there were worried. I needed to call them and apologize for not showing up. But what excuse would I give? Being kidnapped was a huge red flag and would bring me more unwanted attention.

"You're *working?*" Olwyn's jaw dropped. "You can't work while taking classes."

Her bringing up my scholarship agreement shocked me. In class, I often overheard people talking about their jobs off campus, usually at a shop or coffee bar, so many students did have jobs. "Other students work off campus, and my grades are good. Besides, it's volunteer hours."

"But it's stated in your scholarship that you can't have a job," she replied, and Lafayette's head jerked toward her. She clamped her mouth shut.

"That's not a *normal* clause." A vein bulged in Raffe's neck. "Which forces the question as to why it's in her agreement. Did you recognize her abilities when she came here for her admission interview?"

My attendance here was stranger than I'd realized. "I didn't have an interview. Hell, I didn't even apply. I just got an acceptance letter in the mail."

Raffe rolled his shoulders, his hand trembling on my back. He growled, "And Dad and I weren't warned about any of this? How did you know about her?"

For a second, I swore the supreme priestess's face paled, but then she squared her stance like she was readying to fight. She ran a hand over her navy suit. "Skylar's acceptance wasn't something a wolf-shifter royal needed to weigh in on. The decision involved school academics and the board voted to invite a bright, young, promising student with amazing grades to join us."

"How?" Adam snorted. "There wasn't an application to go over. There wasn't *anything* to vote on."

"Unless …" Keith snorted. "Someone completed the application for her."

My head went dizzy, and the world stilled. "But … why would anyone do that?"

"That's what *I* want to know, and furthermore, why didn't Vapor inform me or my father?" Raffe's lip curled.

Vapor? I had no clue who that was, but now wasn't the time to ask. Besides, I didn't want to lose focus on getting the answers I'd wanted since getting the acceptance letter in the mail.

"Vapor wasn't there when the vote happened," Supreme Priestess Olwyn replied. "It was just the two human board members, me, and Demetris. I completed the application on Skylar's behalf because, after what I learned about her from my coven members, I knew she needed to be here."

The more she talked, the more the information didn't make sense. Fog filled my mind like I was in a dream. "Someone from a coven saw my magic fritz?"

"They overheard a wolf shifter talking about how a woman's presence calmed him, and he felt compelled to allow her to help him while in animal form."

"Wait." Hecate gasped. "That was Skylar?"

Keith shook his head. "That's impossible. Wolf shifters are more cautious in animal form. No one would let a human come close to them, no matter how attractive she was or how calm she made them feel."

A deep, vibrating snarl came from Raffe, and the icky feeling of jealousy flared in my chest.

"Dude, why'd you add the attractive part?" Adam shook his head like that was the important detail.

Not wanting to derail the conversation, I snuggled into Raffe's side, making it clear we were together. "I did help a wolf in the woods once, but still, how did you all figure out it was me?"

"Dear, it wasn't that hard when we learned where it happened. Your house was closest to that location, and when we checked it out, we saw you and sensed that you were more than human and not in control of your ability. That's why we wanted to bring you here. When we learned you'd attended a two-year community college and graduated valedictorian, it made it that much easier to bring you here. The stipulation of you not taking a job off campus was to keep you nearby where we could watch out for you." Olwyn placed her arms around her stomach. "I'm sorry, Skylar. I should've explained this to you when you arrived, but you were struggling and so clueless about our world that I didn't want to put too much on you—"

"Did you know what I was?" My blood fizzed, and I couldn't see straight. Not only had the supreme priestess kept so much from me while pretending to be a friend, but she'd also manipulated me. Little had I known that she'd been aware of me and had let me struggle until I'd made a mess of things on my own.

"Let's go to your apartment so we can talk alone. Even though the humans can't hear us, it's clear we're getting upset and could cause a scene," she suggested.

Raffe laughed humorlessly. "You aren't going anywhere with her alone."

How much worse could this day get? Yes, I was free from the underground bunker, but Raffe might have lost everything, including his pack, while I'd learned that the coven members I'd relied on had kept important information from me. At least Raffe had never pretended to be my friend while manipulating me. He'd merely pretended to hate me while secretly wanting me. That was marginally better, right?

"You can join us." Olwyn waved a hand dismissively. "As well as Slade. But that's it."

In other words, she didn't want to be alone with Raffe and me.

"You say that like you have a choice." Raffe sneered.

There was no way in hell I was going anywhere without Raffe. I didn't want to hear any excuses.

I also didn't want to be like all the teachers and principals who'd made snap judgments about me and hadn't bothered to hear my version of a story. I refused.

"Lafayette, I'll let you know if we need anything else but do work on placing more guards around the perimeter and more supernatural reinforcement in the woods. The rest of you are free to do whatever you normally do at this time." Supreme Priestess Olwyn turned on her heels and marched toward the women's apartments, not bothering to see if Raffe, Slade, and I followed.

It wasn't like we had a choice. She was going to my room.

"Man, do you want us to come with you?" Keith asked, arching a brow. "It's not like the supreme priestess has any authority over us."

I didn't like that idea. I wanted answers, and if we fought with her, I'd remain clueless.

"Mom won't talk if anyone joins," Slade murmured, sounding pained. "It's best if you two come alone."

Raffe huffed and rolled his eyes. "Unfortunately, I agree with *him*. But you two can join Lucy in Josie's room. That way, you'll be close by if we need you."

"You got it." Adam saluted.

I smiled. Adam had always been a nice guy who went with the flow.

Zella gave me a little wave, and she and Lafayette headed toward the student center.

But Hecate came to me and placed a hand on my shoulder. "I'm glad you're back and safe."

"Me too," I sighed.

She winked and headed toward the woods. Adam and Keith were already halfway to the apartments.

Slade waited for us. "Are you two ready?"

"Let's get this over with." Raffe scowled.

As the three of us slowly walked toward the apartment building, I moved so that I was walking between the two guys.

Twenty feet from the double doors, Slade bit his lip. "Please listen to her. Give her a chance to explain her decisions. She wasn't sure what to do."

A horrible thought hit me right in the chest. My blood ran cold.

CHAPTER SIXTEEN

I couldn't push the thought away. The thought that my friendship with Slade hadn't started with the best of intentions knocked the breath out of me, and I stopped in my tracks. My blood fizzed.

"Babe?" Raffe asked with concern. "What's wrong? Is it your ..." He scanned the area.

Why he'd stopped talking wasn't hard to figure out. He wanted to ask if it was my magic, but there were humans and other supernaturals close by. I inhaled shakily and focused on Slade as he turned around, realizing we weren't beside him.

I asked, "Is that why you were nice to me on that first day of class?"

Slade's eyes bulged, and he winced as if he were in pain.

I swallowed the question of whether he was okay, not wanting him to use his discomfort as a way of avoiding this conversation.

Huffing, Raffe took my hand, and our intense buzz eased my blood. Losing control here, in front of humans, would be asking for trouble.

"We should go inside." Slade clutched his ribs. "Mom's waiting for us."

"Answer her question." Raffe lowered his voice, the sound more menacing. "Or we're not going anywhere."

Taking a cue from my mate, I leaned into Raffe's side. Slade needed to know that we weren't bluffing and that we were united.

A group of girls walked out of the building, heading toward us.

Slade's eyes flicked toward them. "This isn't the place ..."

"Cut the bullshit." That presence in my chest swirled. "You can answer without giving anything away. It's a simple yes or no question. *Did you know?*"

From his reaction, I already knew the answer, but I needed to hear him say *something* before walking in. I didn't trust Supreme Priestess Olwyn, and I feared I was about to put Slade alongside her.

His Adam's apple bobbed. "I did, but I *wanted* to meet you. I was sincere."

I snorted, the harshness raking my throat. "Oh, I bet." I held Raffe's hand tighter and marched past Slade toward the apartment entrance.

Fortunately, Raffe didn't miss a beat and remained at my side.

A pained grunt came from behind us. "Sky, wait. Let me explain."

"Nope." I didn't pause, and Raffe opened the door for me to enter the building. I retorted, *"This* isn't the *place,"* lobbing the words back at him because I was petty. Not only that, but the discussion shouldn't happen with prying ears nearby.

The corners of Raffe's mouth twitched upward, but he mashed his lips together.

"Ugh," Slade groaned as he continued to fall farther behind.

He could wait for the elevators because I needed a few minutes away from him. I needed time to process that our friendship had been built on a lie.

I hurried to the elevator, and by the time Raffe and I entered it, Slade was coming through the door. Sweat dotted his forehead as he tried to reach us.

"Want me to shut the door?" Raffe smirked and reached for the close-door button.

Even though I wanted to say yes, watching Slade rushing to catch up had my heart aching. I caught Raffe's hand and cut my eyes at him while saying, "You're enjoying this way too much."

"I'm not enjoying that he's hurt, but it's about damn time this came out." He moved his hand to the button to keep the door open. "And yeah, Slade always played the good guy. I won't lie. It's nice to know I wasn't the only one being a complete idiot."

I arched a brow. "Even if it's something you have in common with a *coven member*?"

He grimaced hard and shivered.

I laughed at his exaggerated reaction. The noise caught me by surprise. Raffe had a way of making me smile when no one else could.

"You're right." He gasped, placing a hand on his chest. "Don't *ever* repeat that."

Slade caught up and slid into the elevator. "Thanks for waiting on me," he panted, his face twisting with each breath. "I thought you might not."

"I didn't want to." I leaned my head on Raffe's shoulder, refusing to look at Slade. "But you did save me from the underground bunker." Even if our friendship had changed, I still owed him. He wasn't like his mother, who only gave me her time when it suited her. Slade had befriended and helped me when I had no one else.

"Sky, I swear, I genuinely like you. I chose to hang out with you when I didn't have to." He shuffled, no doubt turning to me. "We share a love of science and nature. The way we got along had nothing to do with me knowing you were different from everyone else."

Some of my anger chipped away. He was right. We'd spent hours in the woods together, and because our majors were so similar, we had all our classes together. "Still, our friendship started under false pretenses."

"When—" he started, but the doors opened to the fifth floor.

Wanting to address the supreme priestess's part in the situation, I stalked toward my apartment with Raffe at my side and found her waiting at the apartment door. Seeing her standing there lifted some of the worry from my shoulders. I suspected she would've let herself into my room and searched through all my things if she could. Lucy must have left the apartment before she arrived. Knowing Keith and Adam had informed Lucy of what was going on so she wouldn't get caught in this mess put me more at ease, and I could only hope Cat-Keith was in Lucy's room so the supreme priestess didn't see her.

Raffe tilted his head. "Waiting *outside*? I'm surprised. I figured you would've gotten her code from Lafayette."

Lafayette handled student housing. He would have the code.

"I didn't want to invade Skylar's privacy." Supreme Priestess Olwyn smiled sadly and glanced at the light-gray carpet. "This is her home after all."

I quickly entered the apartment code into the keypad,

pretending to press buttons in between in case Slade was more focused than before from his spot halfway between the elevator and my room.

Even though I was learning about supernaturals and their abilities, I still wasn't sure how good each species' vision and hearing were.

When the door clicked, I pushed it open and entered the apartment first.

Whew. Lucy's door was shut. Cat-Keith had to be in there, especially since she wasn't growling at Raffe to warn him he'd be attacked upon entering the room.

I went to stand by the two couches but didn't sit down. Raffe was on my heels, followed by Supreme Priestess Olwyn and Slade. The two of them sat on the couch against the wall between my room and Lucy's.

Raffe stood next to me, and we faced the two witches. Raffe took my hand and looped it through his arm so that our sides were touching. The thrum from our connection eased the energy that made me want to climb the walls. I felt vulnerable having the supreme priestess in my apartment, and with what I'd learned, I wondered if she'd asked to speak here on purpose.

A stray piece of hair fell into her face, and she pushed it behind her ear. "Uh ... I thought all apartments came with a coffee table."

This was how she wanted to start the conversation? *Really?* "My power broke it." It happened the night I'd come home to find Keith, Adam, Raffe, and Josie on our couch. Raffe had been sitting next to Josie with his arm over her shoulders. I hadn't known they were only pretending to date, but even if I had, it probably wouldn't have helped.

"Are you ready to address the problem, or are you going to ask how her family is doing and if her classes are going well?"

Raffe waved a hand at me. "Oh, wait. You don't need to ask because you've been spying on her, and Slade is in *all* her classes, which I'm sure is a *mere* coincidence."

That felt like a punch to the gut. Even though Slade and I had similar majors, I'd thought it was odd that we were taking the same electives at the *exact* same time. I'd known this situation was too good to be true. The scholarship they'd offered me was the opportunity of a lifetime and one that guaranteed me a competitive edge once vet school came around.

My face heated. I'd been such a *fool*. How had I missed all these signs? "Am I some sort of experiment? Watch her in unnatural surroundings to see how long it takes her to implode?"

"What?" Slade's voice rose as he shook his head. "How could you even think that?"

"Son." Olwyn put a hand on his arm.

My blood increased to a fizz. "Don't sit there and act like you're insulted by my questions." He didn't get to play the victim here. "You all invited me here, knowing I was different, then planted someone in all my classes so he could *observe* me." I gritted my teeth. "Did you already know what I was? Was the research you supposedly did a lie?" Slade had acted like he'd figured out I was arcane-born after my arrival, but I didn't know what to trust anymore.

Slade opened his mouth, but his mother glared at him. She answered with a clear, steady voice, "No, we weren't sure what you were. I'll be honest that I suspected you could potentially be—" She cut herself off, glancing at Raffe.

Pursing his lips, Raffe maintained an indifferent expression, not ratting me out that I'd told him everything.

I wanted to kiss him, but this wasn't the time.

It *was* time for *all* of us to come clean. "He knows I'm arcane-born and that you have the *Books of Twilight* in a hidden library under one of the residence halls." The wolf shifters had forbidden the witches to keep the books, wanting to cut off their link to ancient spells and their history. The books were supposed to have been destroyed, but the witches had hidden them in the secret library, which only witches could access. I'd been down there once when Slade had invited me, and I'd learned about my heritage from Supreme Priestess Olwyn, two other priestesses, and a priest.

"We trusted you with that information," Olwyn snapped, her calm demeanor slipping. "And you told *him*? Do you have any idea what you've done? I bet King Jovian is on his way now with his man-beast cavalry."

A growl ripped from my chest. I didn't like the way she was talking about wolf shifters, especially since Raffe was one of them.

Raffe chuckled, unfazed by the insult. "I haven't informed my father. But keep on trying to control and manipulate my *mate*, and I won't hesitate to do so."

She placed a hand on her throat and leaned back. "You haven't told him?"

"There's no way." Slade snorted. "He would've told his father the moment he learned. They're playing a game with us, and I don't like it." He focused on me. "How could you do that to us?"

"After you tried to pressure me into kissing you, I needed someone to talk to." Though I'd done what I needed to do at that moment, I couldn't help but feel guilty. They *had* trusted me with sensitive information. "Before I told him, I made him promise that he wouldn't share the information with his dad."

Slade blinked. "That was before I took you to the library."

"I know, and his dad never came, so that should tell you everything."

Supreme Priestess Olwyn crossed her arms. "Well, he

can't hold knowing that over us. Even if the wolf shifters storm the campus, they won't be able to find their way inside the library."

"Unlike your coven members, I didn't withhold the information from my dad to get something from you." Raffe rolled his eyes.

She tilted her head. "Then why didn't you tell him?"

He turned, kissed the top of my head, and answered, "Because Skylar needs answers, and that's the best place for her to find them. I would never risk having *anyone*, including my own species, destroy something that could give her knowledge about how to control her magic and not die. That's the most important thing to me even though you've broken the law."

My heart felt so full I feared it might implode.

"No way." Slade shook his head. "I'm not buying it. You bit her for a reason. It wasn't for love—it was so you could track her wherever she goes. Either you're using her to rebel against King Jovian, or you need her for something else. You've been an entitled, self-absorbed asshole the entire time you've been at EEU. Do you expect me to buy that you suddenly had this drastic change of heart because of *her*? A *human*? I call bullshit."

The rage that slammed through Raffe caught me off guard, and my knees shook. Raffe tried to charge Slade, but I held his hand firmly.

"Don't," I murmured, knowing everyone could hear me. "He's not worth it."

The muscles in Raffe's jaw twitched, and his teeth ground together hard enough that I could hear the creak.

"You two need to leave." I understood the irony of me asking the head board member of EEU to leave my apartment, but we weren't accomplishing anything. I hadn't even been free for twenty-four hours yet. Raffe and I had had little sleep. Raffe had had a huge fight with his father and might have to leave his pack. And now *this*. We needed to rest so we could start thinking levelheadedly, and that included Slade. "It's been a rough day. We should regroup later in the week."

Standing, Supreme Priestess Olwyn smoothed her skirt. "You're right. Between your abduction, Slade's disappearance and one of my most trusted priestesses' involvement in this secret group, everyone is on edge. Let's take some time to get life back to normal, and I'd love for us to meet and talk again." She bit her bottom lip, not appearing like the strong woman she portrayed to the world. "I want you to know I'm truly sorry for hurting you. That was never our intention. We only wanted to help you find your place, put you at ease, and surround you with people similar to you. You're in this delicate place between the human and supernatural world. With your magic, you understand the struggles of our world, and I thought it might feel inviting for you. Hurting you was never our goal."

Raffe sniffed, and I knew why. He was trying to smell if she was lying.

Slade moaned as he awkwardly climbed to his feet. His face paled.

He probably shouldn't have sat down.

Despite her son's struggle, Supreme Priestess Olwyn headed to the door and waited for him impatiently. She didn't hesitate, and I wondered if the thought of helping him had even crossed her mind. What sort of mother was she? Mom would've been at my side, pestering me about breathing too deeply.

Speaking of which, I needed to call her.

Finally, Slade was on his feet. "Sky, I'm sorry, too."

He didn't add a list of excuses, thawing my anger toward him. "Just get some rest."

Raffe's hand tightened on mine, and we watched them walk out the door.

When we were finally alone, I sat on the couch and patted the spot next to me, then winced. "I should call home." I hadn't gotten around to doing that.

"Did you leave your phone in the car?" Raffe edged toward the door. "I can get it."

"Lucy never gave it to me this morning." I yawned, not wanting to get up from my spot on the couch.

Raffe winked. "I'll get it. I know where it is."

I smiled sweetly, batting my eyelashes. "You're the best boyfriend ever."

He pretended to scowl. "That's *mate*. Get it straight." He leaned over and brushed his lips across mine. "Find us something to watch on TV. I'll be right back." He strolled into the hallway and added, "But none of that *Criminal Minds* shit."

I laughed. "Never. That's my show with Lucy." I swiped the remote from the cushion on the other couch. When I turned on the TV, I heard a bedroom door open, followed by a hiss and a loud, "Holy shit!"

CHAPTER SEVENTEEN

I leaped to my feet and hurried after him. I should've realized he was going into Lucy's room and not mine.

Another hiss sounded as Raffe snarled.

If I hadn't known better, I would've thought I was at the animal clinic. But no. The snarling wolf was the man I loved.

When I reached the room, I stopped in my tracks. Cat-Keith had her underside plastered to Raffe's face as she clung to his temples. Raffe's hands gripped the cat's stomach to tug her off. With each tug, my cat dug her claws in deeper, and blood trickled down Raffe's face.

The scent of copper had my stomach churning, and my humor vanished. I hadn't realized she was hurting Raffe, not with how gentle he was being with her.

"*Keith*," I chastised and reached for her.

Raffe jerked. "Don't." His words were muffled. *That damn cat better not hurt her. I don't care if it's her pet.*

The last few sentences had popped into my head. That was the third time it'd happened today. I had to be losing it.

Not wanting to analyze possibly losing my mind, I

reached over and placed my hands on Keith. As soon as I touched her, I tensed, remembering I smelled like a wolf now.

She could attack me, I thought, but the damage was done. I pulled her toward me and whispered, "Keith, it's okay. I promise." I used the same soothing tone I had in the animal clinic when she'd become scared and aggressive around people she didn't know.

I expected her to turn around and attack me, but instead, she retracted her claws from Raffe's face, and I took her into my arms. Her body relaxed as I moved my hair over my shoulder, allowing it to blanket her and make her feel as if she was hiding.

Holding her tightly, I stepped away from Raffe, hoping she'd calm completely. I could only imagine the trauma she'd endured while I was kidnapped, being stuck with a wolf shifter she didn't like and feeling all alone. I wasn't sure if bringing her home had been the right move.

"Damn feline," Raffe growled as he wiped blood from his cheeks. Luckily, she hadn't dug her claws in as deep as I'd feared, but I still didn't like seeing him hurt.

Rocking gently from side to side as if the cat was a baby, I nodded toward the bathroom. "You should clean those cuts so they don't get infected."

Huffing, Raffe bared his teeth at the cat. "I'm fine, but I want to get cat DNA out of my skin. Nothing good can come from that."

As he headed into the bathroom, I went back into Lucy's room. She would do better in here with Raffe spending the night in mine.

I shut the door and placed Cat-Keith on the olive-green comforter, which was neatly tucked into the bottom corners of Lucy's queen-size bed. The wooden end table beside the window held a potted plant along with my phone.

Cat-Keith meowed as I snatched up my phone and looked to see if I had missed texts or calls. I had two texts from Mom, the first from around ten this morning.

Mom: Hey. I hope your classes went well. I miss hearing your voice but understand your throat has been hurting. Hope we can talk tonight.

Even though I hated that I'd have to lie to Mom, I could kiss Lucy for handling the situation for me. If they'd learned that something had happened to me, I wasn't sure how they'd have reacted. They'd tried to have children for so long, and I had become their miracle child after several failed adoption attempts.

Meowing, Cat-Keith jumped onto the nightstand and rubbed against my side. I scratched behind her ear as the sink in the bathroom turned on.

The next message had come in about an hour ago, so around five.

Mom: Sky, I'm getting worried. Please let me know you're all right.

Blowing out a breath, I pressed her number. She wouldn't calm down until she heard my voice. As expected, she picked up on the second ring.

"Sky?" she said hurriedly. "Are you okay?"

It wasn't meant to be a trick question, but it was just the same. "Yeah, sorry. It's been a busy day, and I just checked my phone." Though she wasn't here and wasn't a wolf shifter who could detect my lies, I still hated lying to her. "I saw your messages and figured I should call."

"I'm so glad you did." Mom sighed. "Your father and I have been so worried. Are you feeling better? Do you need me to drive down there and take you to the doctor?"

If only a doctor could solve my problems. "No, I'm feeling better." That was true. Two days ago, I was drugged and locked in a room. "I didn't mean to worry you two."

"I know that things have been hard for you, but you're still our daughter. We will *always* worry about you, and if you ever need us, all you have to do is tell us."

My vision blurred. "I know. And I miss you two as well."

"Dad and I were thinking we should visit now that you've been there for a while and are settled in." Her voice rose as if she wasn't sure she would be welcomed.

"No," I said way too quickly.

She sucked in a breath, her tell when her feelings were hurt.

Lovely.

"Oh, well. I mean, then, maybe ..." she stuttered, searching for the words.

I was an awful daughter, and I wanted to kick myself.

A faint knock came from the door, and it cracked open enough for me to see a sliver of Raffe's face. He whispered, "You should invite them to the game this Saturday."

Game? For a second, I furrowed my eyebrows until understanding slammed into me. He meant the football game a week from Saturday. Between the capture, the drama, and all the fighting, I'd forgotten he was one of the best quarterbacks in the division.

"Mom, hold on a second." I hit mute on my phone and continued petting Cat-Keith. She pressed her entire body against me and purred.

Apparently, that was enough for Raffe to feel comfortable opening the door wider. He kept a wary eye on the cat.

"Do you think it's a wise idea to invite them here?" I couldn't deny that seeing them would be nice. Though I'd never felt super close to them, they did love me. They just didn't understand me. But seeing how often Mom had texted to talk revealed a facet of our relationship I hadn't seen until now. "I mean, with witches, vampires, threats, and me all at the game?"

He smiled sadly. "Weren't you the one who said you didn't want what's happening to make you live your life any differently?"

Touché. And some women said men didn't listen. Clearly, they weren't lucky enough to have a man like Raffe in their life. Still, I couldn't give in too easily. Where was the fun in that? "Those weren't my exact words." I shrugged and *tsk*ed as if I were disappointed in myself while trying to fight a smile.

"Oh, excuse me." He touched his chest. "I was listening for understanding. I didn't realize there'd be a pop quiz later."

I snorted, feeling happy ... and almost normal. "I would hate for something to happen to them. And what if your dad comes?"

"I'll make sure eyes I trust are on you at all times, and my dad won't show up, not after how we left things. He won't risk having a confrontation in front of everyone on campus. That's not how he works. Besides ..." Raffe averted his gaze, looking vulnerable. "I kind of want to meet my mate's parents. We could go out to dinner afterward."

"Okay." There was no way I'd say no after that. I'd never had a chance to introduce a boyfriend to my parents, and the fact that my first was Raffe felt right. "Let's do it."

His head jerked up, and a weight lifted off my chest as if he hadn't expected me to say yes. "Great. It's a noon game, so dinner after works."

Unmuting the phone, I placed it back to my ear. "Mom?"

The front door to the apartment opened. Raffe must have

informed Lucy that Supreme Priestess Olwyn and Slade had left.

"Yeah, honey?" Mom replied, her voice sounding tight.

"You know what? Why don't you and Dad come down for our next football game, and we'll go out to dinner with Raffe after?"

Lucy appeared at Raffe's side and blinked at me standing in her room.

"We'd *love* to," Mom said enthusiastically. "And who is Raffe? Will he be watching the game with us?"

Jaw dropping, Raffe dramatically placed a hand in front of his mouth as if surprised I hadn't told them about him.

I snickered, unable to hide the sound. "Raffe is my ..." I trailed off, searching for the right word. *Boyfriend* didn't hint at the depth of our relationship, but I was afraid to say anything too strong because then they'd be worried. So, I settled on the safest bet. "... boyfriend."

"Well, that's a first." Mom giggled. "I know you were hesitant to attend EEU, but my gut screamed this would be good for you. Though I will say, I expected you to say Slade since he's the only guy you've mentioned."

Cold, sharp tingles of hurt and the icky, slimy sensation of jealousy flowed deep within my chest where Raffe's emotions sat. This was one of those times I wished his hearing wasn't so amazing. I'd hurt him again in less than twenty-four hours. I was doing *great*.

"Slade's just a friend. Raffe and I were kind of dancing around each other." That was the nicest way I could think to phrase what our relationship had been like before. Trying to explain our secret moments together, his assholey indifference in public, and the way he had taken over my thoughts and heart would put my parents on edge. We had to be careful about how we presented our relationship to them. "But we finally got things right." At least, I hoped we had.

"Seriously?" Lucy scoffed at him.

"I'm very excited to meet him. We'll get down there around eleven, so we aren't in a rush to get to the stadium," Mom replied, almost with a squeal.

"Sounds great." I could only hope we hadn't made a huge mistake, but Raffe had been right in reminding me what I'd said. I couldn't allow these people to control my life and make me afraid of doing normal things. If I did that, they'd essentially win.

Mom said, "I'll call you later. I need to tell your father about our plans. He'll be thrilled. I love you, baby."

She hadn't called me by that nickname in years. "Love you too."

When I clicked the end button, Raffe was still pouting.

I wished I could go back in time and tell Mom all about him. "Raffe, I'm sorry. With everything going on, I didn't want to tell them about you, and then—"

"Oh no." Lucy lifted a finger and stormed into her room. "Do *not* apologize. That's not how this is going to go."

I mashed my lips together, unsure what to say. Lucy had no problem being assertive, but she didn't usually get this worked up. "But he's hurt that—"

"Sky, I know exactly why he's hurt, but that's his own damn fault." She stood beside me, glaring at her cousin.

Tilting his head back, he scowled. "How do you figure?"

"Oh, okay." Lucy nodded. "We can do this. First, you were an asshole when she came here. You publicly humiliated her while she was struggling with her magic so that people would keep their distance. It wasn't until after Slade tried to kiss her that you showed her consistent interest, but then you made her keep it a secret because you didn't want anyone to find out about you two."

Raffe lifted his hands. "I was there. I am aware of all this."

"I'm not sure you are since you're over there acting all butthurt about her mom not knowing about you and knowing about Slade." She spun her hands. "So, I'm going to continue."

If I didn't have a fated-mate bond with Raffe and wasn't completely in love with him, I could have fallen for this amazing woman.

"While you two were secretly dating, you had one of your closest friends *still* pretend to be your girlfriend in front of everyone, including Sky. And when Keith caught you two in her bedroom, you didn't make it clear that you wanted to be with her. You were torn. So why would she want to tell her mom about you when your entire relationship was ambiguous?"

I hadn't thought about it that way, but she was right. That was exactly why I hadn't told my mom. I'd considered Slade a true friend, so it had been easy to talk about him and Lucy.

"But we're together, so forgive me if it hurts that my *mate* had to tell her mother who I was." His jaw clenched. "You don't know the other shit she's thought about me, so don't come at me with this lecture."

My heart panged with hurt, and Lucy glanced at me. She asked, "Like what?"

"It's none of your business. I'm just saying you don't know —" Raffe started.

I cut him off and told her about the pictures and what I'd asked him. He'd brought it up, and I wanted her to get off his case. If I wanted to heal things between Raffe and me, I needed to own up to my mistakes.

The more Lucy heard, the pinker her cheeks became.

When I was done, I prepared for her to rip into me.

Instead, she marched over to Raffe and smacked him on the back of the head ... hard.

"What the fuck?" he snarled.

"You're more of a jackass than I realized." Lucy pointed her finger in his face. "And that's really saying something."

I blinked, trying to understand what the hell was going on. "Shouldn't you be mad at me?"

"No," Lucy answered, turning to me. "Did you not list all the reasons why? You two got your shit together right after you almost died and Raffe told us you were it for him. Then you got kidnapped and went missing for over three days!"

She had a point. Though our relationship felt like we'd been together a lot longer, it hadn't even been a week. We'd gone through so much in so little time that it felt like months.

"You were continuously drugged, manipulated, and shown actual pictures. Who in their right mind wouldn't have a seed of doubt after that, especially after how poorly Raffe and Keith treated you?" She placed her hands on her hips and glared at her cousin. "After being back for less than a day, she got into a confrontation with your dad and came back only to be forced into yet another confrontation! I thought fated mates were supposed to be considerate and kind to one another."

The back of my neck tingled, informing me that Raffe was staring at me. I wanted to meet his gaze but kept my attention on Lucy.

"Sky, do you mind if I have a moment alone with Lucy?" Raffe's voice was deep, and his emotions in my chest were a strange combination I couldn't quite put my finger on.

I dropped my hand from Cat-Keith and nodded. Having a moment alone to process everything Lucy had said would be wise. She had a lot of valid points, but I didn't think she was being completely fair to Raffe. "Yeah, but what about Keith?"

As if she knew I was worried, she jumped on Lucy's bed and curled into a ball in the center, then began licking her paws as if she hadn't attacked Raffe moments ago.

Lucy smiled. "She seems okay to me."

"Okay. I'm going to my room to change into pajamas." I forced a smile. As I left, my arm brushed Raffe's, and the buzz sprang to life.

I didn't pause as I went into my room and shut the door, giving both them and myself privacy. I grabbed a pair of lilac pajama bottoms and slipped them on, then threw on a dark-purple shirt. When the door to my room opened quickly, I jerked back, caught off guard that their conversation had gone so fast.

I pulled my hair from under the shirt and turned to Raffe.

His expression was strained, and he shut the door. I didn't feel only anger but a mix of emotions. My breath caught. "Is something wrong?"

He exhaled. "Yes, very." His face twisted in agony, and regret flooded that spot of his, nearly weighing me down.

The walls closed in on me, and for a moment, I didn't want to hear more.

CHAPTER EIGHTEEN

His expression morphed into a combination of concern, confusion, and disgust. My blood jolted, and I considered running out of the room so he couldn't talk to me. What if he'd decided it was best if we weren't together anymore?

She looks scared, he said in my head. *This confirms everything.*

Now, my blood jolted. "You're breaking up with me, aren't you?"

His jaw dropped, and shock resonated through my chest. "What? No! There's no *ending* what we have."

Once again, I knew those words should scare me, but they provided me with much-needed comfort. "Then why are you being so hard to read? That makes the worst-case scenario pop into my mind." It didn't help that, for most of my life, the worst was exactly what had happened to me. I'd been mostly alone until I came to EEU.

"Because I'm disgusted, angry, and annoyed with myself." He fisted his hands.

Hearing him name the emotions made it easier to sort

through them. My blood eased to a jolt, though I wasn't fully comforted yet. "Why?"

He scoffed and closed his eyes. "You're seriously asking me that?" He opened his eyes again and stared at me through those warm cobalt irises. "Even after everything Lucy said?"

"Is that why you're upset?" Even though I loved Lucy for standing up for me, she hadn't been completely fair to him. "Because you've had it rough too. Maybe more so than me."

"No, I haven't, and I need you to stop being so considerate." He closed the distance between us and placed his hands on my shoulders. "Don't let me take advantage of your goodness. You're the one person I never want to do that to. I'm an entitled brat most of the time, and I don't want to be that way with you. You deserve better. You deserve a man who will put your needs, wants, and desires ahead of anything else." He cupped my face, his bottom lip trembling. "And it may take me some time to become that man because, dammit, Sky, I'm *not* worthy of you. But I will try to be. Harder than ever because you fucking deserve it."

My heart was officially warm mush. I'd never dreamed of having anyone—especially someone like *Raffe*—say that to me. Though I loved every word of his proclamation, I couldn't accept it entirely. "We both have our faults, and you're putting too much pressure on yourself." I didn't want him to feel the kind of pressure that his dad put on him about his role. "Maybe I should stand up for myself more with you, but how can I not be understanding when I feel your emotions so strongly?"

His head tilted back. "What do you mean, feel my emotions?"

Crap. I hadn't meant to say that. "When my blood reaches high levels, I can read people's emotions, and ever since you bit me ..." I suddenly found his chest very interesting, not wanting to look him in the eye. I had to sound crazy. "I can *feel* your emotions in my chest when you're upset. It's a sort of warm sensation that grows and can overwhelm me."

"Hey." He placed a finger under my chin and lifted my head so our gazes met. He smiled. "That shouldn't be possible at all, but dammit, I'm so glad it is."

I nodded, relieved that he wasn't freaked out. "When I was kept in the bunker, I could feel your fear and anger. It was constant, and even though I hated that I wasn't with you, it was nice to feel what I hoped was part of you with me."

"That must be why I could track you." He pressed his forehead to mine. "I could sense which direction you were in, and we were able to find your general location. I could feel that you were so damn close, but I couldn't figure out exactly where you were in the woods."

"The bunker was behind a waterfall." I needed Raffe to understand that his inability to find me while I was a prisoner wasn't all his fault. "But that's my point. If I were in your shoes, unsure of where you were and what was going on, I don't think I could have functioned. You went through my kidnapping, Aldric's arrival, Dave's disappearance, and the confrontation with your dad and then the coven." I snorted, wondering what could possibly go wrong next.

Wait.

No.

If there's a higher being out there, that wasn't me issuing a challenge.

I placed my arms around his neck and breathed in his unique scent. "We've both been stressed and maybe we've been taking it out on each other."

He smiled tenderly. "You haven't taken anything out on me, and yes, we've been stressed, but that doesn't give me an excuse to be a douchebag. I'm sorry. I know you called my ass out for always saying that and never changing, but I want to be a better man for you, starting right now."

"It was a different situation." Though I couldn't deny I loved hearing all that. "You were acting hot and cold about us like you couldn't make up your mind. That hurt. But this was about me doubting your character, and I can see why it would burn to have my mom know about Slade and not you. Honestly, you're the one I wanted to tell her about, but it would have led to questions about why we weren't together. I didn't want to have to explain."

"And you had every right to do *both* things." His arms wrapped around my waist. My body buzzed damn near all over from our closeness. "I haven't been a good enough mate to you for you not to have doubts, especially while being drugged and held captive." He grimaced. "I should've realized that. Then, I wondered why you didn't tell your mom about us, and hell, *I* told you to keep me a secret. What did I expect you to fucking do? Not listen when you're one of the most loyal and considerate people I've ever met? This was all on me, and I'm sorry I made you feel guilty for *any* of that. It just proves I need to be a better man for you and for us."

"I don't want you to change, and I don't want to be a stressful obligation to you. I want us *both* to be happy." I kissed him sweetly then forced myself to pull away. I needed him to hear my words and not allow myself to get distracted by his mouth and body. "You're an amazing man, and I don't think you know that. You try to be what everyone expects of you." I'd never considered that Raffe felt like that because he was *the* Raffe Wright, wolf-shifter prince, star quarterback, a son desperate to make his parents proud, and untouchable to almost everyone. But he didn't have to be strong in every way with me. He could be vulnerable and let me in because I loved him for everything he was, not what I wanted him to be.

"Oh, really?" he whispered and nipped at my nose like a puppy. "Now I like the sound of that."

I kept my animal-nerd mouth shut, knowing he wouldn't appreciate the dog reference. "Me too."

Without another word, his lips were on mine, and I opened my mouth eagerly. The strange distance that had been between us was gone. My body heated. I wanted his hands on me again—*me,* not my clothes.

Until Lucy knocked loudly on my door.

"You two, stop it right now and get your asses out here. You had alone time in the car, even if Raffe ruined it, and spent last night together. I need *Sky* time, with or without Raffe. He's optional."

Raffe leaned back, his eyes glowing. "I'll handle this."

I put a finger in his face, trying to hide my smile. "Don't pack-link and leave me out of the conversation. That's rude."

He shrugged. "Fine. Lucy, I swear to the gods, if you don't leave us alone, I'll—"

"Go grab some food for us from the student center?" I arched a brow. Even though there was nothing more I wanted to do than sex it up with Raffe, Lucy was my best friend, and I'd always sworn that, if I ever had the chance, I wouldn't be one of those girls who stopped spending time with her friends because of a guy. Lucy deserved my time, especially after helping Raffe and me reconnect.

He pouted. "Seriously? You're choosing to watch *Criminal Minds* over ..." He nodded toward the bed then slid his hand under my shirt, forcing a gasp from me.

Maybe I could do both—have sex with him *then* spend time with Lucy? That seemed totally reasonable.

"You forced my hand," Lucy said smugly.

Raffe and I froze.

"What did you do?" Raffe rasped, his fingers digging into my skin with a pressure that had me panting.

"The rest of the gang is on their way. You know, *Keith*, Adam, and Josie."

"That's a dirty move." Raffe sighed, removing his hand from my shirt.

I didn't have to ask why. Keith wouldn't leave us alone, especially if he knew what we were doing. I didn't want a repeat of the time he'd walked in on us. No one needed to relive that.

Lucy's footsteps grew fainter as she headed into the living room. "I don't care. I've missed Sky too. You aren't the only one."

Guilt pressed on me, and my arousal ebbed enough for me to remember it was important to spend time with her. "We're coming out. Don't worry."

After kissing me once more, Raffe growled when he pulled away from me. He shook his head. "This is not over, and I'll be getting even with Lucy."

I licked my lips, enjoying the minty taste he'd left behind. "Don't. She just misses us." It wasn't just about me. Normally, she told Raffe he had to stay in my room or leave, but tonight, she'd invited him to join us.

My stomach grumbled and he scowled.

"Food. I'll go get us all some." He headed to the door, pouting about missing sex just because I was hungry.

I was so damn lucky.

I followed him and sat on the same couch as Lucy, on the end closest to the bedrooms.

"Get me a burger and a large fry," she called out seconds before the door shut. She frowned. "He better get me something."

Sometimes, those two acted more like siblings than

cousins. "He will," I assured her, getting comfortable on the couch.

Lucy turned on the TV and scanned the movie options. "I'm assuming you two are good based on the amount of arousal you forced me to smell when I came out of my room."

My face burned. Of course, she'd call me out on that. "Yeah, and all thanks to you."

She turned to me and winked. "You're welcome."

A soft knock sounded on the door, followed by the keypad buttons. The door opened, and Josie entered, wearing black yoga pants and a burnt-orange shirt. Even dressed casually, she was beautiful.

The icky, slimy sensation of jealousy seeped within me as my blood jolted. The last time we'd all hung out like this, it'd been the Josie and Raffe show, and it had bothered me way more than I'd ever like to admit.

"Hey, you two." She smiled, but it didn't quite reach her eyes. She took a seat on the other couch near Lucy. "Any updates on Dave?"

"Not since the last time you asked." Lucy rolled her eyes. "Besides, if there was an update, do you think Raffe wouldn't be over there right now, all growly and upset?"

"Right." I swore her expression dropped for a moment before she turned to the television. "What are we watching?"

"Don't know." Lucy pursed her lips.

Josie lifted her hands. "There's this new reality show that—"

"No." Lucy karate-chopped the air. "When I stayed with you last week, I watched enough of that. Sky and I get to pick something this time."

"Okay." Josie shrugged and sat back, unfazed. She picked at her nails as Lucy continued to scan.

Then, one of my favorite stories appeared. "Oh, let's

watch *All Creatures Great and Small*." I'd loved the books growing up—they'd inspired me to become a vet, and I still hadn't seen the movie. "I've been wanting to watch it for a while."

"Okay." Lucy nodded, selecting it for me.

Our keypad went off again, and from the other side of the door, Keith said, "Are you sure that's enough for Skylar? I can go back and get her some more."

My stomach churned. Was he calling me *fat*?

"She won't even eat half of this," Raffe replied as the door opened.

The three guys entered with three full pizzas, subs, containers of food, and a bag of what smelled like fries. They'd brought enough to feed an army.

Keith homed in on me, brows furrowed. "If there's something else you want, let me know, and I'll go get it. They didn't have any fresh cinnamon rolls, so we had to improvise."

I swallowed. He seemed concerned and wasn't being mean or mouthy. But I had no clue why he thought I'd be upset about the cinnamon rolls. "Uh. It's fine."

"Last time you got one, so I tried—" he started.

"Man, stop ass-kissing." Adam rolled his eyes and set the bag on the table. "You go from one extreme to another."

Keith turned to Adam and murmured, "Shut up, man. I need her to like me, and when I win her over, I'll level out. I can't have her hating me."

I mashed my lips together to keep from laughing. He'd taken Raffe's threat seriously. I almost wanted to be mean and pretend the cinnamon rolls were a big deal. "It's fine. I only got one last time because they didn't have the chocolate cake I like."

"The chocolate cake that I got you, which Keith has been

bitching about." Raffe held out the triple fudge cake that made my knees go weak almost as much as he did.

Close.

But not quite.

I salivated.

Raffe grabbed two plates, put two slices of pepperoni pizza on one, and had the second one overflowing with fries over a sandwich. After snagging two Cokes and two pieces of the cake, he headed into the living room, where Josie scooted over to make room for him.

My heart ached, and I tried to school my expression. I had to remember they were friends, but that presence in my chest churned uncomfortably.

Needing something to do so I wouldn't reach over and yank her hair or punch Raffe for no good reason, I stood and almost collided with him.

He tilted his head and smirked. "I'm down."

I blinked and watched as he took my seat and placed the food on the center cushion. Then he pulled me onto his lap. My eyes widened, but I didn't complain.

The jealousy eased. He hadn't even thought about sitting with Josie.

I laughed. "We're eating. Let me sit next to you." I snagged my plate, cake, and drink while he narrowed his eyes and picked up his own.

"Fine." He settled in. "But as soon as we're done eating, you're right back here. I don't want any barriers between us."

Lucy leaned her head back. "See what I have to live with?" She smacked Josie's leg and said, "Let's get something to eat."

Without meaning to, I glanced at Josie, wondering what reaction I'd find.

She winked at me and looped arms with Lucy. The two of them strolled to the kitchen and got their own food.

"What are we watching?" Keith asked with two plates of food as he took the spot next to Josie's.

I told them our choice.

"What? No!" Keith wrinkled his nose. "That sounds—"

"Skylar picked it," Lucy interjected from the kitchen.

His eyes bulged, and his scowl transformed into a smile. "Different. That's what that sounds like."

"Yeah?" Raffe asked, throwing an arm over my shoulder. "You want to watch something else? You don't sound thrilled about it."

"*Thrilled* is not the word I would use, but there's no fucking way I'm not watching this with everyone." He rearranged his food so one plate sat on the edge of the couch and the other in his lap. "I'm just glad we get to learn about big and small animals."

Adam strolled into the living room and sat on the floor. "Man, sometimes I wonder about you."

I snorted. "This isn't a documentary. It's actually a movie."

"Oh." He exhaled. "Thank fuck for that."

And, for the first time since my capture, things felt normal. I relaxed next to my mate, ready to enjoy time with our friends.

THE NEXT FOUR days flew by. Raffe, Lucy, or Slade was with me whenever I wasn't in the apartment, and I'd begun training with Slade again, though not the other witches.

After what I'd learned, I understood better where Supreme Priestess Olwyn had been coming from, but I didn't trust her. I'd have felt the same about Slade if he hadn't helped me escape the bunker at a huge risk to himself.

When I trained with Slade, Raffe, Keith, or Adam came with me. Raffe didn't trust that Slade wouldn't let one of the other coven members ambush me.

Even Keith and I were getting more comfortable with each other.

Raffe had asked me to take time off from the animal clinic for a few weeks. He swore after football was over, he'd go with me each Saturday, saying the thought of me being ambushed and taken again was unbearable. The thing, I agreed with him.

I stood by the football bus where the team was getting on to go to another campus an hour away for tonight's game. I wanted to go with Raffe, but I was afraid his dad would show up and my blood would activate, so I was staying behind.

He'd tried to miss the game, but I'd insisted he go. He didn't need to give his dad any more ammo for us not to be together.

Raffe's displeasure and concern swelled into my chest. He kissed me again despite the football team and their coach watching. Lucy, Adam, and Keith stood a few feet away from us, but everyone else had boarded.

Raffe muttered, "I shouldn't go."

"You should." I cupped his cheek, enjoying the way his stubble rubbed my fingertips. "You're part of the team."

"Fuck them." He pouted. "You're more important."

"Oh my gods," Keith groaned and smacked Raffe on the arm. "We've got to go. We'll be back tonight. You act like it'll be days."

"Let's go!" Coach Prichard yelled from the bus. "Or I'm calling all your parents, and you can explain why you're benched."

Raffe scoffed. "He'd never bench us."

"Better not test him." Adam patted Raffe on the shoulder. "Lucy will stay with her. Your girl will be fine."

I pecked him one last time and said, "I love you. Now go kill 'em."

He smirked. "Now I have to. I can't make you unhappy."

"Gag me." Lucy shook her head. "Kill me. Something. Just make this stop." The corners of her mouth tilted up.

Sighing, Raffe stepped back, and Adam and Keith dragged him onto the bus. Lucy and I stood there, watching them pull away.

As the bus moved farther away, an uneasy prickle ran down my spine. I already missed him.

"Let's go to the student center and grab some lunch," Lucy suggested, tugging me away.

Hours later, my phone buzzed.

Raffe: We're back, and I'm taking a quick shower. Wanna meet at the student center to get food?

That was enough to get me back on my feet.

"What's going on?" Lucy paused *Criminal Minds*.

"They want us to meet them for dinner." It was close to ten, but I wasn't complaining. We didn't have any food here, and I'd rather sit with Raffe and watch him stuff his face than wait longer to see him.

Lucy turned off the TV and tossed the remote onto the couch. "I could use a snack."

Within minutes, we were heading out of the apartment.

Twenty feet away from the front doors, a woman yelled from the woods, "Help!" She sounded near tears.

We stopped in our tracks, and the world spun.

Two words popped into my head.

Vampire attack.

And the person was screaming for help, which would bring attention to what was going on.

We had to act fast.

CHAPTER NINETEEN

M y blood jolted as I spun around, but before I could take a step, Lucy caught my wrist.

"Go back inside the apartment." Her eyes narrowed. "I'll handle this."

She had to be smoking something if she thought I would run back to safety. "Not happening," I gritted out, my blood already at a low fizz. "Let's go—just tell Raffe and the others to get their asses over here." I wanted to help the person in trouble, but that didn't mean I wanted to be hurt, killed, or kidnapped again.

I took another step toward the fir trees, but Lucy jerked me back.

"Wait," she said, and the new presence in my chest warmed and inched forward. "If something happens to you, Raffe will kill me."

This was the argument she wanted to have when someone was in danger?

I focused on making my intention clear. "Are you going to wait for Raffe to get here before helping?"

"What? No." She blinked several times. "But I'm a wolf

shifter who's been part of this world my whole life, and I can control my magic." She flinched. "I mean—"

My head jerked back, and my stomach dropped. She'd never thrown my lack of control in my face before. "Don't. You meant it, but I don't care. You're my friend, not to mention Raffe's cousin, and I love you. I won't let you go alone."

Lucy frowned, but when another plea for help pierced our ears, she sighed and released her hold. "Fine, let's go, but if something seems off about this person needing help, you leave. You understand me?"

The fact she thought I'd listen was adorable. Nonetheless, I'd humor her. "Understood."

When she sniffed, I knew she was checking for signs of a lie. That was the thing. I understood what she wanted, but that didn't mean I planned to listen. Semantics, but I didn't give a damn. I didn't want to keep fighting while someone was in trouble and potentially outing supernaturals.

With a slight nod, the two of us took off. I expected her to pull ahead, but somehow, I kept pace beside her.

Suddenly, Raffe's voice echoed in my head. *I swear to gods, if something happens to Sky, I will lose my damn mind.*

The heat of his anger and the frigid cold of his fear clashed in my chest, and I nearly tripped. I didn't want to upset him, but I couldn't let someone innocent get hurt either. That went against everything I stood for.

We were close to the tree line when a pained whimper reached me. It sounded exactly like the noise I'd heard the night I found a vampire feeding on a human. Not the screams but the faint sounds of agony.

My blood increased to a high fizz, which was both a blessing and a curse. A blessing because the vampire would attack me, and a curse because, if it was old and strong, it would be a tough adversary.

We ran into the tree line, and the presence inside me vibrated deep within my chest like never before, almost in tune with my blood.

My vision adjusted quicker than normal to the darkness of the woods. Lucy and I darted around trees in tandem. I'd expected her to run faster and leave me behind.

A quarter mile into the woods, panic dug its sharp claws into my chest. How in the hell had I heard the scream and whimpers from this far away? It shouldn't have been possible.

Something *was* off.

"Lucy," I panted, though I wasn't out of breath yet.

A *thwack,* followed by a loud groan, was my response. I dug my feet into the ground and turned to find Lucy on her back, rubbing her forehead as she rolled to her feet and stood.

"Are you okay?" The only thing she could have run into was one of the two firs that were close together, but they had enough space between them for her to run through the middle of them.

She shook her head. "Yeah. It's just weird. It's like I ran into *nothing*." She headed in my direction but slower, with her hands in front of her. Four feet away, she stopped in her tracks.

Her eyes widened. "Sky, come back here *now*. There's a magic barrier."

The woman could still be in trouble, but the way Lucy's chest heaved made me listen.

Pulse thudding, I hurried toward her, but when I reached the same point, I hit the invisible wall. My body jerked back, and my forehead throbbed. At least, this time, it wasn't my nose, like in the bunker.

Reality crashed over me. Someone or something had set a

198 JEN L. GREY

trap. I wanted to stomp and scream for being so foolish, but I hadn't considered a trap because Lucy and I were together.

"No." Lucy ran her fingers through her hair. "This can't be happening. Sky, we've got to get you out of there."

Fuck me. This was witch magic, and I knew someone who could help me.

Slade.

With shaky hands, I took out my phone.

"What are you doing?" Lucy hissed and smacked at the barrier like she might break it. Each time, her hand came back redder than the last.

"Calling Slade." I tried to stay calm. If I let my emotions get the best of me, Lucy could get hurt. "He can get through this." I wasn't sure if he wanted me to give that information away so freely, but I wanted Lucy to know we had a way out of this. "He can help us." I tried to be vague while letting her know all hope wasn't lost.

"What the *hell?*" Lucy paled.

I flinched. "Look, I'd rather it be Raffe, but Slade is a coven member and can—"

Growls sounded from behind me.

I realized Lucy hadn't meant Raffe.

My blood pumped, and I spun around to see three wolves inching toward me like predators stalking prey. The darkest gray wolf in the center bared its teeth while the one on its right hunkered down, its light-gray fur brushing the mulch. The largest one on the dark-gray wolf's left had drool dripping from its mouth.

My blood hummed, and I pivoted and tossed my phone to Lucy. Thank goodness the object passed right through the barrier. "Text Slade *now.*"

The wolf shifters would be on me in seconds, so if I didn't do something, I'd be standing here waiting for my death. They were moving slowly as if to scare me.

My lungs screamed for air, unable to expand, and something *lunged* in my chest. Hard. My blood froze as if it wasn't sure what to do with the strange presence.

Of all the times for my blood to quiet, it would be *now* when three aggressive wolves were about to attack me.

Shit. Had whoever set the barrier also cast a spell to inhibit my blood? Fear strangled me. This had to be the secret society following through on their threat to eliminate me.

I could only hope I could get through to these wolves. It might be my only chance to make it out of this.

I held out a hand to show them I didn't mean any harm. "I'm not here to hurt you. I came out here because I heard pleas for help." I froze and glanced over my shoulder. "Are these wolves or wolf shifters?" I probably should've known how to tell the difference, but this was where I was at.

"Every wolf is a shifter." Lucy didn't look up, typing frantically on my phone.

That answer sat hard in my stomach. I didn't want to think about all the wolves that had been studied and tagged to monitor their habits. Part of my animal knowledge took on a more sinister edge.

When I refocused on the wolves, I noticed that the lighter-gray wolf was standing more normally, as if my message had gotten through to it.

I hoped that whatever had calmed the trapped wolf I'd met that day in the woods oh so long ago was working on these three. "Please, I haven't done anything to you. I don't understand why you're angry with me."

The largest one's eyes glowed, and the lighter-gray one readied itself again to attack. The large one must be the leader.

My heart hammered, and I hoped my blood would help

me. I surveyed the area for a weapon. I didn't doubt that Raffe and Slade would come to my aid—I just needed to hold these wolves off long enough.

My gaze paused on a sizable branch that had fallen from a tree twenty feet away. It was the only potential weapon anywhere close to me.

Great.

This was going to be so *easy.*

I hoped Raffe knew how much I loved him.

"You have to use your magic, Skylar." Lucy pounded on the invisible barrier between us. "They're going to attack."

Fisting my hands at my sides, I screamed internally, *Come on, blood. I need you.*

As if answering my call, my blood jolted, but the presence in my chest pushed forward even more. The two sensations warred with each other.

I'd never experienced anything like this.

"I *can't.*" I hated how my voice rose, conveying my fear. It would make the wolves that much more eager to attack. I took in a shuddering breath and tried to sound calm. "It's not working."

"Fuck," Lucy groaned and placed a hand on the barrier. "I'm going to follow it until it ends. Just stay alive until one of us reaches you."

Stay alive.

"Yeah, I kinda plan on not dying if possible," I snapped. "Not on my bucket list."

"Good," Lucy retorted, her voice farther away. "Now focus on surviving."

Right.

I had to take action. The wolves were thirty feet away, so if I wanted to get that branch, I had to move and stop wasting time begging my blood to surge.

Gritting my teeth, I took off, pushing myself like never before.

Snarls sounded from the three, but I didn't glance back. I pumped my hands fast, remembering a *secret* Dad liked to tell Mom and me every time he brought up his sprinting career. He'd proclaim, *To run faster, you must pump your arms harder. Your legs have to keep up even when your sides cramp.* I hoped it was true.

The trees blurred, and I snagged the branch before the wolves could catch me. When I spun around, they were ten feet away.

So close.

Maybe I could outrun them. The barrier had to end *somewhere.*

I ran in the opposite direction. There was no way I could fight off three wolves without my blood to aid me.

I pushed myself, the wolves hot on my trail. Their breathing was almost as loud as my heartbeat.

The presence in my chest jerked harder, like it was trying to free itself from within me, and I stumbled.

Considering how fast my feet were moving, I couldn't catch my balance, and I dropped the branch as I crashed onto my hands and knees. My body jostled, and my teeth clacked together, pain exploding on impact. Tears burned my eyes, but I grabbed the branch and spun around to find the three wolves springing at me.

Letting instinct take over, I swung the branch with all my strength. The thick middle nailed the largest wolf in the head, knocking him into the darker wolf. The darker one lost its momentum, and both wolves crumpled sideways five feet from me. The lighter wolf flew at me and swiped. I tried to lurch away, but its claws slashed my side.

Cold air hit my skin, and a stinging ache shot through me.

I gritted my teeth, air whooshing from my mouth instead of my nose, and my throat ached. The dark-gray and light-gray wolves circled me. I looked at the largest one. It lay on the ground, its eyes closed.

I'd knocked it out. Since it was unconscious, maybe I could get through to these two. The lighter-gray one had paused earlier. "If you shift back into human form and tell me what this is about, I swear to you—" I started.

A deep rattle sounded from the darker wolf as if it were telling me to shut up.

No talking. Got it.

My blood fizzed, but the damn presence in my chest felt as if it was digging a hole out of me. This was worse than the sensation of implosion when my blood had almost drained the life force out of me. The presence was jarring, like a hammer beating a nail in tune with my pulse.

I wasn't sure what to do, but standing here like a pig on a skewer wasn't an option. I had to do *something*.

Shaking my head, I tried to focus. If these wolves killed me, I would never see Raffe again.

Raffe.

My sense of him in my chest was still strong, but the presence and my blood were all-consuming.

It must be a spell. This presence had manifested in the underground bunker. What if they had placed something in me to attack my blood whenever it grew stronger?

Had the Veiled Circle set this up in case I didn't convert to them?

The darker wolf lowered its head like a bull and charged. The lighter-gray wolf moved sideways as if to attack me when the darker one shoved me into it. I swiveled to the right, my side hitting the wolves. I almost fell, but I used the branch to catch myself and stay upright.

The two of them had already reset. They crouched side by side, ready to strike.

This was it.

I was going to die.

My blood hummed, and the presence in my chest *ripped* out of me. I screamed in agony ... and everything around me changed.

CHAPTER TWENTY

The hum exploded in a quick burst, and a tree fell on the wolves in front of me while something snarled loudly in my head. I clamped my hands over my ears, but the noise didn't ease.

It was internal, the same way Raffe's voice was from time to time.

My skin tingled in a way I'd never felt before. I went to scratch my arms, but as soon as I touched them, I froze.

No. This was impossible.

I jerked my head down and saw thick hair, the color of *my* hair sprouting on my arms.

Not hair.

Fur.

My breathing quickened, and the world teetered around me. What had the witch done to me?

A loud *crack,* followed by intense pain, had the edges of my vision blackening. The top half of my back tilted over despite me standing straight.

I gritted my teeth, my lungs wheezing. If those wolves got

out from under the branch and attacked, I wouldn't be able to do a damn thing to fend them off, and worse, I didn't know how to stop this. I tried to walk away to gain distance from the wolves, but my lower back broke and forced me to the ground on all fours.

Vomit burned my throat, tears poured down my face, and I whimpered. I couldn't move, and eventually, the wolves would get me.

As if they'd heard me, the darker wolf inched out from under the tree, the trunk still on its backside.

My legs and arms shook. Then suddenly, my body shifted, repositioning itself. I inhaled as I watched my arms change shape and my hands turn into paws.

Wolf paws.

What the fuck?

How was this possible? Raffe had told me that people were born supernatural and couldn't be *changed*. Yet, here I stood—on *four* legs. I'd have thought it was a dream, but the pain from the wolf attacking me woke me from my stupor.

This was real. Learning the how and why of it would have to come later ... if at all.

Maybe now I could talk to my attackers and reason with them. But *how?* I didn't know how to link.

After one last jerk, the dark-gray wolf freed himself from the tree. His overly musky smell indicated *male* to me.

He snarled, the sound as loud as if he'd screamed in my ears. Then he charged, though slowly, with his back leg dragging a bit.

At least the tree had done something, but he could still kick my ass, especially since my blood was barely jolting in this form.

How was I supposed to fight him? Unsure what to do, I turned and tried to move away, my legs feeling funny as I adjusted to walking on four feet instead of two. My legs were unsteady for a few steps, but they soon started moving more naturally.

The presence from my chest now brushed my mind. In this form, it seemed familiar.

Maybe the presence had been this wolf all along. Had I been fighting the shifter inside me?

I leaned into the presence and imagined our minds merging into one.

My paws dug into the mulch, and I spun back toward the dark-gray wolf. He was injured—now wasn't the time to retreat. Going on the offensive was my best chance of getting out of this trap alive, and I had to take it. I *had* to see Raffe again ... even if I was in animal form.

Dark Gray snapped, and I watched as Light Gray bounded toward us. Even from my spot fifty yards away, I could smell her lighter musk scent. It reminded me of vanilla.

It was two on one, but the scent of copper wafted from her as well, telling me she was bleeding.

Getting my blood to hum would have helped me, but instead, the energy pumping through my blood seemed to push into the ground, which wasn't shaking.

Dark Gray lunged. The power from my blood continued to flow outward, but a tugging sensation pulled on it as if I were caught on something. Like I was fishing in the mulch underneath me.

Could this night get any weirder?

My magic had distracted me. Dark Gray landed on my back, his claws ripping into the flesh at the base of my back while his tail hit me in the face repeatedly, blocking my view of Light Gray. I could tell where she was by her scent and sounds.

I tried to ignore the sharp sting and rolled him underneath

me, and though his claws dug in deeper, I heard him exhale with all my weight on him.

I bounced a little on him, and he grunted. His claws retracted, and he pushed me away.

Using the momentum, I got onto my feet, but when my back muscles moved, I almost crumpled from the blinding pain. The presence's rage and mine combined, making me angrier than ever before.

I refused to die, not when Raffe and I had just gotten our shit together.

Throwing my head back, I howled, the sound vibrating in my chest. Light Gray caught up to us, and Dark Gray stood, chest heaving. I needed Raffe, Slade, and the others to hear me and come to my aid.

Light Gray's side was bleeding like something had poked her, but that didn't keep her from sidling up next to Dark Gray and staring me down.

I searched the area for something ... *anything* to use as a weapon. But with no fingers and thumbs, I couldn't think of a damn thing I could use other than my blood, which was fritzing in my animal form.

Please, take over, I begged the presence, hoping her animal instincts would get us *somewhere.*

The wolves attacked. Each one lunged for a different side.

I shot backward, ignoring the sensation of the skin on my back ripping open. A whimper lodged in my throat, but I swallowed it as the two wolves landed and leaped at me again.

What were their paws made of? Bouncy balls?

Unable to stumble back farther, I braced myself for pain and targeted Light Gray. I hunkered to the ground and to the right, and Dark Gray overshot me.

I extended my claws and dug my nails into Light Gray's

side, connecting with her wound as she sailed over me and landed on my back. She yelped, and I bucked her off before she could claw my back up again. The agony of her weight hitting me made me want to lie down and never get up again.

Her body crashed to the ground, but something sharp pierced my back left leg. Before I could turn, I was jerked back, and my stomach hit the mulch.

Dark Gray had me by the leg.

He ground his teeth into my flesh and bone, and I yelped.

With my other back leg, I swiped at him and dug my claws into whatever body part I could reach.

Out of the corner of my eye, I saw Light Gray get up again, and I pushed harder with my other leg, trying to cut through Dark Gray's flesh to the bone like he was doing to me.

His jaws slackened, and I curved around and raked my closest paw down his head, ripping his ear in half. He snarled and released his hold, rubbing his face against his front leg.

I opened my jaws, readying to slash his throat.

A howl sounded, startling me and halting my blood haze.

Was that Raffe?

I couldn't kill these wolves. We needed answers.

Somehow, I stopped myself millimeters short of Dark Gray's throat.

My blood hummed stronger, and something surged within me. Something that wasn't *me*, but I wasn't sure what it was. It felt familiar and calm.

Both enemy wolves moved toward each other. Their eyes glowed as they communicated, likely planning their next attack.

I tried to stand, but my left hind leg gave out. The pain was so bad that my vision blurred with tears.

There was no way I could fight.

I'd done my best, but it hadn't been enough.

My blood sang, and I could read the wolves' emotions.

They were angry, but something like curiosity crept into their feelings and morphed into emotions like determination and protectiveness, not from just these two but from many.

The wolves' eyes bulged, but they remained in place. Their gazes shifted behind me.

Ignoring my screaming muscles, I looked over my shoulder. I blinked several times.

What was *this*?

Several owls flew out of the trees and alighted on the surrounding branches, and ten raccoons, eight coyotes, and twelve deer now stood behind me. Even though some were predators and some were prey, they didn't seem wary of each other. Every one of them had their attention focused on the enemy wolves.

The tallest deer's intelligent brown eyes shifted to me, and he nodded.

Somehow, I understood. They were all here to protect me. I'd called for them, and they'd responded. That was what my blood had been doing, though I hadn't understood.

Moving forward, the group split in half, flanking me. The enemy wolves hunkered down and growled, which confused me.

Did they want to die? Or were they acting under a threat that they had to finish me or something bad would happen to them? I'd learned that the supernatural world was ruthless.

I had to stop this. I needed the wolves alive to learn who was behind the attack, and I couldn't let these animals die in their determination to protect me.

My blood power increased to a sing, a level I'd never experienced before, and I could feel it bubbling like it was boiling.

When the wolves ran toward the coyotes in the center,

power exploded from my body. I felt it leave my blood and barrel toward the two wolves.

When it reached them, the wolves swayed on their feet for a few seconds before their eyes rolled back and they dropped to the ground, completely unconscious.

The power continued to sail into the woods.

As if enough shit wasn't strange, all the animals here to protect me were still awake.

A fizzle rushed over my fur, and the power vanished as if the job were done.

One of the coyotes ran to Dark Gray and ripped out the wolf's throat.

My stomach churned. *Stop,* I screamed inside my brain.

The animals all froze. The coyote lifted his blood-covered snout toward me, confusion emanating from him. He had protected me like I'd asked.

It was one thing to kill out of protection, but this was different. The wolves were unconscious, with no way to defend themselves, and I needed the Light Gray and the larger wolf that I'd knocked out first to answer questions.

I also needed Slade and Raffe. Raffe would help me change back into human form and make the wolf shifters shift back to talk.

Thank you for your help, but I'm okay now. I wasn't sure they could understand me, but talking to them seemed effective. *I'm going to find my friends, who should be close by.* I didn't need someone stumbling across me with a herd of animals.

One of the raccoons stood on its hind legs, its black eyes meeting mine.

Understanding washed over me. I should call them again if I was ever in trouble in the woods. They wouldn't be far.

Somehow, I'd become a fucking Disney princess.

My heart skipped a beat as the group dispersed. An owl swooped down and brushed my snout with its feathers as it flew back home.

I watched in awe for a moment, but there were more pressing things to do—like getting back to Raffe.

Raffe.

With my blood calm, his feelings flooded back into me. He was crazed, the sensation adding to my already over-whelming pain. I wanted to lie down and rest, but I couldn't continue to let him feel like this, and I had no clue how long the wolves would be unconscious. The last thing I needed was for Light Gray to find her dead friend and attack me all over again.

"Skylar!" Lucy's desperate cry came from near where I'd left her.

I began to walk toward her voice, but the pain in my leg was so severe that I collapsed. I held it up and hobbled on three legs. The movement was rough, and my back felt as if I was being filleted.

Vomit churned hard in my belly and burned my throat. I wanted to cry out. Instead, I focused on taking one step at a time.

My back bunched and cringed, radiating stinging pain. I couldn't imagine a pain level higher than this. I focused on Raffe's desperation and used it to urge myself forward.

Paw steps sounded—multiple sets—but with all my concentration on moving forward and the pain weakening me like someone wringing out a wet rag, I wasn't sure how many.

My blood jolted ... and a wolf stepped out of the forest in front of me.

Its dark fur blended in with the shadows, or maybe that was just my eyesight because the world began to spin.

The wolf snarled, and I knew it was over. I didn't have any fight left in me, and my animal protectors wouldn't get here in time to save me.

My legs gave out, and I heard a shout. "Wait!"

CHAPTER TWENTY-ONE

he wolf froze and jerked his head to the left just as the
most alluring smell in the entire world hit my nose.

Musky sandalwood and amber.

Raffe.

Home.

Understanding slammed into me like a truck when I realized the wolf in front of me was Keith.

Heavy footsteps pounded from a few trees away, and
when Raffe stepped out of the firs, my eyes burned with
unshed tears.

He was here.

Finally.

Raffe's brows furrowed, and he blinked at me like the
people back in my old town used to do.

Like I was a weirdo.

My heart broke, and I whimpered. I didn't know how to
speak to him like this. I growled, and my blood jolted in frustration, especially since I didn't have the energy to stand up.

Then Raffe ran toward me. His irises turned dark, and his
panic slammed into me.

Skylar? His words popped into my head like they'd been doing but this time loud and clear. *What happened? How is this possible?*

When he dropped beside me, his forehead creased with worry as he scanned my back. Then he noticed my hind leg.

Three wolves attacked me, I said, hoping that the way I'd communicated with the animals worked with him.

But when he didn't respond and gently touched my back, causing me to yelp, I realized he must not have heard me.

What the hell?

"Fuck," he snarled then turned toward my face. "Babe, what happened? Link with me, and tell me everything."

I pawed at the mulch with my front paws, frustrated. I didn't know what to do, but I needed to communicate with him and get him or his pack to find the unconscious wolves. I jerked my head the way I'd come from, hoping he or Keith would understand.

Raffe turned to Keith. "Link with Adam, Lucy, and Josie, and follow her scent—see what you can find. There's got to be something back there she wants us to see," he commanded. "I'm staying with Skylar. I'm not leaving her fucking side ever again. I don't care if I have to quit the team." Determination and love emanated from him.

My fear of him not wanting to be with me disappeared. I never should have doubted his intentions *again*. When was I going to learn? Clearly, this was baggage I carried from a lifetime spent as an outcast. It had more to do with me and less with how Raffe had treated me when I'd arrived at EEU.

Branches cracked not far from us, and I growled, wanting whoever was coming to know that I would kill them if they even looked at my mate wrong.

"It's Slade." Raffe's jaw clenched. He removed his evergreen EEU sweatshirt, revealing his chiseled abs and the curves of his muscular chest.

Despite the pain, I think I started drooling. My mate was not only a caring and loving person but sexy as hell too. Everything inside me wanted to be back in human form so I could feel his body against mine the way nature had always intended.

That was until he leaned over and pressed the sweatshirt to the wounds on my back then lifted me and tied it under my stomach. I bared my teeth and snarled, the agony blinding me. Stars danced in my vision.

"You're going to *freeze* to death," Slade said, pulling my attention from Raffe to him.

Slade stood ten feet away, his mouth pressed into a firm line of disapproval.

I wasn't sure if he meant Raffe being shirtless in the cold or me being in wolf form. If it was the former, I could get behind that, especially with the sweatshirt putting so much pressure on the wound that I wanted to pass out.

"I'm fine." Raffe ran a hand through his wet hair. He'd taken a shower before leaving the gym to meet us for dinner. "You know we wolf shifters have a high tolerance for the cold, and Sky's bleeding way too much to let the blood loss continue."

Flinching, Slade cleared his throat. "I wouldn't believe it was her if it wasn't for the magic radiating off her. It's stronger than ever before."

My mind flicked back to the animals and how they'd come to me.

"I can't link with her, though." Raffe removed one of his shoes and pulled off his sock. "Which doesn't make sense. She's a wolf right now and my mate."

I could feel his worry.

Nothing could be easy when it came to me. Life was like a game of chess, and I had no clue how to play.

Branches rustled nearby, and Hecate stepped up beside Slade. Her eyes homed in on me, and her brows rose. "Can't say I was expecting *this*. How is that possible?"

"That's what we're trying to figure out." Slade slowly stepped toward me, watching me as if I were a science experiment. It was the exact expression he had in labs.

He licked his lips. "Don't wolves who join a pack have to submit and acknowledge the leader as their alpha before they can pack-link?"

"Yeah, but as the prince, I can link with everyone in the United States. Every wolf pack is underneath us, so that shouldn't be the problem." He gently lifted my hind leg.

Pain exploded worse than before, and I gagged. I wanted to thrash, but I wouldn't risk hurting Raffe. When he tied his sock around the injury on my leg, I snapped my teeth, though I made sure not to get too close to him.

"I know it hurts, but I need to stop the bleeding," Raffe rasped and scratched behind my ear.

Even though my leg still hurt badly, I wanted to shake it at how amazing that felt. He must have noticed because he grinned.

"Is that your answer for everything?" Slade wrinkled his nose, ruining the moment. "You're the prince, so my suggestion is irrelevant? After all, you know best, even though you're clueless about what the issue is."

At that moment, not being able to communicate was in my best interest because Slade had a point. They didn't get along in general, but it was worse when it came to me.

"That's what you want to talk about *now,* with Skylar like *this*?" Raffe slipped his shoe back on, sans sock, and glared daggers. "She's a fucking wolf and injured, which means she shouldn't shift back yet, and she can't communicate with me. We should be focusing on how to heal her and get her back in human form."

"You two, *chill.*" Hecate lifted her hands and stepped toward us.

Oh, hell no. She wasn't getting close to my mate, especially while he was shirtless. He was *mine*. I snarled, baring my teeth at her, ready to attack.

Raffe beamed, his eyes warming to the blue that showed only around me, and he waved me forward as if he approved of me attacking her.

The human part of me was slightly appalled, but the wolf in me was ready to tear the bitch apart if she got any closer.

"Get back here." Slade grabbed Hecate, pulling her to his side. "And don't look at him. I don't know why she's acting like that since she's never bitten him, but she's already acting like they've completed their bond."

When Hecate averted her eyes, my reason returned. I wanted to ask how to submit to Raffe, but my wolf surged forward, taking control.

I leaned over and nudged his arm with my snout. His brows furrowed, but when our gazes locked, his brows rose as if in understanding.

We stared at one another, but this was different. This wasn't just pure love; this held an undercurrent. My blood increased to a fizz as if it were preparing for a fight, but there was no way I'd fight Raffe.

"What are you two doing?" Slade asked uncomfortably.

Raffe's breathing turned rapid, and his eyes glowed brightly. The power inside him surged forward. "She's trying to submit like you suggested."

My blood's instinct was to push back, but my wolf howled

loudly in my head. As soon as she quieted, my gaze lowered to the ground of its own accord, then a myriad warm spots popped into my chest. The sensation was less intense than the connection I felt with Raffe, but a piece of my wolf also seemed to float out.

Skylar? Raffe tilted his head.

Hope jolted in my chest, but his speaking to me had never been the issue. So I tried again, using the same method as with the animals, *Raffe?*

His jaw dropped, and he exhaled. *How the hell is this possible? What happened? And why didn't you wait for me before running into danger? I told Lucy to stop you, but clearly, she didn't.*

So many questions, and I was still processing that I was talking to him with my mind. *It sounded like someone was in trouble, and Lucy was with me. That's why she gave you a heads-up. It wouldn't have made a difference if you'd been with me—the wolves that attacked me must be working with a witch who created a magical barrier like the one in the underground bunker. Slade was the only one who could walk through it then. This time, Lucy couldn't follow me, and I couldn't go back. Then, three wolf shifters attacked.*

Whoever did this to you, I get to kill with my bare hands. Raffe's face tensed, making the angles of his sculpted face sharper. *And slowly so I can watch them struggle until they take their last breath.*

That promise had me feeling all sorts of warmth that I didn't want to analyze.

And Slade got here right when the barrier went down on its own. Raffe shook his head. *He and Hecate weren't on campus —we had to wait for them to come back. Adam, Josie, Lucy, and Keith shifted and ran along the barrier, looking for a break in it while I waited for Slade and tried to bust through the damn thing.*

My heart stopped. *The witch must have run off when Slade showed up.*

They didn't want to be caught by the supreme priestess's son. That tracks. He scooted closer, leaning carefully against my side.

"I take it my suggestion worked." Slade tapped his foot.

Raffe scowled. "Yeah. I guess since she was turned instead of born, she was like a rogue."

I didn't want the two of them arguing over something pointless. *He needs to find the coven member who spelled the area. They can't be too far if they've just taken down the barrier, right?* I had no clue how that worked, so I could be wrong.

Raffe repeated what I'd said, but then his body tensed.

What's wrong? At least I could talk to him now like this.

He turned to me, and his eyes glowed.

They can't find anything back there, Raffe linked.

Keith replied, *Yeah, I know, man. That's what Adam just told you.*

Wait. No. *That's not possible. There were three wolves. One was killed, and the other two were knocked unconscious.*

Oh my gods, Josie linked with a faint hint of shock. *I thought Keith was messing with us when he said you were a wolf.*

Josie, focus, Raffe snapped. *My mate is injured, and we've got to find the bastards responsible for it. Keep looking while I take Skylar someplace safe and warm.*

I flinched at his tone.

Okay, we will, but their scents vanish at a certain point, Adam said slowly, like he hoped to prevent Raffe's ire. *But we'll scout farther. See if the scents pop back up.*

Raffe stood and frowned. *I need to pick you up and carry you. We can't stay out in the open.*

The thought of moving made me want to cry, but he was right. If we loitered, that would give the enemy time to bring reinforcements. *Okay.*

"Is everything all right?" Slade asked, rubbing his hands together to get warm.

"No. The scents vanished, which means your coven was definitely involved. You need to help the wolves pick up their trail while I take Skylar somewhere safe and warm."

"Do you think that—" Hecate started.

A menacing growl emanated from deep within Raffe's chest. "I'm taking her home so her wolf can focus on healing is what's going to happen."

Hecate crossed her arms. "Can I finish now?"

"I just need to make sure no one plans to object." He squatted beside me and wrapped his arms gently around my chest and backside. The buzz between us sprang to life, easing some of the pain and calming my blood.

"I *wasn't*." She scoffed. "I was about to suggest that I go with you so I can hide her from sight. I'm sure people seeing you—the elite, untouchable, mysterious quarterback—carrying a wolf into the women's apartments might cause problems on campus for supernaturals."

He sighed. "You'd do that?"

"For *her*, yes."

I tried to smile at her, but all I managed to do was open my mouth and let my tongue hang out.

Then Raffe decided to lift me. My back burned slightly, but not as bad as when I'd been walking and favoring my foot. I realized he'd tied my healthy back leg to my injured one, preventing it from dangling wildly. Overall, being in his arms wasn't that much more painful than when I lay still on my stomach.

"Go. Gavyn and Cade texted and are on their way here to help." Slade frowned. "Sky needs to be safe. She's been through hell." An odd emotion wafted from him, but I couldn't quite make it out.

I wished my blood was fizzing so I could decipher it.

Hecate lifted her phone. "Call me if you need anything."

The three of us made our way back toward campus. The cool air blew, ruffling my fur, but with one side plastered to Raffe's chest and his arms around me, I stayed warm. I was also thrilled that I was covering his chest so Hecate couldn't steal a peek at my man, though I couldn't blame her if she tried. He was amazing.

Should you tell me how to shift so you don't have to carry me all the way back like this? I wasn't sure how it worked, but carrying me must have been awkward for him.

His arms tightened. *You can't, not with your injuries. It'll make them worse. You'll have to rest and heal enough so you can shift back without suffering more blood loss.*

My breath caught. *Wait, I'm stuck like this?* I didn't mind being a wolf shifter because it made everything so much easier for us, but damn, I didn't like not having the option of turning back into human form right away.

Just until you scab over. That's another reason I needed you to stop bleeding. Shifters heal faster than humans, so it won't take long.

Why scabs? If an injury meant I couldn't shift, I would've thought I'd have to heal completely before trying.

He kissed the top of my head, and butterflies took flight in my stomach. I never would've imagined wolves could feel them! An interesting fact I wish I could share with my microbiology class.

As long as your wound isn't fresh and gaping, the magic that shifts you back into human form will heal you in the process, like with scabs. If you do it too soon, though, you risk making the injury worse and, at times, life-threatening.

Made sense ... well, as much as anything did with the supernatural.

When we neared the tree line, Hecate stopped. She wiggled her fingers as if to warm them. "Okay, I should spell her now."

Even with the cloudy darkness surrounding us, I could be seen. Many students would be arriving back late from the away game and throughout the night if they'd gone out instead of coming straight home.

"Fine." Raffe huffed. "But I swear if you try anything funny—"

"I won't." She rolled her eyes. "Sky and I might have gotten off to a rough start, but when the supreme priestess claimed her as one of her own, she became my coven sister, and I will do right by her. Got it?"

My chest expanded. Things had changed between us when I'd been accepted into their coven, and her loyalty to her people and leader spoke volumes about her. *She's sincere. We've become friends.* We'd spent a lot of time together, especially while Raffe and I were broken up, and we'd forged a bond of our own.

Even though Hecate's words made me feel loved, they'd done the opposite to Raffe. The spot in my chest where he lived shrank with distrust and frustration.

"Let's get her inside the apartment," Raffe rasped.

That was all Hecate needed. She lifted her hands, and this time, I felt her magic cover me. It was hot, like fire, the element she could conjure, but it didn't burn.

She gritted her teeth, and her bones popped as she pushed more of her magic toward me. Sweat covered her face, and she blanched and lowered her hands. Her eyes widened. "Something's wrong."

CHAPTER TWENTY-TWO

I f I had a dollar for every time someone had said that lately,
I'd be a millionaire. I couldn't help but *hmph*.

Raffe's arms tightened around me. "Is this a trick?" he
rasped as his anger slammed into me.

"No." Hecate stretched out her fingers. "It's not a trick.
My magic can't coat her. I've never experienced anything like
this before."

I remembered how the air around me had buzzed when
Slade had cast spells near me in the past. This time, I'd felt
only heat and no prickling sensation. *What am I going to do?*

We'll find a spot in the woods to rest until you can shift, he
replied, not taking his attention off Hecate. *I don't know what
else to do.*

I shook my head, whimpering from the agony in my
muscles and down my back. *You're shirtless. You can't stay out
here with me like that. You'll catch a cold.*

Warmth, like love, filled the spot where his emotions
rested within me. He replied, *I love that you care, but were
you not listening to what I said back there? I'm never leaving*

*your side again, and your wolf body's temperature is higher
than mine. You can be my own personal heater.*

That sounded way too damn tempting, but before I could
reply, Hecate spoke. "I'll try again." She rubbed her hands
together and cleared her throat.

Her warm magic enveloped me again, but I didn't feel it
settle over me like a blanket the way Slade's had before. A
lump formed in my throat, and I hacked. I sounded like an
animal trying to cough up a hair ball, and my back screamed
as my muscles convulsed.

"Stop whatever you're doing to her." Raffe's chest stiffened. "She's in *pain.*"

Stomping, Hecate lowered her hands. The intimidating
woman I'd first met at a football game a month ago slipped
back into place as she regarded him. She lifted her chin. "I
didn't make her sound like that. That was all her doing. I'm
trying to concentrate on cloaking her, but it's not working,
especially with you accusing me of stuff."

"It's funny how you suddenly can't hide her. Are you
stalling so someone else can attack us?" Raffe's voice held a
dangerous tone, and his fear and suspicion filtered into me.

"Yes, that's why I followed you so close to campus. So
when wolves come out to attack you, any nearby humans
will hear the growls." Her face flushed, and she crossed her
arms. "That'd be *real* smart, but I'm a witch. The only
species that's actually smart are the wolves, right? That's
why we're having this conversation—because *you* know
best."

Shit. This would escalate because Hecate wasn't one to
hold back, and Raffe couldn't handle people talking to him
like that.

"It just seems really convenient that my injured mate and
I are separated from everyone else, and now you can't help

us." The muscles in his jaw twitched. "What else am I supposed to think?"

"Clearly that I want to hurt one of my sisters, who, might I add, I helped save when *you* were being an ass to her." Hecate arched a brow. "Why would I do that if I wanted her to die? It would've been easier to explain then."

Babe, I did shift into a wolf, which we don't understand. My blood jolted. Raffe and Hecate were wasting time arguing. All I wanted to do was lie down somewhere next to my mate and pass out. I was so damn tired of the constant pain. *Hecate has been a friend to me, so—*

You thought the supreme priestess was a friend too, and we learned she influenced the board to bring you here and then hid it!

His words felt like a slap, and my wolf nudged forward. *That's not fair, and you know it.*

He let out a breath. *I didn't mean to say it like that. It's just... witches are manipulative, and one* just *blocked us from you again.*

My anger ebbed. He was right. A witch had blocked him and the others from getting to me when I was kidnapped, and he'd just gone through hell all over again. *Can we give her the benefit of the doubt for now? 'Cause I'd like to find a way inside.*

"Fine." Raffe gritted his teeth. "If you can't cloak her, is there another option?"

She snorted and tapped a foot. "What? You can't come up with anything?"

I wanted to smack them.

Raffe rolled his shoulders enough to make me grunt, and he froze.

I'm sorry— he started.

It's fine. I just want to lie down and be still.

I can do that. He exhaled. "Hecate, look. I just want to get Skylar inside unseen. Do you have any idea how to do it? Because only a witch can accomplish a feat like that."

And I fell in love with him even more. I understood how hard those words were for him to say. He was putting my needs above his pride and bias ... for the moment.

Hecate's arms dropped back to her sides, and she blinked. She tapped her chin and pursed her lips. "I can't think of anything other than—" She bounced on her heels. "How about this? I run into the apartments and open the door to the stairs, and you take her up that way. As long as we can get her to that door without being seen, I can do an aversion spell so everyone will want to stay in their room."

That was risky.

"What about the elevator?" Raffe asked.

She arched a brow. "Your hearing's decent, right?"

Raffe didn't respond, which spoke volumes.

She smirked, and I believed if we hadn't been in such a dire situation, she would've patted herself on the back for goading him.

Mirth twinkled in her eyes before she turned serious again. "I can spell the area and hold the elevator to make sure it doesn't go down until you get her into her room. The only thing is, with how much magic I used trying to conceal her, I won't be able to hold the aversion spell for long. Maybe a few minutes. You'll need to move fast and get her inside before it wears off. Even if that makes her uncomfortable." She focused on me, saying more with her glare than she had aloud.

She might as well have pack-linked because I understood. *Keep my pain to myself, or he'll worry more about me than getting me inside as quickly as possible.*

I nodded and cringed. Even the little head movement

caused me pain. All my muscles seemed to move through my back.

"Fine, as long as her pain isn't unbearable." Raffe tightened his hold on me. "Let's do it. With wolves and witches going missing, I want to get her somewhere with walls and fast."

Hecate nodded. "Go through the woods to where you can see the other side of the building, and watch for me to open the stairwell side door." She took off toward the front entrance.

During my entire time at EEU, I'd never seen anyone use the stairwell. The school wasn't crowded, and the elevator was so quick that no one minded waiting. This late, no one could enter the stairwell from outside, so we had that going in our favor.

Raffe linked, *If I move too fast, tell me. I'll slow down.* He took off at a quick walk.

I swallowed the whimpers that wanted to escape and closed my eyes, focusing on the cool rain as he continued his path toward the stairwell door.

After a short while, Raffe slowed, and I opened my eyes to find us between the men's and women's apartments.

A group of drunk guys and girls were hanging out between the buildings, almost right in front of the door.

"Fuck," he muttered.

I shouldn't have been surprised that we were facing another damn obstacle. This night had been one disaster after another. *Maybe you should leave me here. I'm close enough that it'd be foolish to attack me, and I can link with you if something happens.* I didn't like feeling like a burden.

If you sleep out here, I will too. I can shift. But after you've been attacked twice in these woods, I don't think I can handle you staying out here.

His worry and frustration knotted in my chest, holding me hostage. I was getting so damn sleepy after everything and feeling this pain constantly.

The stairwell door opened, and Hecate's head popped out. She frowned, taking in the group standing in front of her. Then she raised a hand.

Even though we weren't close, I could feel the heat of her magic faintly.

One of the girls visibly shivered. "It's getting cold. We should go somewhere else."

"Oh yeah." The guy closest to her wrapped an arm around her shoulders. "Why don't we go hang out in my room?"

The group reached a quick agreement and headed toward the men's apartments.

Raffe and I were silent as we watched them go indoors, and my wolf surged forward, listening for others outside.

I could hear TVs playing and people laughing, but I didn't hear anyone outside. Behind us, small animals like raccoons rustled close by.

Hecate scanned the area then waved us on.

Not hesitating, Raffe moved quicker than he had been to get here. *Let me know if you're hurting too much.*

It felt like razor blades slicing through me, but I wouldn't tell him that. I couldn't lie, so I just remained quiet. My heart pounded, and my blood fizzed until we got inside the door. I held my breath until the door shut, and Hecate muttered, "I didn't have magic to spare, so once we get upstairs, move fast."

"Not if—" Raffe started, but I interjected, *I'll be fine. I just want to go home.*

Raffe's displeasure filled my chest, but he didn't say another word.

"I've cast a small spell on the doorway to the stairwell, in case a human decides they want to take it tonight." Hecate rolled her eyes. "You know how humans decide stupid things sometimes."

Now that we were inside, the pressure not to give supernaturals away weighed so heavily on me that I wanted to howl. We were so close to humans. My breathing quickened as Raffe climbed the stairs, Hecate in the lead.

Each step made my anxiety spike higher. We could be caught at any second.

Babe, I swear, nothing is going to happen. And if it does, I'll take care of it, Raffe assured me as if he could make that sort of promise.

After what felt like hours, we reached the top floor, and Hecate slipped out of the stairwell to scope out the hallway. I heard her footsteps stop short.

High heels padded against the carpet. Hecate wasn't alone. An herbal scent floated to us, and Raffe tensed just as the door opened, revealing a frowning Supreme Priestess Olwyn.

Her gaze landed on me, the whites of her emerald-green eyes more visible than usual, as if she was tamping down her surprise. "Is that Skylar?"

"Yes, and she's injured." Raffe's tension increased tenfold, squeezing my chest harder than it had been. "We need to get her inside."

"Fine." She spun and flipped her palms down. After a few seconds, she said, "Take her in *now.*"

Raffe didn't hesitate, stalking down the hallway. When I heard him enter the key code, I wanted to cry from relief, but I refused to do anything foolish, especially with both witches around.

We entered the apartment, and Raffe marched to the

couch, not bothering to hold the door open for the two women.

Someone caught the door, and Hecate complained, "Don't wait on us or anything."

Raffe pretended not to hear her as he set me softly on the cushions, orienting my head toward the hallway so I could see the supreme priestess and Hecate.

Once the pain eased, I became appalled. *Wait, Blood.* I didn't want to ruin the furniture.

We'll pay to get it cleaned or buy a new fucking couch. I want you comfortable. Would you rather I take you to our room instead?

Our room. Every time he called something ours, I wanted to giggle like a schoolgirl. That was how damn happy it made me. *No. I'd rather Supreme Priestess Olwyn not enter our room.* Some places were meant to be safe havens.

I rested my head on the cushion, still in pain but better than I had been. Raffe stood partially in front of me.

"What the hell were you three thinking?" Olwyn hissed. "I wasn't happy to hear you were cloaking Skylar to get her in here, but not hiding her at all was beyond stupid."

"Supreme Priestess, I'm sorry. I tried to cloak her, but it didn't work." Hecate shoved her hands into her jeans pockets. "The spell wouldn't stick to her, so we had to improvise, and my magic was depleted from trying to hide her."

Olwyn's attention landed on me, and she grimaced. "She's a wolf, and your magic didn't work on her. What is going on?"

"You don't think I want to know the same thing?" Raffe spat. His words were controlled, but he had a viciousness to his tone that I'd never heard before. "But we aren't going to figure it out tonight. My mate needs rest and sleep."

"Our magic doesn't work on her, and she's now a wolf shifter with magic in her blood. That's unheard of." Olwyn paled. She stared at me with a neutral expression, but her eyes ... those held fear. "We have to determine—"

"I said *not tonight*." Raffe radiated power. "You two need to leave before you force me to do something rash. There's nothing more important to me than Skylar and her well-being. You two are adding to her stress, and that's unacceptable. So *leave*."

His raw, animalistic magic was strong and made me feel inappropriately warm. I'd always found his commanding presence sexy, but not even that word described how I felt now. He was powerful, and boy, did I like it.

Nostrils flaring, Supreme Priestess Olwyn looked ready to go to war. She sighed and forced herself to relax. "Fine, but I will be back to check on her. I'm on the school board, and I *will* visit our student."

I hate her, Raffe linked as he nodded. "Whatever it takes to make you leave now."

They were at a standoff. Neither wanted to yield, and neither would fully back down.

"Come on, Hecate," Olwyn said sternly and grabbed her wrist. "We need to talk."

I watched as she led my friend out the door, and I wished I could thank Hecate, but that wasn't possible tonight.

The door shut, and Raffe and I were finally alone.

He sat down on the floor next to me and leaned his back against the couch, placing a hand on my fur.

My eyes were closing, ready for sleep to overtake me. *Raffe—*

No talking. We're safe, and I'm staying here. Get some sleep.

I opened my eyes enough to watch him place his arms and head on the cushions and one hand on my front paw.

He was going to wake up hurting, but I knew better than

to try to change his mind. My heart felt so full, and my eyes closed as I linked, *I love you*.

I love you, too, he replied.

Then I fell asleep.

———

A PERSON LAUGHED, and my eyes popped open. The world spun as things came into focus. I was in the living room, my face plastered to the couch's armrest. I jerked to get up and froze, remembering my injuries, but when no pain hit me, I glanced down.

And found myself naked.

In human form.

What the—

I sat up and saw Raffe's sweatshirt tied around my lower waist and upper ass and his sock uncomfortably tight around my ankle. More confusing than anything else, I didn't see Raffe.

Nothing made sense.

I stood on my feet and didn't even feel a twinge of pain. How was that possible, and how had I shifted back into human form? I would've thought this was a dream if I hadn't woken up alone and naked on the couch with Raffe's random articles of clothes tied to me.

Out of the corner of my eye, I saw a note.

I changed the fucking code so that not even Lucy knows it. Don't let anyone in until I get back with breakfast. Your mate—Raffe

I snorted. He'd felt compelled to leave not only his name but the fact he was my mate. As if I wouldn't know it was him.

That was so ... *Raffe*. Claiming everything he wanted and putting his name on it.

The sock and shirt were covered in dried blood, and I didn't want Raffe to find me like this. I had one option.

Shower.

I gathered clean clothes and a towel then got into the shower. The hot water relieved the tension in places I hadn't known were sore. I washed myself three times, and when I finally felt clean, I climbed out of the shower.

The front door opened and shut. Then Raffe linked with me, *Sky? Are you okay?*

Before he was even done with the question, he was standing in the hallway, watching me dry off. He scanned me, and his jaw dropped. "You're in human form and healed?"

"Yeah, I woke up this way." I shrugged and turned to him.

Then something inside me snapped.

CHAPTER TWENTY-THREE

H unger slammed into me, but it wasn't for food. I dropped the towel, not bothering to hide my intention, and stalked toward him. The scruff on his face added an edge of danger, and the way his eyes heated as he took in my naked form made need clench so hard in my stomach that I couldn't handle it.

He swallowed when I placed my hands around his neck. His hair was still damp and smelled faintly of my rose-scented shampoo from the shower he'd taken before getting food.

When I moved to kiss him, he closed his eyes, leaned his head back, and groaned.

"This is cruel, Sky," he rasped, an animalistic growl woven through. "You're making being a good mate hard right now. You need to eat. You were badly injured, and you just shifted for the first time. You need calories."

The presence, which I'd learned was my wolf, surged forward, making my desperation stronger. "Food is the last thing on my mind." My voice was almost unrecognizable. The best way to describe it was feral.

"But—" he started, but when his eyes met mine, he stopped.

I slipped my hand under his blue sweater, and the shock of our bond thrummed between us. I refused to force him to do something he didn't want; I would respect his wishes, but I hoped like hell he didn't want to stop because the fight between my human and animal sides might become a war. "I don't understand it, Raffe, but I *need* you. If you don't want to have sex with me, though—"

Fuck yeah, I do, he linked and kissed me. *Your wolf is calling out to mine.* His kiss wasn't sweet; it was frantic.

My wolf howled in my head as I traced the curves of his abs, causing him to shudder. Our tongues tangled, his taste of mint urging me on.

With his agreement, there was no stopping this. If Lucy could get into the apartment, I doubted even her presence would have stopped me. My head spun as my free hand unfastened his jeans. There were too many barriers between us. I needed him naked and inside me. *Now.*

He caught the waist of his jeans before they fell and chuckled. *Let's get to the bed. Trying to carry you there with my pants around my ankles might cause a hazard, and you've already been hurt too much.*

I heard his words, but they didn't make sense. Nothing but the taste and feel of him mattered.

He slid his free hand down my waist and hoisted me up.

I whimpered, my access to stroking him removed, but then I greedily wrapped my legs around him.

The world spun ... or he was walking. I wasn't sure. But none of it mattered. I moved away from his mouth, needing to taste other parts of him, and gently bit his bottom lip.

He groaned, and suddenly, my back was pressed against something soft ... my bed.

Breaking away from me, he removed his shirt, and I traced his tattoo with my fingers. I watched with heavy lids as his muscles constricted in all sorts of sexy ways. A knot formed hot and heavy in my stomach, fueling my need for him. He quickly removed his shoes, jeans, and boxers, giving me an amazing view of his full naked form.

Not even a marble statue of his body would compare to the real thing, and my body turned into an inferno.

He climbed back onto the bed and lay down beside me.

Raffe, I complained, but his mouth lowered to my breast, and his fingers moved between my legs. His tongue gently flicked my nipple, and I arched my back as he slid two fingers inside me while using his thumb to circle between my lips.

An orgasm ripped through me in seconds, my body shaking uncontrollably.

The urgency intensified.

Again, I commanded, but he moved his hands away and leaned back. I threw a leg over his waist.

He smirked. "That's going to be a problem with you on—" As I slid him inside me, his words cut off with a groan.

His hands went to my hips, gripping me so his fingers dug in like he was having a hard time controlling himself.

"Are you complaining?" I teased and slowly rocked against him.

If you stop, I will. He blinked, and when he opened his eyes, they were glowing.

My own wolf rose higher inside me, thrilled with what we saw. Part of me wanted to move faster and chase after the release I desperately craved, but then everything clicked. Yes, I wanted the release, but here on top of him, with him inside me, was also what I needed.

As he anchored my hips, he scooted up against the headboard and sat. I spread my legs wider, drawing more of him into me, and then his mouth was on mine again.

Our kisses were still desperate, and his body thrust in sync with mine. Each movement brought me closer to the edge, though I didn't rush to the finish. Having him like this with me made me feel the most complete ... like we were one ... like our souls were connected.

When his hand cupped my breast and his finger caressed the nipple, pleasure sparked through me, bringing me so close to the edge.

I tore my mouth from his and kissed down his neck.

"Gods, Sky," he groaned. "You feel so damn good. I want to always be inside you."

Butterflies took flight in my stomach. *That can be arranged because I feel the same way about you.*

When my mouth landed at the base of his neck, where his pulse pounded against my lips, the urge to bite him stole my breath. My mouth opened of its own accord, and my teeth raked his skin as the friction inside my core intensified.

His breath caught, and I realized what I wanted to do.

Claim him.

Is it okay if I ... I wasn't sure how to say it, and my wolf urged me to sink my teeth into his neck. I managed to hold back, though I tasted his blood.

That should've disgusted me, but instead, it made the urge unbearable.

"You biting me would make me more fucking happy than I've ever been in my entire life," he rasped as both hands worked my breasts. "But only if you want—"

I bit him, my teeth sinking deep. As his blood filled my mouth, something *bolted* inside me. The spot in my chest where my wolf usually lived opened and poured from me into him.

He released my breast and gently took my head, lifting it up.

Our gazes connected, his eyes glowing brighter than ever before, and he put his mouth at the base of my neck and pierced my skin.

Pleasure exploded inside me. I gasped. The sensations were more intense than ever as what felt like his ecstasy flowed into me, adding to mine. In that moment, we were truly one, and he groaned gutturally as our bodies quivered together.

Our orgasms lasted longer than I'd thought possible, the two of us gazing at one another, blood trickling down our necks, and our bodies moving in rhythm. Our love for each other mingled, making my chest feel fuller. Somehow, my love for Raffe had multiplied from biting him and marking him as my own.

When our bodies calmed, I laid my head on his chest, breathless, though he was still inside me.

He kissed my sweaty forehead, and his happiness flowed into me so forcefully that I laughed while he cuddled me in his arms.

My hair, still wet from the shower, stuck to my face, the moisture mixing with the perspiration on his chest, but I didn't care. I wanted his scent all over me.

Wait. What?

That was something I would've never thought before; however, my wolf pranced proudly inside my head, and I didn't regret thinking it for one second.

What's that look for? He chuckled.

My face heated. *It's so weird. I never imagined loving you more, but I do. In fact, my feelings for you are so strong that I don't find your sweat disgusting. I want to bathe in it.*

Warm laughter escaped him, the sound more carefree than

I'd ever heard from him, and he leaned his head back against the pillow. His chest shook so hard that I bit my tongue.

If I thought I'd been embarrassed before, nothing compared to now. *Never mind.* I lifted my head and glowered at him. *Forget I said anything.* I moved to slide off him, but his hands captured my wrists.

His face softened, though the smile was wider than ever. He said, "Hey, I'm not laughing at you. I'm just so damn happy. I'd come to terms with believing we could never have *this*, and I've never been so ecstatic to be proven wrong."

My body warmed at the way his hands constrained me, but I sniffed, making it clear I was trying to smell his lie.

But all I smelled was his musky scent, spicy with … arousal.

"Babe, I swear I'm not lying." He leaned up and kissed me. "What you're experiencing is your wolf's influence. She wants to smell like me and wants me to smell like you so that no one questions we're mated. And our fated-mate bond is now fully formed as intended, which allows us to feel more for each other. There's no going back, especially now that we can sense each other's emotions."

My head jerked back. "Well, I mean, I feel yours more strongly now, but still."

His brows furrowed. "You've been feeling every one of my emotions?"

I nodded. "Even when they're faint. How do you think I knew how hard you've been struggling? I sensed it the entire time, and now I feel you as strongly as I feel myself."

"I didn't feel yours before, but it makes sense that I couldn't. You hadn't bitten me yet." He kissed me and linked, *That must be how I was able to track you when you were taken. I couldn't nail down exactly where you were because we were only semi-connected, but I sensed the direction you were in.*

Whatever it is, I need you to make love to me again.

He was already hardening inside me, never having slipped out.

Sounds like a plan, but then we've got to eat.

His tongue slid into my mouth, and once again, we got lost in each other and the moment.

I MANAGED to talk him into two more rounds of sex, but he finally forced us to get up. We took another shower because we were drenched in sweat, and then he went down to the laundry on the second floor to wash my sheets, which were officially stinky. I tried to go with him, but he refused, telling me I needed to eat.

I'd almost argued with him, but his concern had weighed on me.

Instead, I warmed up leftovers, taking my time so we could eat together when he got back.

As usual, he'd bought half the cafeteria, including a large pizza, a hamburger, fries, and the chocolate fudge cake I loved. By the time I got the pizza reheated in the oven and the hamburger and fries warmed up the best I could in the microwave, he was strolling back through the door.

"Now that's a sight I love seeing." He shut the door and leaned against it. "My woman taking care of me and making me lunch."

I rolled my eyes, but my heart fluttered. "First of all, you took care of me by bringing all this stuff, and second, I'm not making it. I'm reheating it."

"Same difference to me." He walked over, pulled me into his arms, and kissed me.

Wanting more, I opened my mouth, but he pulled back a little. He booped me on the nose and said, "More of that after you eat."

This time, I knew I wouldn't win the argument. We took out plates, and I grabbed two slices of pizza and a piece of cake. He took the rest of the pizza but cut the burger in two and put half on my plate.

I shook my head. "That's too much. I'll never eat it all."

He smirked. "Trust me."

Whatever. He'd eat it when I couldn't.

When I took the first bite of food, my stomach gurgled. I needed the food inside me now.

After ten minutes, I'd finished the pizza, the half burger, half the fries, and a piece of cake, and I didn't feel even a bit uncomfortable. "I must have eaten too fast." I frowned. When it caught up to me, I'd be sick.

"You're a wolf shifter." He winked, sitting back. "You need a lot more calories. We burn them four times as fast as a human."

"Seriously?" I must have heard him wrong.

He took the last bite of his double-meat pizza. "Yup. One of the blessings of being supernatural. Between that and how much Keith, Adam, and I work out for football, we have to eat almost all the damn time."

My body warmed. "And all that sex."

He smirked crookedly. "Especially that. I'll need you more often now that you're mine in every damn way. I thought I was addicted before, but I had no idea what both of us claiming each other would do to me."

I tucked a piece of hair behind my ear. "Well, I mean, I've eaten, so ..." I moved to him and straddled him. My eyes locked on the place where I'd bitten him. I could see the faint scab and knew a scar would be left behind.

"Yeah." His hands rubbed up my sides before he went still and groaned, "Fuck." The spicy scent of his arousal vanished in a second, and then we heard a knock.

Adam linked to the two of us, *We need to talk. I know you've been busy with Sky recovering and all, but we learned some new things.*

That sounded ominous.

Raffe kissed me softly and frowned. "This will have to wait."

I wanted to pout, but I held it back. Whatever Adam had to share sounded serious. *I hope they found the wolves and questioned them.*

He flinched as he lifted me from his lap and placed my feet on the floor.

There was something he hadn't told me. *They were looking for them, right?*

Face creasing, he turned and opened the door. *They searched all night and couldn't find them. They've been doing some digging.*

My mouth dropped open. *And you didn't tell me?*

Adam, Keith, Lucy, and Josie entered the apartment and sat around the living room.

Raffe didn't even acknowledge them, instead staring at me with that cocky smirk. He replied, *Oh, I was going to, but someone was naked when I came back from getting food and made me forget about everything but her.*

I bit my bottom lip, trying not to let him know how thrilled I was with that answer. I liked having that effect on him even if it delayed me learning the other stuff. I had been desperate to claim him.

Keith coughed. "Between the stench of sex and the way

they're eye-fucking one another, I'm getting uncomfortable. We could wind up with a show."

Lucy snorted. "I've never heard you complain about a show before."

"I wouldn't, but Raffe would kill me if I saw Sky nake—"

A snarl ripped from deep within Raffe's chest, and he jerked his head in Keith's direction. "Don't finish that sentence. I'm already having to physically restrain myself from killing you."

His anger funneled into me like a hurricane, and for a minute, I considered letting him hurt Keith for hinting at my nudity.

"Raffe, chill." Adam stepped between them. "He was just running his mouth like normal."

"When it comes to my *mate,* he better learn that shit won't be tolerated." Raffe took a menacing step toward Keith, his anger still uncontrollable.

"Man, I don't think about her like that." Keith moved to the side and pointed at me. "She's not my type." His eyes widened. "Not that you aren't hot—you are—but—"

"That's it," Raffe spat.

Josie laughed uncomfortably and reached for his arm. "Raffe, just calm—"

That had me snapping, and I stalked toward her, making a loud, menacing sound I'd never heard come from my throat as my blood jumped to fizz. He was *mine*, not hers.

"Whoa." Lucy stepped between us. She shoved Raffe back a few steps and smacked Josie's hand away. "Everybody, *stop!*"

Lucy touching Raffe didn't bother me, which surprised me. The only conclusion I could come up with was that she was his family.

"We've got a *newly* completely mated couple here, so we

all need to realize that and not touch or say anything about either one of them." Lucy sighed. "And they're fated mates, so they'll be even more possessive of each other. No talking about Sky being hot or touching Raffe. Things have changed, especially around the dynamics of them and the opposite sex." She emphasized that last part to Josie.

"Right." Josie blinked. "Got it." She shook her head and grimaced as she glanced my way. "Sorry."

"Man, I'll never look at Skylar again." Keith lifted his hands. "I'm sorry."

Adam pinched the bridge of his nose. "You can't say you won't look at her again. She's Raffe's mate. It's inevitable. Just don't be a moron."

Some of the tension eased from Raffe, and he moved back beside me, wrapping his arm around me and anchoring me to his side.

The buzz of our connection thrummed between us, settling us both.

Keith marched across the room and sat at the end of the couch, avoiding looking in my direction. Josie followed suit, but she wasn't acting as sheepishly; more like she wanted to make it clear that she understood that we were together.

"You ready to listen?" Adam asked, lifting a brow. "We learned a whole lot of shit that I'm trying to update you on."

Taking my hand, Raffe led me to the end of the couch near the hallway, which was becoming our normal spot. He sat down with me on his lap. The way we were claiming each other kept my heart and blood at a calm, normal rhythm.

"Yeah, what's going on?" Raffe replied.

Shaking her head, Lucy took the spot at the other end of the couch.

Moving to stand in front of the TV, Adam linked to all of us, *It's best if we talk this way in case people walk by who can overhear us. As I told you, we couldn't locate the wolves or coven members in the woods or pick up their trail. But we started asking around, and we found out something very interesting. The Atlanta alpha and four of his pack members came into town earlier today.*

I'd knocked two of them out, and another had died. How had a witch moved all three of them? Either there had been more than one witch, *or* they'd cloaked the wolves and hidden them somewhere.

How did you learn this? And how would they know about Skylar? Wouldn't someone have picked them up from the airport? They shouldn't have been here. Who was supposed to get them?

Josie looked down, picking at her nails.

My blood jolted. I'd never seen a nervous tic from her before. My heart pounded, and my mind raced a mile a minute.

Realization stole the breath from me.

No.

This couldn't be possible.

CHAPTER TWENTY-FOUR

S ilence hung heavily around us.

Raffe remained focused on Adam, who hadn't continued, wary of Raffe's reaction.

Between my quickened heart rate and the way my blood jolted, Raffe must have felt my disbelief. He studied my profile, noting which direction I was facing.

The moment Raffe homed in on Josie, she dropped her hands into her lap and kept her eyes downturned.

"Are you *fucking* serious?" Each word carried more of his anger, the last one sounding more like a bellow than anything. "Aldric picked up the wolves that attacked my mate."

"Dude, calm down." Keith pointed a finger at Raffe. "It's not her fault her dad is involved. I told her she shouldn't be here when you learned this."

More hot rage flowed through Raffe, almost taking my breath away, but thankfully, my blood remained at a steady jolt. At least, Raffe's emotions didn't affect my blood like mine did; otherwise, I'd be screwed.

"Fuck you," Raffe snapped. "I'm not mad at *her*. She didn't have anything to do with it, but I'm *livid* about what that means." His anger switched to hurt. "I can't believe Dad would do this to me."

My chest squeezed tightly with his disappointment and betrayal, and my wolf urged forward, wanting to kill the person behind it all. I took a deep breath to calm down and remain rational. I turned and cupped his face, then linked, *Just because Aldric picked up the wolves from the airport doesn't mean your father was behind it. Maybe they were on their own mission, or the secret society manipulated them into attacking me. We aren't certain what happened, and none of us can jump to conclusions.*

He turned his face into my palm and kissed it. *I love you so much for saying that, but if Aldric is involved, it's very likely that he did this on my dad's behalf.*

Adam dropped his arms. *Skylar's right, though. Your dad could've invited the Atlanta alpha here to update him on your refusal to marry his daughter. King Jovian wouldn't want to leave Seattle right now, and that's the sort of news he wouldn't want to share over a link or phone call. He also wouldn't risk leaving after the turmoil between the two of you and the chaos that could explode if our people learned that the prince was threatening to leave the pack. Add in that if he went to Atlanta after failing to hold up his end of the bargain, he'd be walking into hostile territory.*

And let's be real, man. Keith lifted his hands in surrender. *If I were the Eastern wolves' alpha and wanted my daughter to marry the prince, I'd eliminate the obstacle to fix the problem permanently. Your dad wouldn't even have to suggest it to me.*

Lucy rubbed her hands together. *Josie, did your dad say anything to you?*

Nothing. Josie twirled a piece of her dark, curly hair around one finger. *He checked on me last night, but he always does that.*

I was so damn thankful to be able to pack-link with all of them because I doubted we could've had this conversation verbally. If people were watching us, we'd have to be more careful.

There's one easy solution. I'll call him. Raffe nodded, his emotions still volatile. *If he's behind this, I need to know.*

And what? Add more tension between the two of you so he tries to kill Skylar again? Adam lifted a brow. *If this was anyone but Skylar, you'd say we shouldn't be rash and can't tip our hand until we know more.*

And Sky has a point, Lucy added as she crossed her legs. *The secret society could be part of it. If they knew the Eastern wolves wanted to split, having them attack her would cause problems for all of us.*

Not doing anything would invite him to attack my mate again. Raffe shook his head and wrapped his arms around me. *I won't.*

We don't know the real enemy behind the attack. If you accuse your dad and he's innocent, it'll create more tension between you two and possibly get me hurt again if he thinks I'm driving a wedge between you. I turned to him and pressed my forehead against his.

I had to believe his dad wouldn't do that. Parents loved their children, right? They wouldn't do something to hurt them, even in the name of duty. I shivered, hoping I was right and not misguided.

Raffe growled faintly. *Fine, but you have to be with one of us at all times, and that means no traipsing into the woods near campus alone.*

My wolf whimpered in my head. *But ...*

Babe, I won't deprive you of that. I know your magic and your wolf need to shift. We go off campus to run. He tucked a piece of my hair behind my ear. *All of us together, at least* thirty minutes out. *If you promise to stay with one of us and not venture into the woods alone, I'll agree to be patient until we have something concrete to go on.*

I pursed my lips. *But my blood. I need Slade's help to learn how to control it.*

I know, Sky. He licked his bottom lip. *But dammit, a coven member was involved tonight, and Slade was captured by someone working with the society two days ago. So forgive me if I want the people I trust the most to keep you safe. Can you please agree to my terms? I can't handle you getting injured like that again.* His face creased with worry, and his terror caused my stomach to squeeze.

Yeah, but if the danger isn't resolved soon, we'll have to determine a new strategy. I placed my hands on his shoulders and rubbed my thumbs along the back of his neck. *And I'm only agreeing to this knowing that you'll be with me most of the time to help keep my blood in check.*

Fuck yeah, I will be. He smirked. *Every class we have together, you can sit on my lap if that's what you need ... for stability's sake.*

I snorted. *Is that the angle you're working now?*

He shrugged. *Whatever works.*

"Did he seriously just go from pissed to purring like a fucking cat in seconds?" Keith blinked.

Lucy jumped to her feet. "Oh, speaking of cats, I need to check on Keith."

"What the hell?" Keith wrinkled his nose. "You haven't changed that mangy thing's name?"

"Nope." Lucy strolled past us toward her room. "That's her name *forever*. It suits her."

She entered her bedroom and said, "Oh, Keithy. Did Sky and Raffe scar you with their claiming ritual? I wasn't even here, and the smell will never be erased from my mind."

"Tell me about it." Adam chuckled, taking the spot beside Josie. When he sat down, he placed his hands behind his head. "What's the plan now?"

Even though I loved being in Raffe's lap, we were clearly making them uncomfortable, so I slid down next to him and snuggled into his side. "How about we watch a movie since we're just sitting here to wait?"

"Only if I get to choose." Keith smacked his chest. "I'm not watching any sort of mushy movie with the two of you just inches from me."

Josie, Adam, and Keith debated movies while Raffe and I cuddled, content to be together.

When Lucy joined us, Adam pushed play, and we all settled in to forget all the horrors for a couple of hours.

***

THE NEXT FEW days passed quickly. Besides catching up with my classes, I dealt with the stares as Raffe made sure that the seat right in front of him was open for me, making it clear to everyone that we were together. The only downside to his attention was that even more people were watching me.

Even though I loved that Raffe was open about our relationship, I was uncomfortable with all the attention that came with it. A few people watched as if they expected him to laugh and insult me like our relationship was a joke.

I couldn't blame them. Raffe had made it clear when I started school that he didn't want to be associated with me.

Slade had been pressuring me to meet with him to train, and I understood why. If I could've harnessed my blood on the night the three wolf shifters attacked me, I never would have gotten injured. I explained to him that I believed my blood hadn't activated initially because my wolf-shifter side was trying to surge forward. It'd felt as if the two energies were at war, trying to dominate one another until I shifted, and then they'd synced up or whatever.

But what did I know?

All too soon, it was Saturday morning, and Raffe had talked me into helping him warm up for the game by pleasuring each other. I was on my hands and knees as he thrust into me from behind with his fingers between my legs when our orgasms took over.

With our senses combined, my vision hazed from the intense ecstasy until I was seeing stars. Then, a knock sounded on the apartment door.

Raffe groaned in my ear, and our bodies gave one final shudder when another knock sounded louder than the first.

My hair was a mess, and my breathing was erratic. We disconnected, and I reached for my pajamas.

Raffe's hands caught me by the waist and pulled me against his sweaty chest.

I giggled. "Someone's at the front door. I better answer it."

"We know damn well who it is, and Keith can chill the fuck out," he rasped, nipping at my neck.

My heart fluttered.

Lucy's bedroom door opened. "Are you two serious? You're going to make me answer the door when I was trying to sleep through your sexcapades?"

Even though Raffe kept telling me I had nothing to be ashamed of, I hadn't been raised with overly affectionate parents. They loved one another and held hands on occasion, but if I'd ever heard the kind of stuff we did from their bedroom, I was pretty sure I'd want my eardrums to explode.

The front door opened, and a voice said, "Oh, hi. Is this Skylar Greene's apartment?"

My mouth went dry, and I leaped from the bed and ran to

my closet. Frantically, I grabbed a clean set of underwear and a bra and then snagged jeans and a T-shirt, quickly pulling them on. *Get dressed. Now.*

What's wrong? Raffe asked as he followed my lead, though he wasn't moving fast enough.

My parents are here early. I couldn't believe this was happening. Out of all the ways I'd imagined them meeting Raffe, this was not one of them. *We need to get out there fast.* I ran my fingers through my hair, removing the tangles.

We're together, so— he started, pulling on his jeans.

I spun around and gasped. *Yes, we are. But they're human. They won't understand our bond and how us moving so fast is natural. We need to get out there fully dressed and put together so they don't think we have been doing something!*

His lips mashed together, and I could feel a hint of mirth coming from him. *Yup. Got it.*

If I could have stomped and pouted without worrying them, I totally would have right now. Instead, my blood jolted, and I spun around, but before I could open the door, he grabbed my hand.

His expression looked sheepish. *I'm sorry. I understand this is different, and I'm not making light of your concern. You're just so damn adorable, wanting your parents to like me.*

I gently smacked his chest and replied, *Well, you're kind of important to me, so it'd be nice if everyone got along.*

He nodded. *I'll do my best.* He kissed me before opening the door on my behalf.

My dad and mom were standing in the living room with Lucy still at the door.

A smile broke across Mom's face, but the moment Raffe stepped up behind me, it fell flat. The skin around her russet-brown eyes tightened, and she clutched her white purse in front of her EEU sweater.

Dad scowled, his normally friendly demeanor vanishing. His forehead lined with concern all the way to the top of his bald spot. "Sky ... uh ... we didn't realize you'd have company this early."

I wanted to die. There was no salvaging this. "Oh, well. Yeah. We were—"

"Good morning, Mr. And Mrs. Greene." Raffe breezed past me and smiled. "My name is Raffe Wright. I'm your daughter's ... boyfriend."

Dad didn't smile, but he shook Raffe's hand, whereas Mom glanced between Raffe and me. When Raffe extended his hand to Mom, she gave him a strained smile and shook it.

"It's nice to meet you," she said tightly, flipping her short blonde hair back from her forehead.

Playing with the top button of his green button-down shirt, Dad frowned. "Uh ... we were hoping to have a late breakfast with Skylar, so we came early. We didn't realize we'd be interrupting."

I wanted to die. They knew what we'd been doing. For the first time in my life, I was certain my skin was close to the same color as theirs—fair. It was usually so easy to see that I wasn't their biological daughter with my olive skin and features.

"Actually, I've got to head out. I just wanted to see Sky before the game," Raffe said, taking my hand. "I gotta head over to the stadium for warm-ups."

Mom's brows lifted. "You're on the football team?"

"You could say that." He winked at her, and she giggled.

She fucking *giggled*.

Dad's scowl deepened, which made me believe he might actually have his own supernatural power.

"Are you ready to grab something to eat?" Dad nodded toward the door.

"Oh yeah." I turned to Raffe, unsure of what to say. "Let's go."

"I'll walk with you three over there," Raffe suggested easily then linked to Lucy and me, *Luc—*

On it. Lucy yawned. *I'll change and meet with Sky and her parents at the center.*

Hurry. Raffe headed to the door, leaving it open for the three of us.

Within minutes, we were walking across campus toward the student center. It was a rare sunny day, but a faint chill hung in the air that wouldn't leave until summer.

I listened, impressed, as Raffe talked to my parents, telling them about the campus and informing them of small details I hadn't known.

I could see him using his political science degree. Normally, he was stoic and unapproachable, but with my parents, he was the opposite. He smiled and was open, yet he still seemed unaware and unaffected by the other students who passed by and stared at him, giving him that mysterious edge I adored.

When we reached the student center, Raffe pecked me on the forehead, not giving too much of a public display of affection. Then he sauntered off toward the football stadium, and I had to force myself not to watch him leave.

The three of us headed into the student center, which was loud and brimming with people, and for once, I enjoyed getting lost in the chaos. We snagged something to eat and sat down, and my parents told me what was going on with them, though I could tell they wanted to ask more questions about Raffe.

I kept the focus on them. After all, we had to be safe around this many people.

After we'd eaten and toured the bookstore, Lucy met us outside on our way to the stadium.

"Do you volunteer at the animal shelter with Sky?" Mom asked, glancing at Lucy.

She shook her head. "No. I don't volunteer or work. My entire focus is on schoolwork and watching *Criminal Minds* with Sky when I can steal her away from my cousin."

"Raffe is your cousin?" Dad tilted his head and glanced at me. "Is that how you met Raffe?"

I laughed. "Nope. I met them separately. I ran into Raffe the night I got here, and I have two classes with him." Running into him was putting it mildly. I'd slammed into him. And now, thinking back, I wondered who had been watching me that night. There was no telling, and I couldn't help but shiver. "I didn't know they were related until weeks later when I came home to find him in the living room."

They continued to pepper us with questions, and soon, we were walking through the main stadium entrance, where everyone was being pushed together.

Suddenly, something grabbed me from behind, and a scream lodged in my throat.

CHAPTER TWENTY-FIVE

M y breath caught as the overly musky scent hit my
nose and the power soaked into my bones. Before
even turning around, I knew who it was.

King Jovian.

My heart clenched, and I regretted asking my parents to
come here. I didn't want them on King Jovian's radar if he was
the one trying to kill me.

"Skylar," King Jovian said, voice deep and low.

I turned toward him, knowing there was no point fighting
the inevitable, but I linked with Raffe, *I don't need you to do
anything, but your father is here.* When I faced the king, I
noted that both Queen Tashya and Aldric were with him.

My lungs seized.

As soon as I glanced at Aldric, he averted his gaze. That
was odd, and I wondered if he felt guilty. My blood activated
to a low fizz.

"Ki—" I stopped myself before I finished his formal title.
That would be strange, given that we had no kings in the
United States. I swallowed as the king's eyes turned icy.

What magic did you use to make the bond seem complete?

King Jovian linked, his hands tightening on my arm.

I'll take care of this, Raffe replied just as Lucy exclaimed, "Uncle Jovian!" She hugged him tightly, and the king's eyes widened as he released me.

Lucy looped her arm through his and smiled at the queen, pulling the king a few steps farther away from me as she exclaimed, "What a lovely surprise!"

King Jovian resisted, a frown set hard on his face, and his eyes glowed.

I waited for his voice to pop back into my mind, and when it didn't, I figured he was communicating with Raffe. Part of me wished I could hear the conversation, but the other part was thankful that I couldn't. If his dad had tried to have me killed, I'd rather live in blissful ignorance ... or as close as I could without *actually dying.*

"Skylar," Queen Tashya said kindly as she strolled over to me. Her gray eyes were warm, and her dirty-blonde hair was pulled back into a loose braid, giving her face the essence of youth. "It's so nice to see you again." The corners of her mouth tipped upward. *And I see you've given us yet another surprise.* She tilted her head, emphasizing her curiosity.

Mom cleared her throat, but Dad brushed past me.

His face was flushed as he extended a shaky hand. "Are you *Jovian Wright?*"

Holy shit. My dad knew of Raffe's father. How was that possible?

"Yes, I am." King Jovian flicked a tentative glance at me and asked, "Why?"

"I'm Skylar's father." My dad kept his hand extended. "Robert Greene. I'm the finance manager at Piller Commercial Groups, so meeting the CEO of Wrights Property Group is a little surreal. The way your company moves so quickly despite its size and scoops up properties that no one knows are on the market has everyone intrigued about your methods. It's pure brilliance and, truthfully, legendary."

My dad was fanboying over my mate's father, who could very well be trying to kill me. If this wasn't proof that Fate was real, I didn't know what was. Not only that, but she had a wicked sense of humor.

"Oh, honey." Queen Tashya patted the king's chest. "We get to meet Raffe's, uh, fiancée's parents. How lovely."

Mom choked. "Fiancée?"

I wanted to die. Right then and there. I didn't know what to do, but I noticed Aldric sneaking away in the chaos.

"You're *engaged*? And you didn't think to *tell* us?" Mom clutched my arm, forcing me to face her. Her gaze homed in on my bare ring finger. "Are you hiding the ring? Haven't you been dating this boy for only a week? What—"

"Wait. Raffe is your son?" Dad's admiration fell from his face, and he blanched, almost resembling a vampire. "I knew his last name was Wright, but it's a common name."

"We're not engaged." I raised both hands, wanting the chaos to stop and to get the hell out of here. "Absolutely no engagement has happened." Just an unbreakable fated-mate bond, which made us more committed than marriage ever could, but I would *definitely* be leaving that out.

Raffe's voice popped into my head, and somehow, I felt Lucy in the connection. *Dad is refusing to leave and wants to talk to Skylar and me later. Lucy, don't let Sky out of your sight. Not even for a second. If she needs to pee, you go with her. Got it?*

Don't worry. But when the game is over, we might need to switch to protecting you instead of her. Lucy snorted then tried covering it up with a cough.

I didn't need her stressing him out more than he already was. I glared at her and linked, *Everything is fine. I'll behave.*

A witch couldn't risk putting up a barrier spell here with all the humans around. Just focus on the game.

Easier said than done when I don't give a shit about anything but your safety, he grumbled, his concern flowing into me. *If it wasn't for the pack link with you, my ass wouldn't be down here. If* anything *seems strange, you tell me immediately. I'm tuning in to your emotions.*

"Your silence speaks volumes, Skylar Jane Greene," Mom spat, forcing me back to the verbal conversation going on around me.

A lump formed in my throat. She hadn't full-named me since I was sixteen and accidentally ran my car into a ditch. I had no idea what had been said to know how to answer. *Shit.*

"Clara, this was a misunderstanding on my end." Queen Tashya laughed, a little high-pitched, and clasped her hands in front of her chest. "I misspoke. I meant to say girlfriend, not fiancée."

Dad lifted his chin. "That's quite a mix-up. I know that neither Clara nor I would accidentally say fiancé when speaking about Skylar's boyfriend."

He had a point, but I could understand how the queen had gotten there. She couldn't say *mate*, so she'd said the first thing that popped into her head to convey the sort of relationship Raffe and I had. *Boyfriend* didn't even come close to what we shared.

"We should take our seats." Lucy pointed toward the opening that led to our section. "The game starts in less than twenty minutes, and we don't want to miss the football team's entrance!"

I latched on to the valid excuse to get us out of this situation. "You're right. Let's do that." My heart stopped. *Please tell me we won't be sitting next to them.*

Lucy shook her head. *They have box seats. Don't worry.*

Some of the weight on my shoulders lifted. At least, that was a silver lining, though considering how my parents kept flicking concerned glances my way, the damage had been done, and I couldn't blame them. Mom had only learned about Raffe last week, and she would never understand the bond he and I shared. This seemed superfast to them.

"Well, it was great meeting you." Queen Tashya shook my parents' hands and placed a hand on my cheek. "I'm sure we'll be seeing you soon, dear." She turned to Lucy and hugged her.

Oh yes. We'll be talking soon. King Jovian nodded. *I have some things the three of us need to discuss, and I need you to explain to me how this full bond and her mind-speaking with me is even possible.*

He was already suspicious of me; I couldn't imagine his response when he learned I was now a wolf shifter.

The king didn't shake my parents' hands but told them goodbye. When the four of us moved toward the opening and away from Raffe's parents, oxygen filled my lungs again.

Both my parents were abnormally quiet, Mom's earlier carefree demeanor gone and replaced with the concern that Dad had been trying to hide all morning.

"Come on." Lucy waved us deeper into the stadium, heading toward center field.

The entire place was crowded, and people bumped into us as they rushed to the bathroom, got something to eat or headed back to their seats before the game started.

When we reached midfield, Lucy turned onto the steps to the seats. We headed down to the fifty-yard line, close to the front row.

"Wow. How did you get these seats?" Mom asked from behind me.

Lucy snorted. "Benefits of being related to and dating the

quarterback."

"He's the quarterback?" Dad sounded strained. "Of course he is. He's a *Wright*."

I didn't know how to respond to that, so I didn't and followed Lucy to the front row. She took the fourth seat from the end, so I stayed close to her, not wanting any chance of getting stuck between my parents so they could gang up on me. This way, they knew when they spoke to me, Lucy would overhear.

Mom slid into the seat next to me, leaving Dad on the end. The time on the clock said fifteen minutes, and the cheerleaders rushed to the edge of the field near the band. The last time I watched a game, I'd been distracted. This time, I was able to stay in the moment, waiting in anticipation for my mate to come running out.

Soon, the band began playing, and the cheerleaders danced in rhythm with the song. Josie, in the center. Then the football players raced out with my mate in the very front, Adam and Keith at his sides.

The crowd went wild as they ran onto the field, and I knew the moment Raffe spotted me. The back of my neck tingled, and the warmth of his love filled me even more.

Running out here like this with you there smiling at me has already made this game the best fucking one ever, he linked.

Not missing a beat, he ran to the sidelines where the team would stand, but he pressed past that, and I noticed he held a shirt in his hand. He ran right up to me and winked as he tossed the shirt over the rail.

I caught it, and when I unfolded it, I realized what it was.

My heart leaped into my throat, and my cheeks hurt from how huge I was smiling.

It was his jersey.

He lifted a hand to where his mouth was behind the

helmet and blew me a kiss, linking, *I love you.*

I love you too. I slid the shirt over my head and smelled his scent, mixed with his sweat, all over it. In other words, it was perfect.

He trotted away, and I could feel the daggers Mom and Dad were shooting at me with their eyes. But I kept my head forward, refusing to acknowledge them. I didn't want to ruin this moment.

———

THE ORIGINAL PLAN had been for us to leave campus and eat at a restaurant, but with the horrible traffic, we decided to go to the student center, especially since Mom and Dad needed to leave for home soon.

Even though I loved seeing them, the visit had been tense and exhausting, and with an unknown enemy lurking around, I wanted them gone as quickly as possible.

Lucy pretended to peel off from us after the game, which EEU had won, thanks to Raffe, Adam, and Keith dominating the game, lurking behind us until the three of us headed into the center.

"Should you text Raffe so he doesn't go back to the apartment looking for us?" Mom asked carefully.

I removed my phone from my back pocket, wanting to smack myself. I hadn't even been a wolf shifter for three days, and I'd already forgotten that, around humans, we had to keep up appearances. Even though Raffe had learned about the change of plans the moment it happened, I sent him a text, obliging my parents.

We headed to the cafeteria, which wasn't as packed as I'd feared, and the three of us went through the line. I hated not waiting for Raffe, but I also knew that neither of us could eat like we wanted to in front of my parents without seeming more odd.

I snagged a piece of pizza and a bottled water. Mom chose a salad while Dad got a burger, and we settled at a back table.

Mom and Dad glanced at each other, and when I took a bite of my double-meat pizza, Mom exhaled loudly.

"Sky, we're so glad you seem to be happy here." She picked up her fork and stabbed some lettuce. "This is a great opportunity, and you seem settled, but to be frank, we're worried."

Okay, so this was happening and probably the real reason they'd wanted to eat here—to get me alone before Raffe joined us. "Why? I have friends for the first time *ever*, my grades are solid, and I have Raffe."

"He's the main reason we're worried." Dad interlaced his fingers. "We never heard of him until a week ago, and suddenly, he's in your *bedroom* when we show up in the morning. His own mother says you two are *engaged*, and he brings you a jersey, pretty much claiming you in front of everyone. Whatever this is, it's not healthy, especially with him being a Wright."

My head snapped back. "A *Wright*? You mean the son of the man whose feet you almost fainted at before you realized the connection?"

Dad huffed. "I admire his business tactics. He's cunning and ruthless, which is why I don't want my *daughter* anywhere near that family. You've never had a boyfriend before, and I don't want them to eat you up and spit you out."

Babe, are you okay? Raffe linked, his concern wafting through. *I'm on my way.*

I'm fine. Don't worry. I didn't want him to think I was under attack, though I was. Verbally. It wasn't the kind of danger he needed to worry about.

A chill ran down my spine. *Cunning and ruthless.* Two words that could describe the person who'd been attacking me without leaving a clear link back to him. But I wasn't here to defend King Jovian. I needed to defend Raffe, my mate and the love of my life. "Raffe isn't his father."

"How can you know that, honey?" Mom reached across the table. "You barely know him."

My blood jolted as my emotions became less controlled. "I know him better than you think."

"You losing your virginity to him doesn't mean you know him." Dad hit the table. "This is what I'm talking about. We think you should come home."

I laughed maniacally. "Are you serious? You two pushed me to come here! Remember? I told you it was weird to be accepted when I'd never applied, and you practically packed up my stuff and pushed me out the door. Any way to get your freaky-ass daughter away and get some distance." I'd never told them how I felt before, but they'd never spoken to me this way either. These were whole new relationship waters we were treading.

Mom's jaw dropped. "We've *never* called you freaky. And we assumed you applied and didn't want to tell us. Those accusations right there are not fair."

"Neither is you coming here and judging me. I did come here, and I finally fit in. And yes, Raffe is part of the equation, but he's not *all* of it." I pushed my plate aside, no longer hungry. I didn't like where this conversation was going. "I'm not leaving."

"Now listen here—" Dad leaned over the table.

Mom touched his shoulder, holding him back. "What your father means"—she glared at him—"is that your first love feels like it will last forever, but that's not normally how it goes."

Everything I wanted to say would only elevate the tension between us, so I bit my tongue, trying like hell to keep my mouth shut.

Silence descended for minutes, the three of us not eating and unsure of what to say.

I had to remember that I'd never been like them; I wasn't even human anymore. If I'd been human and didn't have this supernatural connection with Raffe, they would have had a right to be concerned. But I couldn't think of anything I could say to make them understand that there was no way in hell Raffe and I wouldn't be together. Not now. Not ever.

Finally, Mom broke and said, "Honey, we never thought you were a *freak*. I know kids called you that, and I won't lie and say things didn't happen around you that neither Robert nor I understood, but we never meant to make you feel alienated, and I'm sorry if we did."

Some of my anger ebbed. She'd never been honest like this before and had always avoided addressing the issues with my blood. "I didn't understand it either, and I could see your fear. I felt all alone, and now ... I don't."

"I'm glad, but Raffe—he had an entirely different childhood than you." Mom bit her bottom lip.

"She's right." Dad nodded. "He's had a life of privilege, getting what he wants and then tossing it aside. People like the Wrights ... they like something shiny and new. Just like he made a show of giving you his jersey. They like to claim things, but when the newness dulls, they like to—"

Hot anger that wasn't my own scorched through me, and that was when I felt the tingle at the base of my neck. I glanced up just as Raffe reached our table, his face a harsh scowl.

He'd heard everything.

CHAPTER TWENTY-SIX

A nger swirled off Raffe, and I placed my hands on the table.

Dad straightened and forced a smile, unaware that Raffe had heard everything despite the noise in the room.

Damn supernatural hearing.

I didn't want to hide things from him anymore, but that didn't mean I wanted to share something that would openly hurt and offend him.

"Raffe." Mom placed a hand on her chest and laughed way too loudly. "You arrived faster than I expected."

Raffe didn't bother waiting for me to slide over. He sat next to me and threw his arm around my shoulders. Our connection sprang to life, and his freshly clean scent, along with his presence after hours of separation, made me light-headed. As my body pressed against him, I noticed he was damp and smelled more strongly of soap than usual, like he'd rushed from the shower to get here.

Of course he had. He'd felt that I was upset.

With the way my parents were acting, I should have pulled away so they wouldn't give me more grief, but I couldn't. Not that he would've let me; I could feel his wolf radiating from him.

"That's what happens when I'm completely in love with her," he replied, cupping my face with a hand. "I can't help but rush to be next to her."

My heart turned to mush, and the warmth of our love flowed between us, causing me to heat up in a very inappropriate way with my parents sitting right across from us.

Dad cleared his throat rather loudly. "How *nice*. Maybe you should grab something to eat and join us."

I flinched. That was Dad's not-so-subtle way of trying to get Raffe to leave so they could finish saying what they wanted to say to me.

What Dad might not have expected was that Raffe wouldn't miss a beat.

Turning his attention to my parents, Raffe's indifferent expression slid into place. "I will soon, but after playing ball for several hours, I want to sit down for a bit."

Dad scowled, but Mom interjected, "Of course! We were just having a conversation with Sky we hoped to finish is all."

"Alone," Dad added.

Jaw twitching, Raffe linked, *Babe. What do you want me to do here? I heard everything, but I don't want to cause more problems between you and your parents, so if you want me to keep my mouth shut, I'll do it. For you.*

I sighed and despised that he'd even question that I wouldn't stand up for our relationship. Once again, the bond that allowed us to share our emotions caused the other person to feel insecure. Only one thing could make this situation right. Even though I loved my parents, Raffe and I were different halves of the same soul.

"Shouldn't Raffe be part of this discussion?" I straightened my shoulders, though my stomach churned. I'd never talked back to them like this before, and I hated that the first time had to be when the stakes were actually high. This wasn't fourteen-year-old me wanting to argue over clothes or dying my hair. "After all, it's about our relationship and how you want me to leave here and return ..." I trailed off, unsure how to finish that statement. *Home* wasn't the right word anymore, though it was where I'd grown up. Home had always been subjective, but not anymore. Now, home was wherever Raffe and I were together.

His relief poured through me, validating that I'd made the right decision. He wanted us to be in this together. There was no going back with us ... not anymore. We'd sealed the bond and our love for each other.

"Skylar," Mom gasped. "I can't believe you'd do this. We're only concerned about your well-being."

"Which you think I threaten?" Raffe tilted his head, his irises darkening.

This was the man I'd met on the night I arrived, his facade of brooding seriousness in place. Now, knowing him in a way no one else could, I saw the self-control from his kind heart peeking through, as well as his regret that we had to face this. He could be vicious, but he was holding back *for me*.

Dad snatched a napkin and rolled it in his hands. "If this is how Skylar wants to handle it, so be it." Dad tried to stick out his chest, but compared to Raffe, he failed miserably. "Yes, I do think you threaten it. You're rich and have your life set for you, including scouts wanting to recruit you for the NFL. I don't want my daughter getting hurt more than she will be when you graduate and just remember her as one of your conquests. Sky is inexperienced and naive, and you're—"

"Mr. Greene, as much as I want to respect you as Sky's father, you need to stop." Raffe's arm tightened around me as if he thought my dad would try to yank me away. "Skylar means *everything* to me, and it's not because she's shiny and new. It's because of the person she is inside, and for you to think so little of her that you believe she would fall for someone who is callous and manipulative bothers me more than what you think of me."

Face turning red, Dad threw his napkin on the table. "I've known Skylar her whole life, and you've been dating for a week or two, and you think you know her better than I do? I had to watch her come home *every day* when kids were mean to her, or something had happened that she couldn't explain, so forgive me if I want to shelter her from another threat—like *you*!"

"Something you might not be aware of is that Skylar has never fit in *anywhere*," Mom said, rubbing Dad's arm. "So yes, you're charming, *clearly*, and Skylar ..." She winced and looked at me. "Well, she'd fall for anyone who would give her attention."

The lump in my throat blocked me from swallowing, and I felt as if I'd been slapped. I understood that they were concerned, but their concern centered on how poorly they thought of me; they thought I was a weakling desperate to fit in and who would do anything so someone would want me.

Raffe dropped his arm from my shoulders, took my hand instead, and leaned over the table. "Let me be *very* clear. I've been interested in your daughter since the day she arrived. But I acted stupidly and foolishly then, and I would have deserved everything you said about me, but know that when I treated her like that, she didn't try to get my attention or make me like her. She tried to avoid me. But I couldn't let her."

"Son, you're not making this—" Dad started.

"I'm not done," Raffe bit out, his eyes taking on a faint glow. "I let you have your say, and I'm being honest and not putting on a front to make you like me. Your daughter is remarkable and stands apart from everyone, and it's a damn shame that no one acknowledged that before she arrived here. I want you to understand my intentions. Skylar is the love of my life, and I will *never* let her go."

Mom inhaled sharply. "You two are young. You'll be going off to the NFL or working for your father's company, and Sky will be going to vet school. Maybe at this moment, you think that, but there's a whole world out there that you haven't experienced yet."

In a way, she had a point. I hadn't considered what would happen when Raffe went on to play professional ball or work for his dad while I remained in school. But none of that mattered. We'd figure it out.

"Not to mention you're showing signs of obsessive behavior." Dad grimaced. "In fact, I'm worried and think we need to bring Sky home with us to put some distance between you."

Raffe released a low growl, which clued me in that I'd been quiet for too long. I'd been sitting here, letting Raffe go up against my parents. "I'm twenty-two years old. I'm not going anywhere. Raffe isn't the only one who feels that way—I love him, and I *will* spend the rest of my life with him."

"So you're going to give up your future and follow him around while he sleeps with every woman he can behind your back?" Dad spat. "Because that's what guys like him do. My boss cheats on his wife all the time."

My chest heaved, and my wolf surged forward. "If he dared to even look at another woman, I'd kill them both. It won't happen."

"Skylar!" Mom's eyes widened, and she stared at me as if I had two heads. "What's gotten into you?"

"Oh, I know what has," Dad cut in. "Him! There's no doubt what they were doing this morning, and whatever brainwashing he's done on her since she got here is working."

"That's it." Raffe stood, taking my hand and pulling me out. "We're leaving. I won't let you talk to or about her this way. It's disrespectful, and I won't tolerate it. You say you're so concerned with her well-being, but you're making her feel as if you see her as a weak woman and a fool. It's gone on long enough."

"Listen, this isn't a healthy relationship. You're both so possessive of each other, and Skylar just threatened to kill you if you look at another girl." Mom blinked like she was trying to choose her words.

Raffe shrugged. "I'd deserve it, and it won't be a problem because I will never see anyone but her ever again."

We couldn't keep dragging this out. I didn't want to leave things like this, but they didn't understand. They couldn't. This wasn't an unhealthy human relationship, but that was all they could see. They didn't understand that we were fated and made to be with only one another forever. They couldn't understand our world.

Our world.

I'd always felt like an outsider, and after coming here, I finally understood why. I'd been neither fully human nor super-natural. Each species saw me as different from them. With Raffe, I finally fit in. But being with him had put a gap between me and my parents. I couldn't explain this to them without putting them at greater risk. It was safer for them if they left.

"We should go." I stepped into Raffe's side, needing the comfort of our connection buzzing between us. My heart ached at leaving things like this, but it was the right call. "I know all this seems crazy and intense, and I can't explain it, but I promise I love him, and your fears are truly unwarranted. Either way, just know that I love you even if it seems like I'm not listening." I forced a sad smile, not wanting them to think I wasn't the person they knew. Human Skylar was still there, just a little different.

I'm sorry, babe. Raffe's regret swirled inside my chest, making it constrict more tightly. *Had I known, I wouldn't have pushed you to tell them about me.*

No, this was inevitable. I forced myself to turn my back on them. *My life has gone in a different direction than theirs, and I wouldn't change it for the world. Otherwise, you wouldn't be beside me.*

"Robert, I hope you're happy with yourself," Mom muttered. "You had to push her. I told you not to bring this up until later. It's the first time we've seen her in months."

We were already halfway across the room, but I might as well have been sitting with them, given how clearly I could hear them.

"You want to say nothing and let her fall for him more?" Dad scoffed. "She needed to hear the truth. How else are we supposed to protect her?"

"Yeah, that's protecting her, all right. You just pushed them closer, and she's leaving with him, not us. I can't take this." Her hurried footsteps became louder behind us. "Sky, wait."

My feet slowed of their own accord, and I hoped like hell we could salvage the way we'd ended the conversation. Raffe stiffened but didn't urge me forward.

We turned toward her, and Mom's face creased with worry.

"Look, this got out of hand." Mom licked her lips. "The last thing I'd ever want is to cause a rift between us, so I'm sorry."

My lungs worked a little easier. She was as upset as I was. "Mom, I get that what Raffe and I share is intense, but I need

278

you to trust me. He takes good care of me and makes me happy."

"Okay." Mom pressed her lips together, but I could see the wariness in her eyes. "But this is your first relationship, so your dad and I have a right to be concerned. We'll try to be more open-minded."

I smiled, hope growing in my chest and making room for my heart to beat normally once more. "That's all I'm asking."

"And Mrs. Greene, I do love her." Raffe gazed at me adoringly. "Her happiness will always come before mine."

Mom pushed some hair out of her face. "Now I understand why your mom said *fiancée.*"

I giggled. Not only did I like the sound of *fiancée,* but I also liked watching Mom try so hard to accept Raffe and me even though she didn't like it.

"If you give me a real chance, I swear I won't disappoint you." Raffe held out a hand to her. "You're important to Skylar, and that means something to me."

Some of the lines on Mom's face eased as she arched a brow. "You really are sweet on her."

Raffe chuckled, his own relief uncurling more of the knot in the bottom of my stomach. "You have *no* idea." He covered one side of his mouth so I couldn't see and whispered loud enough for Mom and me to hear, "She completely owns me."

Dad remained at the booth, shooting daggers at us.

I pursed my lips. "And I hate that Dad isn't even willing to listen."

Mom rolled her eyes. "You know your father. He worries about you and overreacts. We were surprised to learn you were dating someone. Then to come here and find you ... the way you were, to see how serious the two of you are, and to learn who he's related to ... well, it was unsettling. Your father needs time, and I'll work on him."

That was the thing with Mom. If anyone could get Dad to change his mind, it was her.

"You two, go." Mom nodded in the direction we'd been heading. "I'll get Grumpy Butt and take him back home with me."

"Okay." I hugged her, tears burning my eyes. Now that things were patched up between us, I didn't want her to leave. But she needed to. "Thank you for coming."

"Sorry that the ending wasn't so great." She pulled back and kissed my cheek. "Next time, it'll go better." She cut her eyes to Raffe and said, "You better take care of our girl."

He laughed, a sound usually reserved for me. "More than happy to, though she can be a handful."

"Oh, I know." She patted his shoulder. "I raised her. Now, goodbye."

My steps felt lighter as Raffe and I headed out the door. That cocky smirk was back on his face, but I didn't want to ruin the moment by teasing him.

What are we going to do about getting something to eat? I linked, knowing he had to be hungry. He'd just played football for three hours.

He wrapped an arm around my waist as we headed toward the double doors at the back of the student center. *Let's order pizza. I want to get you into the apartment and away from any more drama.*

I could agree with that.

But as soon as we reached the doors, a familiar musky smell hit my nose, and Raffe stopped in his tracks.

King Jovian stood in a corner near the exit, leaning against the green wall. *Well, that was something to watch, along with at least twenty other supernaturals. I see her parents aren't thrilled about you two either.*

Show's over. We're leaving, Raffe linked, opening the door for me to walk out first.

As we went outside, King Jovian followed. *The three of us need to talk.*

No, we're good. Raffe moved faster.

It's not a question. It's a command. We need to talk about the two of you and the future, he insisted.

Just when I thought we'd dealt with all the drama of the day, more had to show up and prove me wrong. A conversation with his dad, though, was inevitable. *Raffe, he won't leave until he talks with us. We should listen. Keith and Adam are close by, right? Maybe he'll let something slip about the wolves that attacked me.*

Raffe paused, and his emotions grew turbulent. *Fine, but you stay beside me at all times.* He added Lucy, Adam, Keith, and Josie to the link. *Dad wants to talk to us, and I need you to come around to the woods by the student center. He'll want to go into the woods, but I'll make sure we stay close to the tree line.*

On our way, Adam replied.

We turned to King Jovian, who had a grin on his face.

That was where Raffe got it from.

"Your mother is in the bookstore, so let's go into the woods. She wants us to talk, but not in the open." He turned on his heels, expecting us to obey.

Not arguing, we followed him, and a quarter mile in, Raffe stopped and said, "We're far enough."

King Jovian grimaced, and his nostrils flared. "This is our problem now that *she's* here. You're trying to tell me how to run things when I'm still the alpha. That's not how this works, and you know better. If this keeps up, there will be more consequences."

A shiver ran down my spine as hot rage blasted from Raffe. He linked, *Like trying to kill her again?*

CHAPTER TWENTY-SEVEN

K ing Jovian took a step back, and the anger melted from his face. *What?*

"You heard me, but I can say it out loud if that will help you understand." Raffe's neck corded. "Last Saturday, when the football team played an hour away, at least one coven member created a barrier, tricked Lucy and Skylar into thinking someone needed help, and cut Skylar off from the rest of us. Then, three Eastern wolves attacked her—wolves that Aldric picked up earlier that day."

My blood jolted in tune with how my pulse quickened. *Raffe, I thought we wouldn't accuse him of anything until we had proof.* Even though I hadn't expected this conversation to go well, I hadn't been prepared to confront him.

He was threatening us, and I won't stand here and fucking take it, Raffe replied, edging forward so he stood between King Jovian and me.

I had no clue about any attack. King Jovian shook his head. *The wolves Aldric picked up were the Atlanta alpha and four members of his pack. They came to discuss your betrothal to his daughter. I had to tell him it wasn't an option after all and let's just say it didn't end well. I'll handle them.* His eyes hardened and focused on me. *We need to discuss a more pressing matter. How is it that Skylar smells like a wolf and has made it seem like you two have a completely formed bond? She shouldn't be able to pack-link, yet she is. The rumor of my son mating with a human has already begun circulating due to your brazenness, and having anyone learn that a human can link with us and form a completed bond is dangerous. What sort of magic are you using? Are you trying to ruin our family name?*

My mouth went dry, and my blood pumped, edging into a fizz. He truly thought the worst of me, and I had no clue what I'd done to warrant it. Raffe's hands fisted, but I didn't want him interjecting on my behalf, so I snapped, "I'm not *ruining* anything." I didn't bother to pack-link. I wanted him to hear my tone.

He chuckled darkly. "All the evidence says otherwise. You're human, and it was bad enough that Raffe claimed you —now you're trying to fool us into thinking you're a wolf. That's impossible. No one will believe it."

"You better back off," Raffe growled and pointed at him. "She's my mate, and no one talks to her like that, especially someone who tried to have her murdered."

"I never gave any such order." The king's eyes glowed, his wolf edging forward. "And what you two are doing is risky, not only to shifters but to all supernaturals."

Raffe crossed his arms and sneered. "You don't *give* the orders. I know how it works. Plausible deniability."

I understood Raffe wanted to push the topic, but unless we addressed his father's accusation, he'd keep pivoting back to me. Only one thing could end this argument once and for all.

I marched toward a gigantic fir surrounded by thick bushes.

Dammit, Sky. What are you doing? I told you to stay beside me! Raffe's anger swirled through my chest, but I could also feel his hesitation.

Addressing your father's accusation. I reached the tree and stepped behind it.

"What's wrong, son?" King Jovian asked smugly. *Your mate suddenly doesn't want to face the consequences of using magic like that?*

She's not running anywhere, Raffe replied equally smugly.

I removed my clothes, the chill in the air returning now that the sun was about to set. It'd been warmer than normal, thanks to the partially sunny day, but with the wolf-shifter magic running through me, I didn't get as cold as I used to.

Once I was naked, I stood, ready to shift.

Nothing happened.

A knot formed in my stomach. Why wasn't I shifting?

"Raffe, what are you two up to?" King Jovian asked, sounding tired.

What's wrong? Raffe asked.

Clearly, I'd jumped the gun. *Uh, it's not happening.* My heart clenched. What if something was wrong with me? Maybe King Jovian was right.

The breeze kicked up, reminding me that I was naked near campus. Keith and Adam would be close by at any second, and Raffe would kill them if they stumbled upon me.

"She's shifting to show you she can." Raffe's voice sounded clipped. *Tug on where you feel your wolf's magic and let her know you want her to shift. She'll understand you.*

King Jovian snorted. "I can't wait to see how she pulls this off."

I felt the same way. The whole point was to prove him

284 JEN L. GREY

wrong, but I feared I'd been misguided. *I didn't have to ask or tug her the first time I shifted.* I knew I should've practiced shifting before now, but between the attack, Raffe's football schedule, and the makeup work from the classes I'd missed, we hadn't been able to get away.

Because you were under attack. She took over. This time, she doesn't feel imminent danger.

I wasn't so sure about that, but I kept my smart mouth shut. I closed my eyes, feeling foolish but needing to focus. I searched for the spot in my chest where the magic flared whenever my wolf became excited about something. That was when I noticed a ball of warmth next to the spot where Raffe's emotions stayed.

Unsure what he'd meant by *tug it*, I imagined yanking at the warmth in my chest. Thankfully, my wolf responded, and the magic became thicker as if she'd been asleep. Unsure what to say, I stated the obvious. *I'd like to shift ... please.*

Just like that, she responded. Magic soared through my body and brushed my mind. My skin tingled, and I glanced at my arms to see black fur sprouting. *Okay, it's happening.*

Keith popped into our link. *The cavalry has arrived. We're coming up on you now.*

Stay fucking back for a second, Raffe replied. *Sky's shifting, and you better not see her naked.*

My back broke just like last time, and King Jovian asked, "How long is this going to take?"

"Give her a second," Raffe bit. "She's only shifted once before, and it was during the attack."

As my body contorted into animal form, I gritted my teeth. The shift still didn't feel natural or comfortable. After what was only seconds but felt like minutes, I connected, *I'm in animal form. All is well.* Even though King Jovian was out there in less-than-ideal circumstances, being in full wolf form felt nice.

"You can see for yourself." Raffe sounded assured.

"Oh, I can't wait. I heard your friends approaching just before this happened. You do realize I'll know it's not her when whoever it is comes out."

When I trotted from behind the tree, King Jovian's smug grin fell. He walked toward me, but Raffe grabbed his arm, stopping him.

"Stay right here. I don't trust you near her," Raffe snarled.

King Jovian scowled. "This can't be real. I need to get closer to her. This has to be an illusion."

Not wanting to give him a reason to say we'd manipulated him, I trotted to him, my blood fizzing. The power within it wasn't funneling into the ground yet, so I hoped like hell that meant I wasn't calling the forest animals to me. If King Jovian had a hard time grasping that I'd shifted, I didn't need him freaking out even more over a horde of animals rushing to me.

The closer I stepped toward him, the wider King Jovian's eyes became.

When I was ten feet away, Raffe linked, *Don't come any closer. I don't trust him.* He hadn't taken his gaze off his father.

Humans can't be turned. King Jovian sniffed, trying like hell to find proof that I wasn't real. *Something is very wrong with her.*

Pain sucker punched me. Once again, I stood before someone who thought I was abnormal and didn't fit in. Even as a true supernatural, people wouldn't accept me as one of their own.

Nothing is wrong with her. Raffe bared his teeth. *She's a wolf shifter, so you have no reason to have her killed.*

286 JEN L. GREY

King Jovian winced. *Son, this isn't natural. Nothing about her is natural.*

The rejection I'd felt all my life swirled throughout me, and my blood hummed. *Raffe, my power.* It churned inside me like when I'd called the animals. *I need you.* I froze as fear weighed down my legs.

Something like awe spiraled into me as Raffe stepped to my side. He linked, *I can feel it coming off you through our bond and sense how it unsettles you.*

He threaded his fingers through the fur on the back of my neck, our bond buzzing and easing the hum. My lungs expanded more easily.

"Your mother wanted me to come here and make things better between the three of us, but do you know the impact she could have?" King Jovian lifted his hands. "Son, you've got to put your people first—"

"If you and the pack won't accept my mate, then I don't need any of you." Raffe's face twisted in disgust. "*She's* the best person I've ever met with the kindest heart, despite people like *us* treating her like shit and fearing her. But not me. Not anymore. She's my fated mate, my claimed mate, and the woman I'll die protecting from you or whoever you send our way."

King Jovian rubbed a hand over his face, and he pried his focus away from me to his son. "Raffe, you're my only heir. I need you to see things for what they are. Your mother and I were chosen mates, and we're happy."

I snarled, my wolf surging forward. I wanted to rip out his father's throat at the mere mention of Raffe with someone else.

"And that confirms everything." Raffe sneered and linked to me, Keith, Adam, Josie, and Lucy, *Sky, Shift back to human form while I handle my father. I don't want to risk us getting*

*separated. I want to get out of the woods in case a witch is on
standby to harm you. The rest of you, keep a lookout for
anything strange. If Sky gets hurt, you'll all have hell to pay.*

I hated to leave his side, but there was no point in talking
with his father. He wouldn't accept me, just like my dad probably would never fully accept Raffe. I trotted back behind the
tree.

"You did hint for Aldric to place a hit on her, didn't you?"
Raffe pushed.

After a moment of silence, his dad sighed. "I ... I don't
know if he misunderstood me. Either way, Skylar may be the
best person in the world, but she's not fit to be queen. She
wasn't raised our way, and—"

"We've *claimed* each other, and even if we hadn't, it
wouldn't change a damn thing." Raffe's determination and
resentment strengthened.

The sensations radiating from him were just as strong as
his wolf power, stealing my breath. My blood activated again,
but I pushed away my concern, needing to get back into
human form. Using what Raffe had suggested earlier, I tugged
at my mind and asked my wolf to retreat. Just like before, she
listened. The transition eased my blood, and my body shifted
back into human form.

"If you want me to remain your heir and part of the pack,
it will be with Skylar at my side. There's no room for negotia-
tion. This isn't a business decision or a strategy on my end. It's
simple. She's my entire fucking world, whether you like it or
not. When I said I'd leave the pack, I meant it, and if one hair
on her head or strand of fur on her wolf gets injured due to
your influence, accidental or not, I won't be your son anymore.
I'll be your enemy."

Butterflies took flight within me, and I hurried back into
my clothes and shoes. The magnitude of his love astounded

me, but I also didn't want him to give up his future over me. My blood returned to a hum, and I needed Raffe's calming touch.

"Is this how you want things to be between us?" his dad whispered.

When I rejoined them, King Jovian's shoulders were hunched, and he didn't look like the commanding man I'd come to know.

Raffe didn't pause, coming to my side and taking my hand in his. His jaw worked as he linked, *No, it's not. But you're not willing to listen to your own son.* With that, Raffe and I turned and headed toward the apartments where we'd be visible to humans.

I'm sorry, I linked, letting my remorse flow toward him. *I wish our relationship wasn't the cause of the rift between you and your dad.*

He smiled sadly. *Like I am with your parents.*

True.

Still, that didn't mean either one of us had to like it. I stepped closer to him, letting our sides touch, and replied, *But you have to give up your future.*

No, I don't. You're *my future and the only one I care about.* Raffe kissed the back of my hand. *Sure, I'd love to lead the shifters, but there's no way in hell I'd do it without you by my side. I'd rather be poor and work hard every day for the rest of my life, as long as we're together.*

Even though it should have been impossible after our day, I laughed. *Spoken like a rich kid who's never had to struggle.*

We're spreading out and staying in the woods to keep an eye on things, Adam replied. *If we see anything strange, we'll let you know.*

Uncle Jovian is heading back toward the student center, Lucy added. *I'm surprised he didn't try to alpha-will you.*

Oh, he did back in Seattle. I was able to fight it. Raffe grimaced. *He knew better than to try again, especially with Sky's and my completed bond.*

We stepped out of the woods, the lights of campus on for the night.

I hoped that being a shifter would make things better. That was why I'd wanted to show him after all.

Me too, but I'm not shocked. Raffe released me and wrapped an arm around my waist. He said, "Dad's old school, and he doesn't like women who are stronger than him. And that's exactly what you are."

I rolled my eyes. "More like I'm someone who might implode and take the world out with her."

"As long as I go with you." He scrunched up his nose and smiled. "That's all that matters to me."

"Stop." I stuck out my tongue. "This world needs you in it." The apartments were fifty feet away, and my footsteps quickened. We needed to get inside before something else happened. We'd dealt with enough drama.

No, Josie linked, sounding scared. *Guys, I need you here now.* Her tone turned frantic. *I'm farther back, but I can hear Dave, and he's in pain. I can smell his blood.*

Dave.

The vampire who'd drugged me. He could give us answers.

Releasing me, Raffe gestured toward the apartments. "Go. I'll be there in a minute."

"Like hell I will!" I didn't pause; I just ran toward the woods.

Dammit, Sky, Raffe linked, his frustration slamming into me. *This is what happened last time when you got separated and hurt!*

I'm a strong woman, remember? I tossed his words back at him.

We kept pace with each other, and he groaned. *Stay close to me, and let me stay in front, so if we meet a barrier, you won't run through it.*

That's no problem. I didn't want to get into a situation like that again either.

A broken howl rang through the woods.

Josie.

I pushed myself harder, keeping pace behind Raffe.

He faltered, and my gaze shot in the direction he was facing.

My heart lodged in my throat.

Dave lay on the ground, his face paler than ever, while a woman I'd never seen before was stabbing a dagger into his chest.

No! We needed answers only Dave would know. *Raffe, please tell me we aren't too late.*

CHAPTER TWENTY-EIGHT

My blood and emotions heightened straight into a hum as blood trickled from the corner of Dave's mouth.

A sign of impending death.

A death that would rob me of answers about why he'd drugged me and who had asked him to do it.

Stay here, Raffe snarled as he pulled ahead, racing toward the blonde-haired woman leaning over Dave's body, holding the hilt of the dagger lodged into his chest. Raffe's fear and uncertainty swirled through our bond, adding to mine, and I struggled to take a deep breath.

The power ravaging my blood poured from my feet and into the ground, causing it to quake as Josie howled mournfully.

The woman jerked her head toward me, her dark-brown eyes widening. "It's not what it looks like."

"Get away from him!" Raffe growled. His six-foot-five frame towered over the shorter woman, and the muscles in his back were so tense I could see the outlines through his polo shirt.

She lifted her hands, the dagger remaining in Dave's chest. She'd made it stick.

Acid burned my throat. We couldn't lose him ... not when he could provide us with answers. *We need to keep him alive long enough to talk.*

The ground shook harder, moving toward Raffe, and a lump lodged in my throat.

If I let my power increase, the ground might crack, and Raffe could get hurt.

As if something inside me understood, my power eased, though my emotions were getting more volatile.

Strange. That had never happened before, but it had to be due to our mate bond.

"Listen, if you don't get the dagger out of his heart, there's no chance he'll recover." The woman's hands were coated in blood ... Dave's blood. "Not that he'll survive necessarily, but getting it out will allow his supernatural side to attempt to heal him." Her attention homed back in on me.

Raffe laughed jadedly. "Like we'll believe you have good intentions. If you keep looking at her, I'll kill you without a second thought."

She averted her gaze and wrapped her arms around her body. "I'm not a threat."

"I'll be the judge of that." Raffe's anger boiled hot between us.

We're here, Adam linked as two dark-brown wolves rushed from between two firs behind the woman.

From their musky scents, I knew they were male: Adam and Keith. But their eyes were the easiest way to tell them apart; the one farthest from me had milk-brown irises, which meant that it was Keith, and Adam's honey-brown eyes were on the woman.

Keep an eye on her, Raffe commanded as he pushed the woman back several feet, and the two wolves circled her.

With the threat handled and my blood under control, I ran the remaining distance to Dave and dropped to my knees beside him.

Dave's hazel eyes fluttered open, and his gaze landed on me as his teeth extended. A low hiss came as he tried to sit up, desperate to taste me.

My damn blood. I'd thought that since I'd become a wolf shifter, vampires wouldn't find my blood as alluring because it could kill them, but this proved me wrong.

"Dammit, Sky," Raffe groaned as he appeared across from me and shoved the vampire's shoulders against the ground. His frustration slammed into me as he asked, "Do you want him to bite you before he dies?" His crystal eyes narrowed into slits as he glared at me. Did he think his stern look would force me to walk away from this?

That wasn't happening.

Deciding no answer was best, I focused on Dave. His eyes were closing as the blood from the corner of his mouth thickened. He was fading fast.

I scanned him, confirming what the woman had said. She was right—as long as the dagger remained lodged in his heart, he would die, and removing it was the best way to give him a chance to survive.

A threatening growl came from behind me, and I glanced over my shoulder to find Adam standing between us and the woman.

We've got to try to save him. We need answers. I swallowed and grasped the hilt of the dagger, ignoring the way the cool, sticky blood slid between my fingers. I gritted my teeth and tugged just as Dave's eyes opened. He reached for me, causing the blade to dig deeper into him.

294 JEN L. GREY

"Shit," I groaned. I wanted to remove the dagger to help him heal, not make the injury worse. Sometimes, I felt like I was cursed. "Can you hold him still?"

Raffe looked at me and arched a brow. He linked, *What do you think I'm fucking trying to do here? He's a vampire and stronger than his scrawny ass looks. But let me tell you, if he dies, I won't be upset. I just hope we get answers before he croaks.*

Hurried footsteps came from beside us, and I tensed. A human sob that sounded familiar reached my ears.

Dark fur flashed past me as Keith hurried in that direction, but when a naked Josie ran out from between the trees, he stopped in his tracks.

Even though jealousy was the last thing I needed to experience at this moment, my wolf howled and demanded to break free. I tried like hell to fight the tug because shifting wouldn't help anything.

What the hell are you doing? Raffe asked and jerked his head back toward Dave's face so fast that my wolf eased.

I didn't understand what was going on, but one thing was clear: I needed to get the damn dagger out of Dave's chest and maybe stab Josie with it. Wait ... I hadn't meant to think the last part.

I need to help him. Josie's long, dark, wavy hair flew behind her as she dropped down at Dave's head and leaned over his face. Her hair covered some of her nakedness, and her bronze skin contrasted with Dave's, revealing just how pasty he was.

Blowing out a breath, I gripped the dagger. Dave tried to bite me again. I stood and placed a foot on each side of his body, then leaned down. I gripped the hilt again, and when Dave tried to rise, Josie smothered his face with kisses.

"I'm here," she whimpered. "You're going to be okay. We just need you to calm down."

"Josie, get back!" Raffe exclaimed. "He's going to bite you."

Instead of fighting harder, Dave relaxed.

"She must be covering my scent." I exhaled shakily and yanked hard on the dagger. The sickening sucking sound of the blade leaving his bone and flesh made bile roil in my stomach.

Finally, I lifted the dagger over my head, and blood from the edge splattered on me, including my face.

I was going to be sick.

With all the dissections I'd done in my science classes to prepare for vet school, I'd believed I was past being squeamish, but clearly, that wasn't the case.

Blood gushed from Dave's chest, and I didn't have time to worry about being nauseated.

With my hands soaked in his blood, I squatted and placed pressure on his wound. "I need clothes or something to pack this and slow the bleeding. My hands will work, but they'll get too slippery."

"What do you want me to do?" Raffe's chest heaved. "I'm holding him down."

"Fine." My shirt was ruined anyway. Ignoring that my hands were coated with blood, I removed it.

What the fuck? Raffe linked. *Adam and Keith can see you.*

I'm trying to get answers about who's trying to kill us, I replied, bundling my shirt into a ball and using it to put pressure on Dave's wound.

The cold October Portland air whipped around me, raising goose bumps across my skin. I wasn't nearly as cold as I would've been if I'd been human. "Is there anything vampires can do to heal?"

"Feed, but that isn't an option," Raffe gritted out. "Our shifter blood will kill him."

I could only think of one thing we could do: get answers from him before he died. I hated to be that callous, but we hadn't put him in this situation.

Turning my attention to Dave, my breath caught. He and Josie were staring at one another while tears streamed down her face and onto Dave's cheeks. She bent and placed her forehead on his as her body shook with silent sobs.

I hadn't realized they were close.

"Dave?" I bit my lip, unsure what to expect.

When his glassy eyes turned to me, my head jerked back. He was so close to death.

"Why did you attack me?" I tried to keep my emotions level, but some hurt broke through. "I thought we were friends."

"We ... are." He paused and swallowed. "Had ... to."

Raffe's hands tightened on Dave's shoulders, and his jaw twitched. I could feel the unbridled anger swirling off my mate, but he kept his mouth shut.

"Why?" I couldn't imagine doing something like that to one of my friends. Maybe I would if Raffe asked—he was my fated mate, and I'd do anything to protect him—but Dave was single and didn't have that kind of connection with anyone. "Why in the world did you believe you had to do that?"

"I ..." He shook his head and gurgled. "Can't ..." He wheezed, and his chest rattled.

"Stop making him talk." Josie straightened and cupped his face. "Leave him alone. He needs to rest so he can get better. You can ask him all this stuff when he's healing."

My heart stopped and my jaw dropped. I wasn't sure what to say. I wasn't sure how she could assume he'd get better.

"Josie ..." Dave's eyelids closed slowly. "I lov—"

"No." Josie smacked his face. "Don't go to sleep."

What the hell is going on here? Keith linked from his spot behind me, where he was watching the strange woman. *They've never even talked to each other. Did she fall and hit her head?*

I ... I don't know, Adam replied, sounding as perplexed as Keith.

"Sorry ..." Dave sputtered, and his eyes closed.

"We need to take him somewhere." Josie smacked his cheeks again. "He's lost consciousness."

Dave's breathing turned more shallow, and Raffe released his shoulders.

I was at a loss. "Josie, he's not—"

"Don't." She jabbed a finger at me. "He's going to be fine." The whites of her eyes were red from crying, and she sniffled. "You're not a doctor, and you just became a supernatural, so don't even pretend you know anything about this world."

I tensed. She'd never been even slightly rude to me before, and it caught me off guard.

"Listen here," Raffe damn near bellowed, but he kept his eyes on anything but Josie.

Calm down. She's upset, I linked. There had to be more to her and Dave's relationship than anyone knew. They were acting as if they were lovers, but with how tight this group was, if they had been, someone would've known. It hadn't taken long for Keith to catch Raffe and me when we'd been dating secretly. *Give her a pass.*

Dave's heartbeat slowed and became sporadic.

"He needs blood and lots of it if you want him to survive," the woman said loudly from behind me.

I spun toward her and sniffed. How did she know this? She was human, yet she clearly knew about the supernatural.

298 JEN L. GREY

One plausible explanation came to mind—the secret society. Were they recruiting humans? Hell, maybe they had been the entire time. We knew nothing about them. Or maybe this woman was a witch and cloaking her scent. "Where do you suppose we find that?"

She moved toward us. "Me. I'm human. I can feed him."

Adam and Keith growled, the fur on the napes of their necks rising as they advanced toward her.

"Fuck no." Raffe shook his head, removed his shirt, then tossed it to me. "You were trying to kill him. You want to finish him off so he doesn't give us answers. We're not that stupid." He then linked, *Put that on before I have to kill Adam and Keith for looking at you ... even by accident.*

Don't forget Josie is naked, not five feet from you! A growl escaped, though I hadn't meant it to. *At least I'm wearing a bra and pants.*

I can't help it. Raffe glowered. *You took off your shirt.*

We were wasting time bickering like this. I put on Raffe's shirt to appease him and tried not to focus on his bare chest and muscles.

Maybe I can lure another human into the woods so we can use them to feed him. Keith edged a few steps back toward campus.

Who's going to erase their memory? Adam shook his body, ruffling his fur.

My emotions swirled inside me, and my blood rose to a fizz. I hated how each time I thought we were getting somewhere, we got more behind.

Dave's heartbeat slowed further.

"Forget that," Josie rasped.

I spun around to find her biting into her wrist and placing it over Dave's partially open mouth.

Raffe clenched his fists. "Josie, that won't help. It's going to kill him faster."

She didn't budge, keeping her wrist over his mouth. "At least I'm trying *something*."

I wasn't sure if that was the best, and Raffe hung his head. *Should we stop her?*

Raffe wrapped his arms around me and pulled me to his chest. *No, it's done. We need to focus on the human. Maybe she can give us some answers.*

I nodded, turning so my back was against his chest.

"What are you doing out here? How did you get Dave here?" Raffe asked, turning toward the woman.

A deep groan came from behind us, and my blood ran cold.

CHAPTER TWENTY-NINE

I spun around and grew light-headed as I listened to Dave make sucking noises as he drank from Josie's wrist. Even though he remained pale and motionless, his Adam's apple bobbed with each tug.

I blinked, trying to make sense of the situation. His heartbeat strengthened, reinforcing that the groan and sucking noises were coming from him.

Isn't wolf blood supposed to kill vampires? I asked. Maybe I'd gotten my facts wrong. I'd become privy to so much, and maybe I'd jumbled things together, though I was certain I wasn't wrong.

Raffe's eyes widened, and shock swirled off him.

As Dave drank greedily from her wrist, Josie smiled though tears still streamed down her cheeks.

Uh ... it's supposed to, Keith replied. *But hell, humans aren't supposed to be able to shift into wolves, so who fucking knows anymore?*

That was the first statement he'd made that I could fully agree with, which was saying something. My relationship with Keith was still rocky at best, though he was trying to make things better, thanks to Raffe and his threats.

"What are you doing?" Raffe shook his head. "You know we aren't supposed to let vampires feed from us. What will you do when he dies more tragically?" His shock changed to fear.

Between that and him looking in Josie's direction, my blood jolted, and my wolf yanked forward to take control. I clung to my human side, reminding myself that Josie was a friend to all of us and was pack.

"I had to do something," Josie replied, watching Dave. With her free hand, she ran her fingers through his dark-auburn hair. "At least, if he dies, I'll know I tried."

Nostrils flaring, Raffe spun back around and marched toward the human. "What did you do to him?"

As soon as his attention was off Josie, my blood calmed, and my wolf settled.

"I ... I didn't do a *damn* thing," the woman replied forcefully.

I turned halfway so I could keep an eye on Dave and the strange human woman before us.

"You must have done *something*." He gestured with his thumb over his shoulder as Keith and Adam inched closer to her, baring their teeth. "He's near death and can feed from a wolf, so what did you and the witches from the society do to make that possible?"

My limbs grew heavy. He was right—maybe the witches had done something to Dave, but that dagger was in his chest. I glanced at his blood on my hands. I had no doubt he'd been near death, but *why?*

"I don't know what happened. I came here because I was informed that Skylar's life would be threatened in the woods tonight." The woman ran her hands through her hair.

"Nothing happened, and when I headed toward the campus to see if I had the location wrong, I came across *him*." She pointed at Dave. "He was bad off, and I was trying to remove the dagger from his heart before dragging him to the campus."

Raffe's ice-blue eyes glowed as his wolf surged forward, and he cracked his knuckles. "How do you know my *mate's* name?"

"Mate?" The woman arched a brow, glancing at me. "You're the one she's fated to?"

How does a human know about all this? Adam was tense and ready to strike. *Even someone in the secret society would be stupid to expose us like that.*

My blood jolted, and an eerie sensation had my skin crawling. Combined with Raffe's suspicion, I wanted to climb out of my skin. "Who are you working for?" I asked, my voice sounding higher than I wanted. It wasn't that I feared *her* but more about everything we didn't know. How could we defeat a secret organization when we had no clue who was part of it and while Raffe was at odds with his dad?

"I'm not working for anyone." The woman sighed and glanced skyward. "I came here out of concern."

"Concern?" I crossed my arms, examining her from head to toe. She was middle-aged, probably midforties. Something about her looked familiar, though I was certain I'd never seen her before in my life. "I don't even know you."

"Look, can we go somewhere to talk?" The woman spread out her arms. "If someone wanted that vampire to die, they might come back to finish the job. None of us should be here for that."

Raffe laughed loudly, startling me.

"You think I'm taking you back to our place so you can see where we live?" Raffe shook his head, his mouth twisting. "I'm

304 JEN L. GREY

not taking you anywhere that could expose my mate to a greater risk than she's already in."

"I would *never* hurt her." The woman placed a hand on her chest and faced me. "I realize you don't know me, but I'm one of the few who has your best interests at heart. That's why I had to come here to help you."

She had to be mentally unstable, or maybe she was a witch cloaking her powers. Something about this situation didn't feel right. "We know nothing about you, including your name. Do you expect us to just trust you? You haven't given us *any* reason to, so forgive me if I completely agree with my mate."

"My name is Octavia." She licked her lips, her brown irises warming to a cognac shade similar to mine. "And I know what you are."

"It's becoming more widely known, so that doesn't give you much credibility." Raffe wrinkled his nose. "The secret society knows all about Skylar, so if you're working with them, you would know too."

Octavia stomped her foot like a child. "How many times do I have to tell you I'm not a witch? You'd know if I were lying. You're all wolf shifters here."

"Not if you're cloaking the scent." I'd learned that witches had all sorts of tricks up their sleeves to deal with us.

Suddenly, Josie moaned and dropped to the ground. Even with her collapse, she kept her wrist at Dave's mouth. The vampire was now eagerly slurping and holding her wrist.

Something was wrong, and it wasn't Dave who was struggling. Was this a trap?

"What the hell have you done?" Raffe bellowed, stepping closer to Octavia. "Did you get him to inject her with something?"

He could handle that threat while I helped Josie. My wolf

inched forward as I rushed to her side. I noted that, though Dave was still pale, even by his standards, some color had returned to his face.

Josie's blood was helping him, and there was no telling how much he'd drunk. His heartbeat had strengthened, something I'd missed while talking to Octavia, and his breathing was steady though a little shallow.

"I've already answered this question. No matter how many times you ask, the answer will be the same." Octavia grimaced. "I didn't do a damn thing to him or her. He was like this when I found him."

Once I reached Dave and Josie, I removed her wrist from his mouth, and Josie linked, *No. It's helping him.*

At your expense. I squatted next to her, noting that her skin was glistening with sweat despite the cold, and her breathing was shallow. *How much has he drunk?* I ripped off the bottom of Raffe's polo shirt, wrapped it around Josie's wrist multiple times, then tied it tightly.

Not enough. He needs more. He can't die. I can't survive it, she whimpered and tried to jerk her hand out of mine, but it was barely more than a flinch.

She couldn't survive it? If I hadn't known better, I would've thought they were in love, but I'd *never* seen them so much as talk to each other. They'd mentioned each other in passing, and Josie had seemed sad and off since Dave's disappearance, but a relationship between them was impossible. They were different species.

My stomach roiled, and I pushed the thought aside. It couldn't be *that*. Things were complicated enough. I must be paranoid and thinking of the worst possible scenario.

What's wrong with her? Raffe linked.

Blood loss. I glanced around, realizing that Octavia was right. We couldn't stay out here with Dave like this and Josie damn near passed out. If we were attacked, we'd be screwed because they'd go after our weakest. If Dave had any chance of surviving this, he needed to remain with us. I trusted Raffe to get answers for us. *We've got to move. Josie needs to warm up, eat, and rest.*

Then that's what we do, Raffe replied solemnly and added Lucy to our connection. *Lucy, are you on your way back?*

That was an excellent idea. In all the chaos, I'd forgotten about Lucy.

Uh, yeah. About halfway there. I saw the others' clothes where we left them, and I snagged them, she replied. *I'm starving, so I'm hoping you guys already ordered pizza or something. I'd rather not head back to the student center with Uncle Jovian and Aunt Tashya around.*

I wished that was our main concern right then. *We need you to hurry. We're half a mile inside the woods from the apartments, near where the Eastern wolves attacked me. Josie passed out, and we can't carry her inside until she's dressed.*

What? She paused. *Okay, I'm on my way.*

Even though I couldn't feel her emotions like Raffe's, I could hear the shock and fear in her tone.

What are we going to do with her? Adam asked.

I didn't have to turn around to know he meant Octavia.

Kill her? Keith suggested.

I wasn't sure if he was kidding or being serious. With him, anything was possible.

I'd like to, but if she's with Dad or the secret society, she could have information we need. Raffe exhaled noisily. *I'd hate to kill her until we've learned everything we can.*

Okay, Keith had been serious, and Raffe was basically going along with the suggestion. I waited to feel horror, but it never came. Instead, my chest tightened. I was horrified that I wasn't horrified at the suggestion.

Had becoming a wolf shifter changed me so much in so little time?

I didn't even know who I was anymore, but if we killed people for the hell of it, we were no better than the people coming after us. At the end of the day, weren't we all the heroes in our own story? But we needed an ethical line. I refused to become like the people who'd bullied me my whole life and tried to force other people to conform.

My chest loosened, and I realized I hadn't changed completely because I still strongly agreed with that last statement.

But that meant we needed to determine what Octavia was. I didn't want to get Slade involved. He'd tell his mother, and she'd want control over the situation if Octavia was a witch.

I remembered something.

I could sense witch magic. If Octavia had a spell cloaking her, maybe I could tell.

I went to Raffe's side, and he took my hand. The buzz of our fated-mate bond sprang to life.

What are you doing? he asked, his icy-blue irises locking on me.

I'm going to see if I can feel coven magic from Octavia. I rolled my shoulders to loosen the tension throughout my body. *I've sensed it before.* Slade had told me I should be able to feel it within each person who had it. I just needed to figure out how. *Whether it's inside her or swirling around her from a cloaking.*

If anything feels off, stop immediately. Raffe arched a brow. *Promise me.*

I smiled and kissed his cheek. *Promise. Besides, you feel my emotions now. Remember?*

When the spot where his emotions resided in me

expanded and warmed, I realized how tense we'd all become, and I was glad that my words had provided comfort.

He released me, and I moved to stand in front of Octavia.

She lifted her chin, though she was only an inch or so shorter than me, and asked, "What are you doing?"

"I'm going to see if I can feel magic on you." I tilted my head, taking in every inch of her face, waiting for a change of expression. "I want to see if I can find the truth."

Turning her hands palms up, she nodded. "Sounds good to me. Let your arcane power search me."

If only that was how my blood worked.

If this woman makes one wrong move or breathes in a weird way, we take her out, Raffe commanded. *Make sure Sky doesn't get hurt.*

Got it, Keith and Adam responded in unison.

Raffe stepped close to me, and I placed my hands on hers. I closed my eyes, needing to focus on my other senses.

When our skin touched, nothing happened. Her skin was colder than mine since I now ran at the hotter shifter temperature, and I didn't feel the weird sandpapery sensation that usually accompanied coven magic. But maybe it went deeper than that. I needed to look inside her.

How?

I tried summoning my blood like Slade had told me, similar to how I tugged at my wolf, but nothing happened. My blood was barely a jolt. I had to heighten my emotions.

There was only one way to accomplish that well.

I imagined someone trying to take me away from Raffe. I remembered the way it had felt to be kidnapped and trapped, not seeing him, and just as I expected, my blood jolted.

As soon as my blood activated, something inside the woman tugged at me, and my blood swirled more. The sensation increased from a faint jolt to a hum. My power surged through me, more uncontrollable than ever, but it moved in a new and different way.

Something's wrong, I linked to Raffe, following through on my promise.

Fuck, I knew better. He growled.

He gripped my wrists and tried to remove my hands from Octavia's, but my power linked us.

My power flared like a spark, and then an echoing faint jolt answered.

It felt identical to my own.

Understanding washed over me, and the connection between us ended, allowing me to jerk my hands away. My eyes popped open.

This couldn't be true.

I swallowed, my throat and chest equally tight from disbelief. My voice, when it came, was barely above a whisper. "Are you my biological mother?"

ABOUT THE AUTHOR

Jen L. Grey is a *USA Today* Bestselling Author who writes Paranormal Romance, Urban Fantasy, and Fantasy genres.

Jen lives in Tennessee with her husband, two daughters, and two miniature Australian Shepherds. Before she began writing, she was an avid reader and enjoyed being involved in the indie community. Her love for books eventually led her to writing. For more information, please visit her website and sign up for her newsletter.

Check out her future projects and book signing events at her website.
www.jenlgrey.com

ALSO BY JEN L. GREY

The Forbidden Mate Trilogy

Wolf Mate

Wolf Bitten

Wolf Touched

Standalone Romantasy

Of Shadows and Fae

Twisted Fate Trilogy

Destined Mate

Eclipsed Heart

Chosen Destiny

The Marked Dragon Prince Trilogy

Ruthless Mate

Marked Dragon

Hidden Fate

Shadow City: Silver Wolf Trilogy

Broken Mate

Rising Darkness

Silver Moon

Shadow City: Royal Vampire Trilogy

Cursed Mate

Shadow Bitten

Demon Blood

Shadow City: Demon Wolf Trilogy

Ruined Mate

Shattered Curse

Fated Souls

Shadow City: Dark Angel Trilogy

Fallen Mate

Demon Marked

Dark Prince

Fatal Secrets

Shadow City: Silver Mate

Shattered Wolf

Fated Hearts

Ruthless Moon

The Wolf Born Trilogy

Hidden Mate

Blood Secrets

Awakened Magic

The Hidden King Trilogy

Dragon Mate

Dragon Heir

Dragon Queen

The Marked Wolf Trilogy

Moon Kissed

Chosen Wolf

Broken Curse

Wolf Moon Academy Trilogy

Shadow Mate

Blood Legacy

Rising Fate

The Royal Heir Trilogy

Wolves' Queen

Wolf Unleashed

Wolf's Claim

Bloodshed Academy Trilogy

Year One

Year Two

Year Three

The Half-Breed Prison Duology (Same World As Bloodshed Academy)

Hunted

Cursed

The Artifact Reaper Series

Reaper: The Beginning

Reaper of Earth

Reaper of Wings

Reaper of Flames

Reaper of Water

Stones of Amaria (Shared World)

Kingdom of Storms

Kingdom of Shadows

Kingdom of Ruins

Kingdom of Fire

The Pearson Prophecy

Dawning Ascent

Enlightened Ascent

Reigning Ascent

Stand Alones

Death's Angel

Rising Alpha

Printed in Great Britain
by Amazon